Fortunes of
A Misbegotten War

A Novel

by

Thomas Hofstedt

Table of Contents

Western Montana, October 2001

It was not an affair of state, nor was it the smoky back room so beloved of conspiracy theorists, but both the men and their purpose would have fit well within either of those venues. There were three of them, unlike in their professions and personalities but united by their outrage at the idea that a dozen fanatics armed with nothing but box cutters had killed thousands of their fellow citizens and humiliated their country.

The two men in suits were waiting for Barry Wilder. He had flown in to Glacier National Park Airport in a corporate jet and, once on the ground, was met at the foot of the ramp by a Range Rover with lettering on the front doors saying *Flathead Mountain Guides* and a driver who said no more than half-a-dozen words. They drove for well over an hour, through Whitefish and to the northwest. Their destination was a barn that was built in 1910 and refurbished in 1990 in the manner of a rustic hunting lodge, although it did not take in the public and had only a single staff member. Other than a quite serious fence, there were no signs to indicate that it was part of the several thousand acres of Montana belonging to the Strategic Missile Wing of the U.S. Air Force or that a Minuteman ICBM silo was not so very far away.

The three of them sat at a rectangular table at one end of what had once been the hayloft, the two of them facing Wilder and clearly evaluating him on some dimension that only they knew about. Wilder was the oldest of the three and the only one who seemed at home in the hunting lodge atmosphere. He sat quietly, uncaring about either their assessment or any conclusions they might draw from it. *They need to think they are in charge, that they are important. Let them.*

The distinguished looking man spoke first, the one who looked like someone accustomed to chairing meetings like this one. To Wilder, he looked like an insurance executive or a college professor. *Classic CIA, probably an assistant director level. Ivy League tight-ass.* "My name is Chapman. For the purposes of this meeting, you should view me as an entirely *unofficial* representative of the U.S. government."

He paused, clearly expecting a reaction. When none was forthcoming, he shrugged and went on. "The good news: The NSC is crystal clear about our short-term goals and they are both concrete and doable. We want to destroy the Taliban and get Osama bin Laden, and we want to do it fast. The bad news is that we have to wage war in Afghanistan in order to achieve these goals. If we do it ourselves or with our usual allies – think NATO and Kuwait in 1991 – it's a long, slow buildup. Much too long."

Wilder shrugged. "I heard the President's speech. Shock and awe, he said. A nice sound bite, but in my world, I tell my clients that they can have it done good, fast or cheap. Pick any two."

Chapman waved his hand. "Cheap is off the table entirely. And it doesn't need to be pretty. But it has to be quick. And effective."

So they know what they want in the short run and they're willing to pay for it. That's good. I wonder if they've thought about the long run. "Like it or not, the Taliban governs the country. If you succeed in destroying them, you'll own Afghanistan."

"We don't want it. The Afghans can have it."

Sure. That's what the Russians said too. "So how are you going to get the NSC what it wants?"

"We'll get Bin Laden as soon as we can find him. Either from the air or with a Seal team. But getting rid of the Taliban ... that's going to take old-fashioned methods –"

Either Wilder's patience ran out or he'd had enough condescension. "Like actual people on the ground, carrying guns and getting killed. You're going to need people like Massoud, Khalili and Noor." Chapman was visibly startled, but Wilder was pleased to see the man sitting next to him smile very slightly. *So he doesn't like Chapman particularly and he isn't surprised that a civilian knows the names of some of the major commanders of the Afghan opposition.*

Chapman didn't seem to mind the interruption or Wilder's obvious impatience. He nodded at the other man. "This is Colonel Ward. He was in Afghanistan until two days ago. I'll let him talk about that."

The third man spoke for the first time. He was the youngest, somewhere in his mid-fifties. "I'm curious. How do you know those three names?"

"My companies did some construction work in their regions and Pakistan in 1989 and 1990. After the Russians left. I met several of the tribal chiefs, particularly in the north and east."

"Then you know that, those names you mentioned, they're the big three. What you don't know is that I've just finished meeting with each of them and half-a-dozen others like them. They call themselves the Northern Alliance or, more generally, the United Front. But it's a very shaky alliance and there's nothing very united about them."

He paused, clearly expecting questions from Wilder. When they didn't come, he went on. "As you know, it's a pretty ragtag collection of tribal militias, each dominated by a particular tribe and warlord. They're Tajik, Hazara, Turkmen and Uzbeks. Even some Pashtun, although most of those align with the Taliban. But they've been fighting a defensive war against the Taliban government since 1996. We can use them."

Wilder asked a pair of questions that he already knew the answers to. "Can they fight? Will they fight for us?"

"Can they fight? Ask the Brits or Russians. They left a lot of good soldiers buried there. Will they fight for us? Yes, if we make it worth their while."

"How do we do that?"

"Three ways. First, we give them what they don't have – air power, and more and better weapons. With that, they can defeat the Taliban. A matter of a few months, in my opinion. Second, we pay them. They like U.S. dollars."

"And the third way?"

The man looked like someone with a nagging stomachache. "We keep quiet about their opium operations." He glanced at Chapman. "That's not my department, but maybe we even help them a little bit in that area, every now and then."

"What do you want from me?"

The colonel leaned forward over the table. "With the United Front, we have an instant army. In place and highly motivated. But we have no infrastructure. We need instant logistics capabilities ... help with transport for arms shipments, some hard assets on the ground for bringing in supplies and gathering troops for training. We'll have a few hundred special ops people in-country and we need to support them. Your companies have a lot of experience doing that sort of thing around the world. You work fast and get things done."

Chapman had been sitting quietly, clearly attentive to the dialogue between the two other men. Now he leaned forward and said, "You've got friends in high places, Mr. Wilder. Bush, Cheney and Rumsfield all agreed. They said, 'Talk to Wilder.'"

'Friends' is not the right word but it's nice to see some return on all that investment! "What about security for my people?"

"Hire your own. You know how to do that. I suggest you contract with one of the local tribal chiefs. Put it on your expense account."

The other man – the colonel just back from Afghanistan -- smiled in the way of a man accustomed to being betrayed. "Just make sure he's on our side."

Northern Afghanistan, December 2001

The man called Archer sat in the heavy-duty pickup truck at the edge of the hilltop, marveling at the blackness and coldness around him, properties so much in contrast to the daytime brilliance and heat. He held a tactical radio resting on his knee, keyed to a very specific frequency, and watched to the north. It was a uniform blackness except for the occasional firefly flash of gunfire, so quick that he mistrusted his vision.

"They're getting closer fast. I don't think Omar is doing what he's being overpaid to do." Vargas' voice startled him, so loud in the surrounding silence. When he looked, all he could see was the glint from a pair of steel-framed glasses. *I wonder how long he's been sitting there watching me? But he's right. Those flashes are closer. And I can hear the heavier weapons now. This is going to be very tight.*

Not for the first time, he wondered what he was doing here. His usual milieu was a walnut-paneled executive office and the way he got things done was to tell other people to do them. *So why are you sitting here, in the middle of the night, waiting on a hilltop in Afghanistan with some kind of ex-commando for a companion, while the warlord recruited by the CIA may or may not be keeping the Taliban from killing you?* It was a long and purely rhetorical question for which there was an easy answer: *Because the man told you to be here.*

As usual, the order was transmitted in an abrupt phone call. "I want you – just you, no flunkies – to pick up a package and make sure it gets delivered to the right parties. You'll need a forklift and a small truck. I'm sending a man named Vargas; he'll give you the details." *He didn't mention the CIA or the fact that the delivery was to take place in the middle of a war zone. And Vargas hasn't shared much more about what we're doing here.*

As though triggered by his doubts, the radio came to life. "This is Foxtrot One. GPS says I'm a mile out from your coordinates. Time for some light. You have ten seconds to acknowledge or we're going home."

He pressed the transmit button. "This is Teller Two. All I've got for you is a pair of headlights. Coming on now." He reached out and turned on the lights, and was immediately struck by how puny they seemed against the blackness. "You've got a hundred yards of hard level ground directly in front of the lighted area and no obstructions on the way in or out. We show no wind."

"Hostiles?"

Will he abort if I tell him there's a flock of Taliban fighters coming fast? Or is he one of the hot dogs who's been longing for a war to fight? Why take the chance? "All quiet," he lied. "But it's not a good neighborhood." The man standing alongside his window laughed softly.

He could hear the aircraft now and he turned the ignition key and released the handbrake. The diesel engine seemed startlingly loud in the night. The combination of the headlight glare and the engine noise meant that the muzzle flashes and sounds of the firefight disappeared and he had no way of measuring how much time he had left. *Enough. It has to be enough. Omar told me he could hold them. But he didn't look at me when he said that.*

"It's not a good neighborhood." The answer caused the man at the controls of the UH-1N Iroquois helicopter to wonder for about the thousandth time in the last few months why he was doing this yet again … delivering off-the-books cargo to anonymous people in hazardous dark places and fourth-world countries. *It must be the hundred thousand bucks that gets deposited in my account every month. Or maybe I really believe all that stuff about 'doing good.'* But he knew better. Self-delusion was one of the luxuries that he had left behind in the Vietnamese highlands.

Sam Goodwin didn't think of himself as a mercenary. It was true that his infrequent bouts of employment were highly compensated and corresponded with some small war in Africa, Asia or South America, but he had never fired a weapon other than in his basic training at Fort Ord more than forty years ago. He just happened to be very good at flying helicopters during an era in military history when helicopters were essential to fighting wars. So when the CIA was managing America's war against the Taliban in those early days after the attack on the World Trade Center, it was easy to find work, even for an aging veteran like Goodwin.

"Headlights. At one o'clock. Seven hundred meters." The co-pilot spoke in quick bursts and Goodwin wondered how much of that was nerves. He didn't know the man, other than that his first name was Skip. The Huey usually had a crew of four, but tonight it was the two of them and one other, a nameless CIA spook who came with the cargo. It was a single pallet, an approximate cube measuring four feet by four feet by four feet and tightly wrapped in a blue tarpaulin. When it was being secured to the deck, Goodwin asked the spook how much it weighed. When the man just looked at him, he said, "I need to know. It affects fuel consumption and how this flying piece of junk handles."

"It's about the same weight as a two bales of marijuana. Or six live marines with full gear. But much more valuable. So your job is to get me and this pallet where we need to be."

Goodwin let it go. The man was classic CIA. Maybe thirty years old, clad in a black jump suit with what looked like an Uzi across his chest and a handgun in a shoulder holster. He reminded Goodwin of the pair that he was transporting in the late stages of Vietnam; the ones that threw three suspected Viet Cong out the open door of his Huey when they were at four thousand feet over the Central Highlands.

He changed the pitch to bleed off his forward speed and the copter lurched and emitted a series of squealing sounds. Goodwin smiled, feeling some affinity with the Huey. *The thing is forty years old, probably carrying a lot of deferred maintenance along with it. But it flies.*

The CIA was checking the terrain below them, standing braced in the open door. He toggled his microphone. "There's a firefight going on down there. Mostly small arms, but a lot of them. Not that far from your LZ. You need to go in and get out real fast." The man's voice was calm in Goodwin's headset. *I think he's done this before.*

"You want to abort?" It was a pro forma reaction, not really a question at all, and the response was instantaneous and unsurprising. "No. This cargo gets delivered. On time and in the right place. Tonight. Down there." Goodwin switched to the other channel, the one to the man on the ground. "Teller Two. You've got the wrong kind of people headed your way. Maybe seven or eight clicks directly north of you. You need to keep them away? Can you do that?"

There was a pause while the man in the cab of the truck looked at the man by his open window. They were on the same level because the man was now sitting on a small forklift. There was only a faint glow from the headlights, but enough to see outlines. Archer was holding the radio at arm's length, the volume turned up. "Did you hear that?" There was that same soft laugh and the voice in the dark said, "Don't worry. Omar wants what's on that bird. He'll give us space."

If he can stay alive. But the man nodded and keyed the radio. "Come on in. We've got at least twenty minutes to ourselves. That's plenty."

Goodwin came back quickly. "Kill the headlights as soon as I'm down. No need to show them the way. And I won't need any runway lights when I leave." He threw a quick look over his left shoulder. The spook was bracing himself against the blue tarp, already beginning to release some of the securing straps that held the pallet in place. Goodwin had a last flash of resentment before he turned back to his instruments. *They could at least tell us what's under the tarp, given that it may get us all killed.*

The Huey descended from out of the blackness and was invisible until it was on the ground, but the sound of the rotors and the dust cloud that it raised gave ample notice of its arrival. The man in the truck turned off the headlights when the skids were a foot from the ground and found the darkness to be comforting. The only light came from a weak light in the interior of the Huey.

"Go!" shouted the man in the truck at the driver of the forklift. "And watch the rotors!" He'd made the calculations a dozen times. They could get the pallet out easily, but it wouldn't fit under the rotors if the tines were raised more than five feet from the ground. He got out of the truck and turned on his flashlight. He had little to do for the next new minutes. *This is why Vargas is here.*

In the cargo area of the Huey, the man was undoing the last of the restraining straps from the pallet, working with the dim light from the headlamp he had strapped on. Once the last strap was removed, he put his Uzi on top of the tarpaulin and he and the two helicopter pilots lined up and used their combined weight to push the pallet to the open doorway, so that the edge of the pallet projected a few inches beyond the line of the door. Then they stood watching as the forklift maneuvered itself, slid the tines under the pallet, smoothly drew it out of the helicopter and lowered it to within a few inches of the ground.

Sam Goodwin and the co-pilot never left the copter, turning to go back to the controls as soon as the cargo was cleared. As the rotors began to turn faster, the black-clad CIA man jumped to the ground, took his Uzi from the top of the cargo bundle and shouted at Archer, "Let's go! We have –"

The shot came from behind him, snapping his head forward and propelling him against Archer, who instinctively caught him before letting him slide to the ground, leaving a trail of blood and brains smeared on his shirtfront. He stood, stunned in place, as Vargas stepped around the body, picked up the Uzi and jumped back into the cargo area. From there, it was two quick steps to the front.

Sam Goodwin already had his headset on and his hands and feet in position on the controls. The main rotor was approaching liftoff rpms. Even with the headset, he heard the series of popping sounds and turned to see his co-pilot jerk forward in his seat as the bullets slammed into his back. He watched the muzzle of the Uzi swing toward him. His immediate reactions were– *It's been a long time coming* – and then a final act of defiance. He pushed the collective hard to the right and jammed the right rudder to the floor. His last thought was one of regret about doing that to the Huey.

Archer stood alongside the forklift watching the Huey cartwheeling away from him, its rotor chewing up the rocky ground even as the fire engulfed the aircraft and turned it into a spinning fireball. He tried to step forward but the black clad body was still leaning against him in a kneeling posture. He stepped back but even then the corpse remained upright with head bowed, a penitent for unknown sins. He looked down at his shirtfront and touched the black blood and brain matter on his chest as if to verify that it was not his. Then he reached out and put his hand on the blue tarp that was covering the cube that had just gotten four men killed in the last ten seconds. The surface was cold and solid and perhaps it was those sensations that snapped him back to the reality that he was alone and that his self-imposed time window was about to close.

He moved quickly and purposefully. He drove the forklift to the rear of the truck and slid the pallet onto the bed. He closed the back gate of the truck bed and fastened another very heavy canvas cover over the load using the tie-downs around the rim of the cargo area. Then he got back on the forklift, pointed it at the intense fire burning forty yards away, put it in gear and once it was underway stepped off. The machine lumbered about halfway to the fire before its right-side wheels caught in a small trench and it fell over, its drive wheels still spinning slowly. By then, Archer was in the truck and driving, in a direction opposite to the muzzle flashes and increasingly loud sound of automatic weapons and the dull thump of grenades.

He drove for about three miles along the rude track, really no more than a pair of parallel ruts, until he came to where the ruts intersected a one-lane dirt road. According to Vargas, the drop-off point for the cargo was about six miles to his left. He stopped the truck and shut off the engine. The silence was complete. He sat, closed his eyes and replayed in his mind the events on the mountaintop and the phone call that had sent him there.

The old man wants whatever's on that pallet. Never had any intention to deliver it. He sent Vargas to kill the CIA and the pilots. I wonder if I was on the list too? The question bothered him, but he knew that he was never going to know for certain.

He got out of the truck cab, climbed into the truck bed, loosed one of the tie ropes on the tarpaulin, and pulled it back to expose the front half of the cube. He stood looking at it for a full minute, thinking about – and discarding – his options. Then he moved decisively. He took a large jackknife from his pocket, opened the blade and made a six-inch cut along each of the three axes that converged at the upper left corner of the package and peeled back the material so that he had a small aperture to view the contents. He used the knife once more to extract a small piece of the cube that he looked at for a long time before carefully inserting it back where it had been. He pulled the covering tarp back in place and returned to the truck cab where he resumed thinking about his choices.

After that, it was pure improvisation. But even after fifteen years of rethinking the alternatives and his choices, he could not come up with a better plan than what he had done in those frantic few hours. Even the choices that he made for the wrong reasons turned out to be right in the longer run.

He drove the truck to the deserted construction site and parked within the wire fence surrounding the heavy equipment. He picked up keys from the trailer for a large Caterpillar front-end loader that he then maneuvered into the twenty-foot-deep trench that was fifty yards downhill from the trailer. It took more time than he thought it would, but it had been a long time since he had actually operated heavy equipment and the controls were different than he remembered. The trench would be a major component of the septic field for the police headquarters and barracks that his company was building for the Afghan government. It took two hours to extend the trench another twenty feet on the uphill side, to drive the pickup into that end of the trench, and finally to refill the extension, completely covering the truck and its cargo. The sun rose as he was finishing.

He used his satellite phone to call the man, using the number that was reserved for special transactions. He hesitated before touching the last digit, thinking again about those ten seconds on the hilltop and the same question: *I wonder if I was supposed to wind up like the rest of them?* The man answered immediately. "Is it done?"

"No. Vargas started killing people and the helicopter totaled itself."

"The cargo –"

"Barely got off the copter. Last I saw, it was sitting on the forklift. I imagine the Taliban is picking through what's left of whatever was in the package. They showed up about the same time Vargas started shooting. I took off."

"What about Vargas?"

"He was in the copter when it turned into a ball of fire. I'm the only one left."

There was a long silence. "OK. Someone will come around in a day or so. They will be representing the people that were responsible for the cargo and its delivery. Tell them the same story, but leave out the bit about Vargas. Tell them that the Taliban got there at the same time as the bird."

The call was terminated by the man at the other end, leaving Archer to stand looking at his improvised burial site and finally begin to question his actions. *What have you done?*

The man sitting in the lawyer's office in Dubai stared at the phone in his hand for a long time, replaying the dialogue in his memory. *It's a good story. I wonder if it's true? Vargas told me that everything was in place ... but he couldn't speak for the Taliban. If it was Vargas telling me the story, I'd wonder, but Archer doesn't have the balls to play that kind of game.*

I probably should be pleased that it didn't work. I told them it wasn't a good idea ... that much temptation in one shipment. And in a place where anything can happen. But they didn't care ... said things like 'time is more important than money' and 'this will get us into Kabul.' They were asking to be ripped off.

But there are more immediate issues to deal with. The conference room where he was sitting had floor to ceiling glass walls and he could see the two Pakistani officials waiting for him to finish his call and resume their meeting. He waved them back into the room and when they were seated, he began, *"About our project … There's been an unexpected delay in the funding …"*

It took two more days, but the CIA came around to ask Archer about that night. This time, it was a man in a suit, although he pulled the tie loose and took off the jacket even as he was walking to the door into the Quonset hut that was Archer's office. He managed to look impatient, suspicious and angry, all at the same time, and his first words matched his looks.

"You screwed up."

He'd had a lot of time to think, even rehearse what he would say. "No. I did exactly what I was supposed to do. Your people were the ones that screwed up. You told me 'Omar will hold them. You'll have plenty of time.' Well, Omar didn't hold them. The Taliban got there ten seconds after the Huey touched down. We had just pulled the pallet out. There were thirty or forty of them. I got out of the truck and ran. I heard the shooting and saw the fireball, but that's all."

The visitor had been to the scene and picked through the wreckage of the Huey. He listened to Archer, checking for inconsistencies with what he saw on the ground. He couldn't find any. "What did you do then?"

"When I went back, the truck was gone and the Huey was still burning. All they left was the forklift … and the body of your man."

The man in the suit got upset about that. "What you call 'the body?' His name was Donavan. He had a wife and two kids in Ohio and he was a friend of mine."

"Sorry." He waited long enough that the single word stood on its own. Then he asked, "What was it in that helicopter that was important enough for him to die?"

The man thought about it and said, "Nothing. Nothing important enough for anybody to die for. Like this whole god damned country and everything in it."

Archer asked, "You done?"

"Yeah."

"We got the forklift back, but you owe us for the truck. I'll send you an invoice."

"Yeah. You do that."

Two days later, Archer called his wife at their home in Vancouver. It was a ritual of theirs. No matter where he was, even in the most remote spots, he found a way to talk to her every few days for at least a few minutes. In this case, it was easy. The company provided communication linkages for all of the senior people in the field. In his case, he had a satellite phone and a secure place to talk.

"Something happened this week."

They'd been married twenty-nine years, one of those rare couples that find everything they need in the other person. They had no close personal friends, disliked their respective parents and siblings, and did not want children. Each was sufficient for the other. They wanted the same things, thought the same way and shared everything. They were like a pair of identical twins that never grew up.

So when he said, "Something happened this week," she understood without asking that the 'something' was both important and dangerous in some way that required them to be careful about how they talked about it. So she merely said, "Oh?"

"I picked up a shipment. For delivery to a third party. A big package. But both the buyer and seller are gone. I have no idea how to find them and I don't know what to do with the package."

"Is it valuable?"

"Very."

"Will someone finally miss it and come looking for it?"

"Yes. They've already been here, but they don't know that I have it. They think it's gone for good."

She thought about what he was saying. And not saying. "Can you repackage it and send it somewhere? Maybe here, for safekeeping."

"It's very heavy and bulky. Not easily moved. It would attract a lot of attention."

"You should be sure to put it somewhere safe ... somewhere that you can retrieve it when the times are quieter."

"I was hoping you'd say that. I've already done it."

"Good." After a few seconds, she asked, "Does Daddy know about this?"

Toronto & Afghanistan, 2014

It seemed strange to the man called Archer to be sitting in a restaurant that rotated on its axis a thousand feet above the ground, causing the view of the skyline and lake to constantly change. But his wife liked that sort of thing. He'd planned it carefully, booking a time such that they would start with appetizers in daylight, watch the sunset come and go during a leisurely dinner, and finish with dessert with all of the bright city lights of Toronto beneath them.

He told her, "It's a triple milestone dinner." It was their forty-third wedding anniversary and his sixty-fifth birthday was in two weeks, which would be the day he retired from the company where he had worked for the last forty years. He didn't know it when he made the reservation, but it would also serve to mark the end of another phase of his life.

They almost didn't go. The call came while they were in the taxi on their way to the restaurant. When he glanced at the caller ID, he knew he had to take the call. He held the screen up so that she could see who was calling. When she saw the name, she grimaced.

"Yes?"

Then he listened for thirty seconds, said "Yes" once more and turned the phone off. He gazed out the window, staring blankly at the passing street, and she knew what he was thinking. So she said, "Only two more weeks to put up with this kind of crap." And then, "Do you have to go now?"

"He's sending the Gulfstream, the big one. I have about six hours. Still plenty of time for dinner."

"What is it? The Indonesian thing?"

"No. It's Afghanistan. And it's bad. Six of our sub-contractors were killed by their Kurdish interpreter two hours after they arrived in-country. It's a total mess on the scene. The construction site's been shut down, everybody put on standby, and he wants me to go fix it. I think it's pretty serious." *The whole project has been one long screw-up. Getting six people killed will get us all kinds of attention, and we don't need that ... not on this project.*

They sat in silence for the remaining fifteen minutes in the cab, but thinking very different thoughts. He was remembering all the dinners cut short, birthdays missed and all that time spent fixing problems all over the globe. For him, the phrase 'only two more weeks' represented an interminable period of waiting before he could start the rest of his life with this woman. For her, however, 'only two more weeks' was like a nano-second. *We need more time. We need to wait for the conditions to align. In two weeks, we lose the opportunity!*

When the waiter handed them the menus and left them, she asked, "The construction site ... that's near Kunduz, isn't it?" And midway through the salad course, "The Taliban hasn't been very active in that province recently, have they?" So that when she pushed her half-finished main course to the side and started to ask, "How far is the site from –" he knew where she was going and finished the question for her. "From our retirement funds? Twenty-two miles."

They'd discussed it many times. The problem was infuriatingly simple, but intractable. The logistics were straightforward: Extract and transport a very large package over seven thousand miles. The problem was how to do it in such a fashion that nobody else would know that they had it or where they got it or that they shipped it or where they put it.

They ordered a soufflé for dessert, one of her favorite dishes. It took half an hour to prepare, long enough that the outside view changed from twinkling city lights to the vast dark space of Lake Ontario. They talked of starting the next phase: the move to California where no one knew them and they would finally have all the time to themselves.

She ordered cognac, something she had never done before, and he knew that she wanted to prolong their time in this slowly revolving glass-enclosed bubble so far above the ground. She sat staring out of the floor-to-ceiling window but he knew she was not seeing. When they finally stood up to leave, she asked, "You said that six of your sub-contractors were killed. What do they do with the bodies?"

Fourteen years and three months. It looks different in the daylight.

The mangled fire blackened wreckage of the Huey was still there, vivid proof that recycling and reclamation are not high priority needs for a country that has been at war within itself and against the major military powers of the world for the better part of a century. There were still burned-out hulks of Russian tanks from the eighties scattered around the countryside. To compound the irony, they'd given him a truck that was virtually identical to the one that he'd been driving on that night. *I wonder if anything ever changes in this place?*

That question became even more poignant when he got to the project that they'd been building almost fifteen years earlier. Like many of the ambitious 'nation-building' projects from those early days, the police station and barracks were never finished. A forlorn first story of unroofed concrete walls ran along the hillside, with rebar sticking out in every direction. The walls had pockmarks from machine gun fire and the occasional gap where a rocket-propelled grenade had struck. The trench for the proposed septic field was still an open gash in the hillside, with two very large plastic cylindrical tanks taking up most of the space. Even they were bullet riddled.

His wife had worked out the details in the two hours that elapsed between the time they left the revolving restaurant and when he boarded the Gulfstream. *"Both sites are deserted. You can operate the equipment by yourself. Transfer the goods. Once it's repackaged, we're home free. I'll manage the reception at this end."* It was a simple plan but he trusted her judgment. He had spent most of their married life making her plans come true. As she put it, "I'm strategy; you're tactics. I'm a planner; you're the doer. We work well together."

He'd arranged for a front-end-loader at the site, and it was sitting on its flatbed trailer transporter near the uphill end of the trench. Despite his explicit instructions, the local manager sent an operator along, an Afghan who spoke no English other than to introduce himself as 'Mohammed,' which was fine with him. Using hand gestures and the little bit of Pashtun that he knew, he got him moving dirt and they uncovered the rear end of the buried truck after less than an hour of digging. Based on a quick inspection, it looked like the cargo was as he had left it; about what you'd expect of packaged goods long buried in a semi-arid high desert landscape. The canvas tarpaulin had rotted away in spots, but the plastic blue covering beneath it was as unblemished as ever except for the small incision in the upper left-hand corner. It took another twenty minutes to transfer the pallet from the half-buried truck to his truck. He had calculated that the loader could do the job, but it was right at the limits of its weight-bearing capacity. It called for some skill and, in the end, he was glad to have Mohammed at the controls.

As the Afghan was closing the tailgate, he shot him twice in the back of his head, slamming him against the truck. He had reasoned his way through all of the options, but could not come up with any other choice that was acceptable. *We didn't anticipate an operator showing up. Probably not an issue: when he doesn't show up back at the barracks; they'll assume he's gone back to raising opium.* But the shooting brought back the image of that night, when Vargas shot the CIA guy and left his brain and blood smeared on his shirtfront. *His name was Donavan. He was a family man from Ohio.* He nudged the body at his feet. *I wonder if he has ... had ... a wife or children?* He dragged the body into the trench and dumped it alongside the long-buried pickup truck. Then he used the loader one more time to put back all of the dirt and rocks they'd removed, until once more the site was pristine, indistinguishable from the surrounding landscape.

He got the loader back on the transporter, lashed it down and hitched the trailer to his truck. He had twenty-two miles to go; to another construction site where the company was contracted to provide logistical support for an Afghan battalion and its U.S. military advisors. It was empty of men and had very little machinery sitting around. It was judged to be too dangerous until the army cleared the province of the roving Taliban bands. The proof was the six bodies that were laid out on the concrete floor of the only building on the site. They were civil engineers who had signed on for a six-month tour with the company, having been assured by the Afghans that the area was safe. Unfortunately, they overlooked the interpreter. He executed the six of them in the two hours after they arrived.

Except for a small forklift, the bodies were the only objects in the room and they were put there by some one who appreciated symmetry. The room was square and the group of corpses was centered within the room, a set of aligned and blanketed shapes with only the booted feet poking out from the end of the blanket. Leaning against the wall were six coffins. They looked metallic, gleaming in the faint light from the open doorway.

He opened the massive overhead door and backed the pickup truck with its blue cube into the space, positioning it alongside the bodies. He used the forklift to pull the pallet off the truck bed. It fell heavily, tilted to one side.

One more burial. He lifted each of the six bodies into the bed of the pickup. He found himself handling them carefully, as if they were still capable of feeling pain or indignity. When he drove back into the building almost an hour later, he looked older, less committed to the plan. He had not engaged in much real physical work for a number of years and the combination of the hard labor, the jet lag and the psychological toll of dumping six men that he had personally hired into a hole in the ground was beginning to show.

Almost done. He dragged the six metallic coffins over next to the blue cube. Then he used a large razor knife to slice through the blue tarp along the top and the two sides of one its faces. He found himself looking at a solid wall made up of small rectangles. It could have been a shipment of bricks, except he remembered quite well the single sample he had extracted fourteen years ago. He used the tool to make the same cuts to the plastic shrink wrap that held them together and even before he finished the last cut, a cascade of individually-wrapped packages slid out onto the floor, leaving him knee deep in brick-sized packages. It was a strange sensation, but he did not stop to consider it. Using a large scoop shovel, he shifted all of the little bundles into the six coffins.

She did the basic arithmetic on a paper napkin while they were sitting in the restaurant. More than a ton of stuff to be spread out in six coffins. Each will weigh more than three hundred pounds ... probably about right given that coffins usually look heavier than they are. And nobody's going to be looking inside, that's for sure.

At about that same time Archer was filling the coffins, his wife was calling the next-of-kin for each of the six victims. Offering condolences from the two them and on behalf of the company, of course, but also reminding them that the company's standard contract did not include the shipment of remains for burial and that, in keeping with the local customs, burial followed shortly after death. She also reminded them that the company provided for a hundred thousand dollar life insurance payment to them, contingent only on their acceptance of these final arrangements.

Two hours later, the man called Archer watched the six coffins being loaded into the cargo area of the Gulfstream by eight Afghans, each dressed in an immaculate ABL uniform. He and the four-person crew of the Gulfstream stood solemnly in a row attending to the small ceremony. One of the flight attendants was crying.

Thirty hours later, Archer and his wife sat at their kitchen table staring at the small rectangular object placed precisely in the center of the table. She finally asked, "How much is it?"

"Ten thousand dollars. Exactly a hundred bills, identical except for the serial numbers."

"And how many are there like this?" She pointed at the brick-like object.

I was standing knee deep in all those little packages. "Thousands."

She shook her head. "So much! It was easier to imagine it as a bulky cargo on a pallet. A big package that needed a small crane to move around. Something ... tangible ..."

He picked it up, seeming to judge its weight, and let it fall lightly back onto the tabletop. "It's tangible. You can pick it up ... feel it."

"We can't deposit it in a bank, can we?"

He just smiled.

"Can we spend it? Pay our bills with it? Buy dinner? Go on vacation?"

He thought about it. "In small amounts and in different places. It's hard to do and it will attract attention ... from both sides of the law." *And it would most certainly get Daddy's attention.* "It wouldn't make much of a dent in the total." *And there's nobody we can leave it to.*

She nodded and then smiled at the joke. "So we're rich, but we can't spend the money?"

"We are rich, yes, and we can spend the money, but not just yet. We'll have to make some arrangements. It will take a while, but you're good at solving problems like that."

"Is it in a safe place? Did you do what I suggested?"

"To the last detail. It's in a high-security, climate-controlled self-storage facility in Colma, California. Not far from where we'll be in a few months."

"Still in the coffins?"

"Yes, except for this sample," he said, pointing at the small package of bills in the middle of the table. "As you recommended, the storage unit is rented by a company called Interment Products Limited and holds dozens of coffins of various qualities."

Even as he heard himself talking, he was marveling at what he had learned in the last few days about this woman sitting opposite him. *We've been a couple for fifty years. She's been homemaker, executive wife, community volunteer ... all the trappings of upper-middle-class correctness, right up through managing our retirement plan. I thought I knew her, but then she turns out to be a criminal genius. There must be genetic transfer going on, but it's been dormant for a long time.*

As usual, she was tuned to his thoughts. "We work well together, don't we?" He reached out his hand to her and she put her hand in his. "Yes we do. But I have no idea what we do next."

"I have some ideas. Once we're in California ..."

His cell phone rang. Once again he showed his wife the caller ID before he answered.

"Yes .... Yes ... It's taken care of, the Afghans are – No, I didn't know that ... That's not good ... Damage control, yes ...OK."

He put the phone onto the tabletop very gently and sat looking out of the window. She didn't say anything, knowing that he would tell her everything. He always had.

"We may be retiring sooner than we had planned," he said. "They're starting an inquiry into the Afghan incident and he thinks that will lead them to look more closely at the UN contracts in West Africa."

"But he's ... we've ... been through this before. It can –"

"He says this time is different. He wants to shut it down. Everything. Go away for good. Now."

They looked at each other and then at the rectangular prism in the center of the table. Suddenly, it seemed bigger and more important, less innocent.

Northern California, 2017

How in the world did we get to this point? Graham Dodd found himself asking this question more and more these days. At first, it was just a generalized puzzlement, the kind of headshaking question that older people pose to themselves when something reminds them of how much the world has changed around them while they were just going about their lives. Lately however, he was treating the question seriously. He prided himself on his 'go with the flow' mentality and deliberately avoided any probing into its origins, especially when his daughter Alison was deep into what she termed "her spiritual phase" and sought to convert him to her belief that "everything happens for a purpose." But finally the very absurdity of the decisions they were debating intrigued him and he tried to reconstruct the path that brought them here. *You're a prizewinning investigative journalist. You've untangled multilayer conspiracies ... exposed intricate corruption schemes. Surely you can understand what's happened to your own marriage?*

Part of the answer was easy: We got rich. The idea of throwing the various parts of your life up into the air and starting over is not all that scary if you've got almost fifteen million in your checking account along with a few other millions of assorted investments. And I suppose another part has to do with getting old. Not that sixty – or fifty-eight for Valerie – is 'old' these days, especially if you're healthy and have good genes. But still, the New York Times obituaries begin to seem ominous and I find myself more aware of birthdays, more conscious of uneven sidewalks, wet surfaces and dark stairwells.

So. Old, wealthy and risk averse. A lifetime trifecta of sorts. Then there's the serendipity factor, the cosmic wild card. The Palo Alto real estate market goes through one of its periodic manic phases, with twenty-five year old nerds wandering the streets with fistfuls of stock options and wanting to live within biking distance of this dot com and that dot com, driving up the price of housing. We turned away the real estate agents, but could not have anticipated the knock on the door at nine o'clock on a Saturday night.

The kid standing there looked like the others that moved in packs through the streets of Palo Alto and Mountain View and San Francisco – intense, with a three-day-old beard, dressed in black jeans and a T-shirt. He spoke with a accent that may have been Russian and may have been slightly drunk, but his words were perfectly clear. He said "I'll give you ten million in cash for your house, as is. Tonight." He stood there, swaying slightly but clearly expecting a response.

Valerie and I looked at each other. Later, she would say, "I didn't think he was serious," but we both knew that he was. And I was complicit, simply by doing and saying nothing. So Valerie said, "Fifteen million. As is. And you can have the furniture."

The kid blinked and leaned sideways to peer around us. We were standing in the doorway and all he could see was the hallway with an umbrella stand and a coat rack. "OK," he said. "Do you want the check now?"

I think we both knew that the kid was real and that we both wanted it to be true. But Valerie spent a good part of every day dealing with mentally ill walkabouts, or maybe her Midwestern upbringing required her to give every sucker a second chance, so she said, "That's a lot of money for a house you haven't even seen yet. What's your name and why do you want our house?"

He looked startled, as though he had not thought about what might follow his one-line sales pitch. "I am Andreovitch. Sergei. I am a software engineer. I am getting married next week and I have promised Sonia a house in Palo Alto."

"You've been drinking, Sergei."

"A little, yes. But I have the checkbook –"

Valerie stepped out of the house, put both hands on Sergei's shoulders and turned him around. "We'll be here with our lawyer tomorrow morning at ten. If you feel this way then, bring your checkbook and we'll sell you our house for fifteen million dollars. You might want to bring a real estate agent or a lawyer with you." She gave him a gentle push. He took one involuntary step and turned back to face them. "I'll bring Sonia. She'll like this house."

Sergei and Sonia were on the doorstep at ten the next morning. He and I sat in the kitchen, drank coffee and talked about the future of the internet while Valerie and Sonia walked through every room, talking – as far as I could tell – about children and Ukrainians in America. By noon, we had sold the house, deposited the check and – in keeping with the absurdity of the entire transaction -- agreed to be out within a week.

So we were suddenly homeless, after a fashion, and confronting the perennial dilemma of the displaced: What next? Where do we go? It lacked the life-or-death quality of a Biafran refugee fleeing genocide or an Iraqi Kurd marked by Saddam's death squads, but it had the same the-world-as-I-know-it-is-over-and–what-do-I-do-now quality to it. The positive thinking crowd would call it an opportunity.

Then there was what the AA bunch calls 'the elephant in the living room.' The marriage wasn't working, limping along waiting for one of us to finally say what we were both thinking; that it might be marginally better to be sad and alone rather than sad and together. It was a thought that had been building for the last *several years, slowly working its way to the surface through more than three decades of shared history.*

So when the kid asked the absurd question, "Do you want the check now?" Valerie and I looked at one another and thought the same thought: What the hell? Let's give it another shot! As though our issues were monetary in nature. What we did not appreciate at the moment was that "new opportunities" were not the problem that we should have been trying to solve.

Graham Dodd was a nice-looking sixty-year old white American male. He had thinning, sandy hair and eyes somewhere between green and brown. Six feet tall and still thin, although it was due to genetics rather than diet or exercise. He really had only two distinguishing physical characteristics. One was the limp, a result of an IED – "improvised explosive device" – that targeted an armored personnel carrier just ahead of the one he was riding in on the outskirts of Baghdad, shredding its six occupants and then incinerating their remains while he sat staring at the jagged bone sticking out of his right leg.

Six months later, he had a new knee, a Pulitzer Prize in journalism and his second distinguishing feature -- a perpetually skeptical expression. On their better days, Valerie likened it to what she called an 'informed curiosity.' He had no idea what that meant and did not worry about it. For him, the expression was a 'keep away' signal, a way for him to stand off and observe rather than engage. That same habit often irritated others around him, particularly Valerie.

Valerie could have been cover girl of the century for the AARP magazine. And she conducted herself as if she was aware of it and did not want to lose that status. Her hair, wardrobe, and makeup were carefully constructed each morning and maintained until she went to bed at night. Her ash blonde hair was shoulder length and never out-of-place; her skin as translucent and almost as unwrinkled as when they first met. She worked very hard at not changing. She and Graham had been married for thirty-two years and the many pictures of them over those years puzzled him because he seemed to age, even shrink, while Valerie looked the same year after year, right down to the smile and the crinkles in the corners of her eyes.

Thirty-two years was a long enough span that their daughter Alison and their close friends assumed they were good for the duration, that either affection or inertia would suffice. But they would have been wrong. As a couple, they caromed between emotional extremes, sometimes in love and totally dependent on one another and at other times wondering why they stayed with such an infuriating partner, always just short of the tipping point.

It had worked – or not failed – for a long time. Like other upwardly mobile couples of their generation raised by middle-class parents, they bought into the idea of lifelong marriage, of a relationship that, although imperfect, was good enough, and maybe even 'the best we can do.' They played their roles without thinking of the alternatives, at least for the first twenty years. Graham was working his way to the top of the professional heap while Valerie played second banana and raised Alison. The arrangement began to fray when Alison moved out at the same time that Graham got his Pulitzer, went free-lance and started hanging around the house rather than flying off to some small war in Africa or disaster area in the Balkans. Proximity and dual careers brought out all the petty aggravations that are inevitable between two strong-willed individuals, each of them believing that 'now is my time.'

Fidelity was never an issue, although each of them suspected that the other was susceptible and may even have acted on the occasional opportunity. The sex was always good, particularly when they traveled together. It was as though new surroundings mandated new beginnings. But at home there were weeks-long stretches of simmering animosity, an icy civility that was somehow worse than outright screaming at one another.

It helped that each of them had moments when they suspected that they were slightly inferior to the other, that they were married to someone better than they deserved, and that they had the best possible spouse for them. To be ungrateful was to be unrealistic about your options or – perhaps worse – run the risk of being alone and sad.

The last several years were helped by Valerie's career. When Graham started staying home, she began volunteering at local agencies and parlayed that into a meteoric rise through the ranks until she was the CEO of one of the most prominent social service complexes in the US. Graham was proud of her and bragged to their friends, "Everywhere I go, people point at me and say, 'He's Valerie's husband!'" For those same friends, the two of them were the ultimate power couple – accomplished, attractive and committed to one another.

They were annoyed with one another much of the time. Never about anything major. She liked to be on time, meaning to walk in at the precise instant and therefore every contingency had to factored in. He wanted only to avoid being so late as to be impolite. They disagreed about whether to take the freeway vs. local streets, about whether to eat in or out, about how big their donation to the Cancer Fund should be, about what he should wear when they went to movies assuming they could agree on what movie to see. It was a series of low-level skirmishes, but it was building to the point where each of them was composing speeches in their head; speeches with lines like "You no longer meet my needs." "You don't understand me." "You're not listening to me." "I need some space."

Then Sergei, the Russian engineer fresh from his IPO, knocks on their door and buys their house for fifteen million in cash, enabling them to reconfigure their lives once more. Neither of them said it out loud, but they were thinking the same thing as they stood in the hallway deciding how to answer the absurd question, "Do you want the check now?" *We could do whatever we want, for the rest of our lives.* It was a natural step from there to *we might as well stay together,* as though they believed the money would reknit all those frayed old emotions from another time.

A Hint of Fraud

It was Day Three of what Graham thought of as 'The Transition Period,' the phase that came immediately after the seven-day 'Moving Out Period.' Neither he nor Valerie had sought to renegotiate that part of the contract with Sergei, thinking that the physical act of moving would be trivial, given that all of the furniture was staying behind. It was also the case that the whole transaction seemed so unreal ... the idea that the house they had bought thirty years ago for two hundred thousand dollars should be worth fifteen million dollars today ... that it was hard to be rational about lesser choices.

The problem was what they came to call 'the other stuff.' It included sports equipment dating back to their college days, filing cabinets filled with legal documents and correspondence, shoeboxes stuffed with slides, photographs and souvenirs from trips they couldn't even remember, tire chains for cars long gone, Alison's baby clothes, partial stamp collections, and an entire trunk filled with dog toys. Then there were the books: high school yearbooks, college texts, an entire set of encyclopedias curiously missing the 'Q' edition, National Geographic magazines dated from 1983 through 1993, and every hardbound and paperback that either of them had ever read. One of the books – one of Winston Churchill's memoirs -- had fourteen twenty-dollar bills scattered throughout its pages. Neither of them remembered putting the money there and they laughed at their lack of concern about whether there were more such stashes. As Valerie said, "It's amazing how fifteen million dollars changes your priorities."

It was a treasure trove of memories disguised as junk. They cleared a space in the garage and began sorting. The plan was to put everything in one of four piles – "sell," "take," "throw" or "store" -- and they agreed that every item would require them to agree as to the classification. Two days after beginning, they realized it would require another six months and that one person's "throw" was the other's most treasured possession. And it made them sad, because the sorting process resurrected memories of happier times, so different from the current 'day at a time' mentality that defined their present relationship. So when Day Seven of the Moving Out Phase arrived, almost everything in the 'other stuff' category was trucked off to a self-storage unit to await another and more leisurely triaging. Neither of them said what they were thinking, that such an activity would never happen.

They were out of their house, living in the Sheraton and evaluating their options. They had developed a couple of absolutes to guide the real estate portion of the 'what next' decision process. First, the realities of aging must be part of the decision … no stairs, close to good medical care, somewhere between urban and suburban, no more lawn care or remodeling projects. Second, they weren't going very far. They agreed that Northern California was their natural habitat and Alison was here, promising future grandchildren. In any case, Valerie's job was here and neither of them wanted to walk away from that.

Valerie was touring with their realtor, a full day of 'looking at neighborhoods.' Graham was perfectly willing to leave the early-stage reconnaissance to Valerie, so he made a date to meet their daughter at the Starbucks near the courthouse. Alison was a homicide detective for San Mateo County with a highly uncertain schedule, so he made it a point to meet her wherever and whenever she found the time. Usually, they spent the time fending off each other's attempts to pry into their respective personal lives. In Alison's case, it was her parent's concern about her love life. Or lack of one. In Graham's case, it was his daughter's solicitude; distasteful because it implied that he was getting old enough to warrant it.

But this time was different: Alison had an agenda. "Dad, there may be a problem at Mom's work." She sat back and looked at him, obviously relieved at having it out in the open.

"NEW SF? She hasn't mentioned anything to me."

"That's part of the problem. I don't think she knows."

"So why aren't you talking to her rather than me?"

"I can't. I'd be fired. And you can't say anything either, because you heard it from me." After a pause, she added, "And I thought you might have picked up some signs of what's going on."

Graham thought about it. *Alison works for the San Mateo County Sheriff's office, so whatever she's heard must be part of some kind of criminal investigation into NEW SF.* He chose his words carefully. "I'm surprised that they would share anything with you. Everybody in the department knows your family connections."

She shook her head. "There's talk of an investigation, but it's coming from the state level, not the county. An agent from their tax unit was in our office and I overheard him asking questions about NEW SF. Later – this was yesterday – a friend of mine who works specifically on financial crimes told me that the guy was requesting that the local cops – that's us – provide them with some backup surveillance support."

Graham shook his head. "Why surveillance here? NEW SF is in San Francisco."

"But the CEO and the CFO live in San Mateo County. That's Mom and Jay Gould. And NEW SF does have some small storefront programs in San Mateo, drop-in centers for teens, resale shops, that sort of thing. "

OK. If the investigator was from the state tax unit, then it's about financial stuff. NEW SF is a big not-for-profit. Doesn't pay taxes as long as its activities stay within the boundaries of what's permitted. But why would they put surveillance on the executives? Unless they think there's some fraud going on inside NEW SF ...

"Dad? Do you know anything at all about what's going on?"

He shook his head. "NEW SF is a complex business. Lots of moving parts. And it attracts a lot of attention – and political enemies – because a lot of its clients are undocumented immigrants. My guess is that somebody with a political agenda is pushing for a quiet inquiry into how they spend their money. Part of that could be a check on the life styles and habits of the key executives. It's sneaky and not very nice, but I'd guess they can do it." What he didn't say was that, if he was right, all of that presumed a criminal investigation. *Valerie's at risk.*

"Let me see what I can find out with some below-the-radar inquiries. And I don't think either of us should say anything to your mother just yet –" Just then, Alison's cell phone buzzed. She took a quick look and said, "Gotta go. But let me know what you find out."

Let's see what we can find out about local scandals. He sat staring at the Google logo on the screen and then set the search parameters for "articles" and "last 12 months" and typed in 'NEW SF.' Half the screen was immediately filled with a list of about thirty items. He scanned the titles quickly, but none of them hinted at any impropriety, scandal or investigations being opened. They were uniformly positive. *Puff pieces. Valerie must have a really good PR person. All this stuff makes NEW SF sound like the solution to most of the intractable urban problems out there.*

He erased the search history, viewing the action as a constructive form of paranoia. He had developed the habit after facing a congressional committee that badgered him to reveal his sources for a story highly critical of a particular lobbyist.

Time for some old fashioned techniques. He scrolled through the contacts list in his iPhone and dialed a number, halfway expecting the "That number is no longer in service" recording. But it rang and the woman with the familiar gravelly voice answered.

"This is Watson. My caller ID reads 'Dodd,' but the only Dodd I know quit calling me after he got a Pulitzer. Got himself an upgraded set of friends, I heard."

"Brenda. It's good to hear your voice. I miss you. And I'm glad that they haven't replaced you with a search algorithm or an eighteen-year old in Mumbai. And I wouldn't have that Pulitzer if you hadn't saved my impetuous ass a dozen times."

Brenda Watson was a disappearing breed. She had started as a 'fact-checker' for the Washington Post and had carried on the same trade for the Wall Street Journal and then the

New York Times. She was both relentless and completely objective, a rare combination. She worked free-lance for the last several years and only for a very small set of editors who she knew personally and called on her for highly sensitive stories, where 'getting it right' was sometimes necessary for the paper's survival, not just its circulation. Along the way, she accumulated – and retained -- more information than any other person Graham had come across.

"It's a brand new world, Graham. Politicians have gone from extravagant exaggeration to outright lies. *Alternative facts*, for crissakes! But I heard you're retired, out of the game."

"Not quite. Your sources confuse 'old' with 'retired.' Look, I need to find somebody who knows a lot about ferreting out financing irregularities in large social welfare organizations."

"Not for profit?"

"Yes."

"Governmental or non-governmental?"

"Non."

"Foundation or some other form of organization?"

"Not a foundation."

"Domestic or international?"

"Domestic."

"Renee Delgado."

"Huh?" *I'd forgotten how Brenda's brain works. You can almost hear the clicking sounds of the synapses.*

"Renee Delgado. I'll send her contact info to your email. She's with Treasury. Focuses on the large not-for-profits. Knows more about wrong-doers in the do-gooder industry than the rest of the world does. And there are a lot of them out there. Wrong-doers, that is."

"Thanks Brenda, I'll –"

"And Graham? If there's a real story, I know a couple of reporters that would give it the attention it deserves. Just in case you're serious about being retired."

Am I? I wonder? But I sure as hell can't write this story. He envisioned the headline: "Disgruntled husband blows whistle on executive wife." It was easy for him to promise Brenda that she would be his first call if he thought there was a real story.

His email 'pinged' thirty seconds after he ended the call. It was the promised contact info for Delgado. It was a Washington DC address and area code. He dialed the office number listed. "You've reached the voice mail of Renee Delgado. Please leave your name and number and I will return your call as soon as I can." The voice was businesslike and uninflected and he could not help thinking of the phrase "a faceless bureaucrat."

He recited his name and cell phone number and added, "Brenda Watson suggested that you could help me with some questions about not-for-profits. Please call me." His phone rang twenty minutes later. "This is Renee Delgado returning your call. Are you the husband of Valerie Dodd, CEO of NEW SF?"

Meeting With a Bureaucrat

So this is what a faceless bureaucrat looks like. So much for my stereotyping skills!

Renee Delgado was a tall – almost six-feet – and athletic-looking woman dressed in a pin-striped pants suit that would have blended well with any corporate boardroom in the country. Graham guessed that she was in her mid-fifties but didn't trust his judgment very far. She wore no jewelry other than simple earrings and she was carrying a large purse that probably doubled as a briefcase for meetings like this. She had straight short hair, black with marked streaks of grey. Her dark brown eyes and an olive-tinged complexion hinted at a southern European or Latin ancestry somewhere in her past. She was a formidable looking woman, enough so that Graham did not appreciate that she was quite attractive until she smiled when they shook hands.

Only eight hours had elapsed since her phone call, when she asked, "Are you the husband of Valerie Dodd, CEO of NEW SF?" The question left him suddenly aware that he may have started something that was now out of his control. *This is a high level Treasury official who may be conducting a criminal investigation into my wife's activities!* He was actually calculating the consequences of saying "no," and the silence became uncomfortable.

"Mr. Dodd?"

"Yes, I am the husband of Valerie Dodd. But I –"

"I'm in LA at the moment. I'd like to meet with you and can be in the Bay Area within a few hours. Are you available, say at six this evening?"

"Yes, but I –"

"Could you meet me at the Delta Lounge in the San Francisco Airport? I'll reserve a meeting room for us in my name."

"OK, I guess, but you should know –" He intended to go on to tell her that she was wasting her time talking to him; that it was ridiculous to think that he would help her investigate his wife. But she cut him off abruptly. "That's great. I appreciate your flexibility and I look forward to meeting you. And please don't mention the meeting to anyone else. That's important." She disconnected the call before he could respond, leaving him staring at the screen of his cell phone and marveling at the one-sidedness of their call. *She'd make a great cold call marketing rep ... or an investigative journalist.*

They sat on opposite sides of the oval conference table in the small room. The walnut-paneled surface was empty except for her cell phone and the business card that she slid across the table to him. It had the logo of the U.S. Treasury Department and her name and office number ... no job title or address.

He nodded at the phone. "Are you recording this?"

"No." She picked up the phone and put it in her bag. "Perhaps later, with your permission. But for now, this is entirely unofficial and off-the-record. You are a journalist, so you will appreciate the importance of that."

"And since I am a journalist ... highly experienced, mind you ... I cannot help but wonder what in the hell is going on?"

"You called me, remember? Why?" She smiled slightly as she spoke, in a way that told Graham that she was fully aware of her non-responsiveness.

"I'm chasing a rumor based on a speculation derived from a conjecture." He was pleased with himself and his impromptu response. *Tells her nothing and leaves me an out if she pulls out a subpoena.* But even as he congratulated himself on his evasiveness, he was thinking about how dumb it was to use his own name to question someone that Brenda had warned knew more about his wife's business 'than the rest of the world.'

She leaned forward on the table, narrowing the distance between them. The smile was gone. "I called Brenda. She told me you were asking about financial irregularities in large not-for-profit agencies …. social safety net kinds of organizations like your wife manages."

Time to go on offense. "Who are you, Ms. Delgado? Nobody at your level drops everything, flies off to a meeting with an unknown who is unlikely to talk to you in any case, based on an inquiry that will turn out to be perfectly innocent. Who are you and why are you here?"

"I am a senior Treasury official with a broad set of responsibilities. I try to –"

Graham stood up. "This is a fun dance, Ms. Delgado, and I'm sure you're better at it than me. But I've done it too many times with too many ill-defined 'senior officials' who are always 'off-the-record.' Have a good stay in the Bay Area." He turned for the door, wondering how far she'd let him go.

It was only half a second. "Sit down, Mr. Dodd." When he hesitated, she added, "Please," in a way that made the word a genuine plea. And the look in her eyes reinforced the single word. He sat back down, but kept his chair pushed back from the table to make the point that she was on probation.

She took a deep breath. "OK. First, I really am a senior Treasury official. I am part of a small but very elite group of investigators of financial crimes. As Brenda told you, I specialize in not-for-profits, but I also get involved along the whole economic spectrum." She paused and looked at him, as if leaving a space for questions. He said nothing.

"Second, NEW SF is being investigated. It started as a routine IRS audit, but they picked up some curious transactions and it got routed to me for follow up. I thought I was the only one who knew of the investigation, but then you call me about a rumor based on a speculation derived from a …. I'm sorry, I've forgotten the third leg of your very clever but evasive answer?"

"Conjecture. You said 'curious transactions.' What kind of transactions? Why are you investigating NEW SF?"

Her reluctance was obvious, but she finally said, "Money laundering."

Graham almost laughed out loud. *Here I was expecting tax irregularities or technical violations of some obscure government contracting provision. Money laundering?* He did not even try to disguise the sarcasm. "So how does that work for a cash-poor not-for-profit agency? I associate money laundering with Russian oligarchs and drug cartels, so I'm having trouble with the idea of struggling safety net organizations in the inner city in that business."

She leaned forward. "Look, Mr. Dodd, you're a relatively famous investigative journalist. You must have come across this kind of stuff somewhere in your career."

Actually I have, but it would help if she thinks I'm financially illiterate. So he shook his head. "Most of my expertise is about ordinary corruption ... politicians taking bribes, CEOs rigging stock options, outrageous tax frauds ... I really don't know much about your money laundering schemes."

"OK then. Here's the 'Money Laundering for Dummies' tutorial." She put her left hand palm down on the table, her four fingers spread in front of him. "There are four pieces. It doesn't work with three; you need all four."

She folded her index finger into her palm. "First, you need an individual or organization with lots of cash that they want to be able to spend without drawing attention to the fact that it was obtained illegally. This person or individual is usually the primary villain –"

"Because of the illegal manner in which they got the cash."

"Yes, and he's usually the one managing the fraud." Another finger folded under. "Second, you need a legitimate business enterprise – the washing machine, so to speak – that takes in lots of cash and that either can't or won't identify where it comes from. Its customers are anonymous in every sense. Casinos, taxicab companies, restaurants, gas stations, toll roads, bars... mostly small businesses, except for casinos."

"And a disappearing breed, what with credit and debit cards."

"Yes, but we're still a long way from the so-called cashless society. So, Party A – the one with all the cash – begins to funnel some of that cash into Party B – the legitimate business, making it look like ordinary cash revenues from providing whatever services it is that Party B is selling. For example, maybe thirty-thousand dollars gets slipped into a casino's nightly take, on top of the ordinary gaming revenues."

Graham nodded. "But it can't stay there. The whole idea is that the cash makes a round trip."

"That's where our third actor comes in ... Party C, that is usually owned or controlled by Party A. Another business entity, often more than one. A kind of business that would plausibly be a vendor to Party B. They sell their products or services to B, but they either fail to deliver them or they sell them at a super-inflated price. Maybe a ten-thousand dollar invoice from a consulting firm that never provided any real advice, or a fifteen-thousand dollar purchase of some office furniture that normally sells for three-thousand dollars."

Graham continued to play his role as diligent student. "So A gives thirty thousand to B, who then gives twenty five of it back to C – who is really A in disguise. But that money now appears to be legitimate business profits, legally earned."

"Yes. It's been washed ... laundered... and is now 'clean,' spendable without raising any eyebrows about where it came from."

"And the five thousand? The difference between the thirty that went in and the twenty-five that came out? That's the fee paid for enabling this swindle?"

She nodded. "And that's about the usual percentage. Fifteen to twenty percent, assuming that both parties A and C are able to avoid paying much in the way of income tax."

"That's three parts. You said there were four."

"Party D. There has to be an insider at Party B, usually someone that has access to the organization's financial systems so that the unusually high cash inflows and the absurdly expensive outlays don't raise red flags. And that's where your hypothetical five-thousand dollar fee goes. To the enabler."

Graham was thinking. *NEW SF would clearly qualify for the Party B role. It takes in millions of dollars in cash from the Bingo games, resale shops, moving company. And donations. But why would they take the chance –"*

She was ahead of him. "I know what you're thinking. Why would NEW SF knowingly play that game? But imagine yourself as a not-for-profit that is doing tremendous good for society. You're passionate about your mission and you know that you could do so much more if you had more resources. One day, you are approached by a well-dressed banker type who says he represents a philanthropist who wants to remain anonymous but wants to help you expand your budget by twenty percent."

"I'd be ecstatic, of course. But Valerie would never collaborate –"

"She doesn't have to collaborate. Not if there's a Party D already placed in her organization."

Valerie's never been a numbers person. That's always the first thing she delegates to others. And that would be her CFO, Mr. Jay Gould.

Time to end this. He reviewed what he had told her since she walked into the room. *Nothing about Valerie or NEW SF. She's done all the talking.* "I still think you're on a classic wild goose chase, but I can guarantee that my wife is not involved in any such fraudulent activity."

"Whatever. Right now, what I am most interested in – and why I called you -- is finding who else knows about this investigation and how they know."

He ignored her. "Ms. Delgado, you're wasting your time talking to me. You obviously know that I'm not going to say anything whatsoever that would incriminate my wife even if she was a master criminal, which she's not." He looked at his watch. "In fact, she's getting home about now. What's to stop me from warning her that she – and NEW SF – are about to become the object of a federal investigation?"

Delgado seemed distracted, only half listening to Graham. When she started talking, Graham had the feeling that it wasn't really what she wanted to say. "As we both know, there's nothing to stop you. But she's going to know of the investigation within the next couple of days anyway, as soon as I make if official. As to why I called you ... Look... Mr. Dodd ... You're obviously concerned. You leaned on Brenda to get my name. You called my office. Why wouldn't I call you back? Maybe you're angry at your wife and want to make trouble for her ... Half of the whistle blowers that I deal with are angry spouses."

This has nowhere to go but downhill from here. He leaned forward, preparing to stand up. "That's not good enough. I'm not going to help you with your investigation into my wife's agency. So ..."

"What do you think of President Trump?"

What do I think of President Trump? The question was so out-of-context that it stunned him into sitting back in his seat and staring at the woman. As for her, she seemed to relax, like someone who had crossed a line, one that set her on a course where she was along for the ride, no longer in control of the vehicle.

She waved her hand. "You don't need to answer. I've read most of your stuff and made some informal inquiries. I know what you think of him and I agree with you."

"Ms. Delgado –"

"Just listen to me. I'm entitled to that much, given that I've just put my entire career into your journalistic hands."

Her question about Trump, along with the sudden harsh language and change in her demeanor signaled that this was her real agenda, and he felt the familiar thrill go through him. *This is a reporter's fantasy ... A senior insider about to vent her innermost negative feelings about the administration.* Much later, Graham would remember this initial reaction and be ashamed because of it. But that was later. And even in the moment, he tried to give her a second chance.

"You should stop now, Ms. Delgado. I can decide to un-retire at any time. I'm still a reporter ... one who would be ecstatic to quote significant insiders telling stories out of school about the moron who happens to be our president."

She wasn't even listening. "I'm a holdover from the Obama administration, kept because the administration needs ... wants ... experienced investigators to go after enemies of the White House. They particularly like the idea of what I'm telling them about the inquiry into NEW SF. It's the kind of agency that doesn't fit with the 'Make America Great' mantra. It's not white enough and it is embedded in a 'sanctuary city,' one that they would like to discredit any way that they can. I've got free rein on this one."

"You could resign."

"I was close to doing that. But there are a couple of problems, maybe three. The most obvious one is that I like my job and I'm good at it. And we've got a team, most of whom feel like I do about the White House. If I leave, it would be like an infantryman who deserts his buddies under fire."

She looked at him sympathetically. "There's a second reason, and you're not going to like it. Despite what you think, NEW SF is genuinely dirty. It's violating about twenty different banking laws and it needs a severe intervention, no matter how much good it's doing. I'm confident of that. It will take a lot of time and legwork for me to get ready for indictments, but it *will* happen."

Everything about Valerie is business as usual. No signs of distress. She talks about her job the same way she always has. She just doesn't act like someone who's worried. Delgado was watching him closely, apparently able to trace his thoughts. She shook her head. "For what it's worth, I don't think your wife is in on the scheme. I don't think she even suspects what's happening. I may be wrong, but I don't think she's guilty of *criminal* negligence, but ..."

That's an eloquent pause. So Valerie may not go to jail, but her reputation is ruined and she'll be blamed for the agency's failures. Graham was hooked, and he knew that she knew it. He said, "So that's two of your reasons for not resigning – loyalty to your team and a genuine passion for justice. Very commendable. What's the third reason?" He heard the undertones of his own hostility to this woman and wondered at it. *You still have this instinct to protect Valerie from the consequences of her own actions. Some emotions have a long half-life.*

Delgado was clearly bothered by the question, beginning to emit very slight symptoms of nerves. He tried to help her. "Look. The White House ... every administration ... has always had an enemies list. Some of them, like Nixon, were more explicit about getting at them, but they all do it. If you go after NEW SF, you're doing it legally rather than illegally. I know it may not feel good to somebody that voted for Obama, but –"

"That's not it. This White House has got two objectives – attack its enemies and protect its friends. What I'm doing – the inquiry into NEW SF – it helps them on the enemies side, but it can do much more damage to them on the friends side. If I keep on doing what I'm doing, I'm going to call attention to some activities that they would rather not make public. And they don't know that … yet."

Most of the White House staff members are paranoid. Partly because so many of the insiders are either family members or cronies. And we've already got a Special Prosecutor zeroing in on exactly those people. And this woman is somehow caught in the middle.

"OK, you've got my attention, but this is all a little vague for me. Your boss has a secret list of enemies and friends, both sides doing bad but unspecified things. They want you to expose their enemies and cover up for their friends. You feel conflicted but are committed to doing your job. Sounds like an ordinary day at the Justice Department."

"Treasury, not Justice," she said. She was staring at the window opposite her, watching a Korean Air jumbo jet being pushed back from the jetway, but Graham doubted if she was even processing external stimuli at the moment. When he shifted slightly in his chair, she seemed startled and it took a second or two for her to refocus. *She doesn't know why she's here or what she wants from me.* So he asked the same question that he had when she came in the room.

"Ms. Delgado, why are you here? Really."

She stood and walked to the window looking out onto the tarmac. The KAL jet was still moving away from her. "NEW SF is engaged in significant money laundering and various other financial crimes that are associated with that activity. I'm quite sure of that based on evidence I've already seen, and I think I can prove that to a judge and jury."

She paused, going inward once more. Graham prodded, "And the Trump administration is all in favor of that."

She nodded, "Big time. It fits nicely with their "Make America Great" theme. We've got undocumented aliens sucking up taxpayer dollars, a sanctuary city aiding and abetting fraud, one of Hillary Clinton's pet charities going rogue, and a glaring example of why their 'drain the swamp' chant is a compelling campaign slogan."

She stopped, clearly engaged in some sort of internal debate. He cleared his throat and said, "But then there's the part they don't know …" *This is going to be a long conversation if I need to prompt her for every line.*

"It's where the money is coming from, the funds being laundered."

She's scared. And Graham began to wonder if he should be as well.

"Ms. Delgado –"

Before he could finish, she stood up, looking like she was regretting the entire meeting. "I've got to go. But I'm going to be in the Bay Area for the next few days for some first hand checking on what I think is going on. But we need to continue this discussion. I'll give you a call." And she was out the door.

Volunteer

The Delgado meeting bothered Graham, and it wasn't just because of the threat to Valerie's reputation. The woman had forced him to reconsider past decisions, ones that he had put into the "Well, that's done" category. The most obvious of these was his loyalty to Valerie. *How far am I willing to go to support her if she is in fact knowingly managing a criminal enterprise?* Just thinking about it triggered flashbacks to all those press conferences with stoical wives standing next to their famous husbands as they made apologies for their crimes. *Bill Clinton, Bernie Madoff, Bill Cosby.* The sinned-against-but-still-supportive spouse was always the woman; he couldn't think of a single instance of a man playing such a role.

The other question that Delgado raised for him was the same one that he had been struggling with for the last five years. It could be phrased in a number of ways, but its most basic form was, *how do you want to spend your time?* For most of his life, Graham thought he knew the answer. His father had worked forty years for one company, retired on his 65th birthday, and died eighteen months later, providing Graham with a determination to avoid just such a life.

So he picked a career – investigative journalism – that engaged him and ensured a continual diversity of interests. He pursued it passionately and when he won a Pulitzer at age fifty-four, he decided to go free-lance, work no more than half-time, and stay away from airplanes and wars. The economics were favorable. Valerie was earning real money, their house was paid for, Alison was launched and on her own and their investment accounts were doing well. The Pulitzer came with a check for ten-thousand dollars and he chose to interpret that as the equivalent of the literal gold watch that his father had received from the bank that had employed him for forty years.

So he taught an evening journalism course at the local community college, volunteered at a couple of non-profits, wrote some long feature articles on subjects that interested him and could be researched using nothing more than the internet and telephone, played occasional bad golf, and annoyed Valerie by being underfoot. He thought about writing another book and went so far as to engage an agent on his behalf but resisted her efforts to actually start writing.

OK, it's been a six-year-long experiment. And then Delgado waltzes into my comfort zone and teases me with the possibility of a Watergate-scale story. Am I bored? Over the hill? Do I still need to prove something to somebody? If so, what? And to whom? I don't know the answers, but I know it's time to ask the questions once more.

Once a week, Graham spent four hours working in a homeless shelter in San Francisco. It was one of the larger operations that NEW SF ran for the city, featuring two hundred dormitory style beds for men and a hot dinner served for all comers. Graham worked as a greeter, recording names and directing the stream of individuals to the various social service tables scattered around the cavernous space. He sat behind a large table that displayed a dozen small stacks of literature, each dealing with some solution to a particular inner-city pathology – homelessness, addiction, abuse, needle exchanges, AIDs, etc. A large fishbowl sat prominently on one corner, a receptacle for cash. The meals were nominally priced at "pay what you can afford" and that's what the fishbowl was for.

One of Graham's 'jobs' during his four hour shift was to watch the fishbowl, to make sure nobody took money out, and at the end of the evening to count the money along with the shelter director. After his visit with Renee Delgado and her allegation that NEW SF was laundering cash, that fishbowl loomed very large, so he paid special attention.

Less than half of the clients paid anything at all for the meal and, so far as he could tell, that was only a dollar or two, maybe even a smattering of dimes and nickels. Some of the half-dozen volunteers working in the shelter, including Graham, put in ten or twenty dollar bills and a couple of times people would wander in from the street, drop some cash into the bowl and then leave. *Valerie said they get a lot of cash donations. She called it street-corner philanthropy. But it's small potatoes; no self-respecting money launderer would be interested in a goldfish bowl with a few bucks.*

The director of the shelter was a very large black man named Nate. He was covered with tattoos and had several prominent scars. He seemed to know almost every man that came through the doors and – depending on the context – exhibited either empathy or encouragement or sometimes disapproval in ways that seemed to make the person he was talking to feel better about himself. And he did this in both Spanish and English with equal facility.

Graham had mentioned him to Valerie. "Your guy at the shelter? Nate?"

"Impressive, isn't he? He was one of the first clients to go through our prison reentry program. And you'd never guess that he has a day job as a stockbroker. He manages some of our money for NEW SF and he's very good at it."

"So why does he –"

"Work five nights a week at a homeless shelter that pays him a pittance? Aside from his belief that we saved his life, he had a sixteen-year-old son that lived on the streets and died of a Fentenyl overdose in a doorway."

That night, when Nate dumped the contents of the fishbowl onto the table and they began sorting the coins and bills, Graham said, "I hear you're a stockbroker by day." Nate looked at Graham sideways but kept on with his sorting. Finally, he said, "I hear you're a journalist. Your wife says you're really good at it."

He used the present tense. Does Valerie still see me as a working journalist? "I think maybe she's better at what she does than I ever was." He gestured at the vast interior of the shelter. "You – and she – do real things for real people. I just write ... wrote ... stories."

"We don't do enough things for enough people. But this helps." He put a very large hand on top of the paper money that he had arranged in three stacks, one and five dollar bills, and a lone twenty that Graham had put into the bowl.

He counted the money. It didn't take long. "Just over two hundred and twenty dollars. A little more than usual." He pushed the small stack of bills and coins over to Graham to verify that the count was correct. Then Nate wrote the amount in a small notebook that he took from the drawer of the table where they were sitting. Finally he bagged all of it in one of those heavy canvas bags with "Wells Fargo" stenciled on it.

"What happens to it now?"

"I drop the bag in a night depository at the NEW SF building. After that, I have no idea."

"You said that it's 'a little more than usual.'" He gestured at the notebook. "Do you keep a running tally?" Nate flipped open the notebook to show Graham two facing pages with two columns on each page. The first column was labeled "Date," the other "Amount."

"The accounting people say I don't need a record, that once it's bagged and deposited, everything is automatic. But you never know. Some anal city auditor might come along one day, take one look at me, do some racial profiling and think, 'He's skimming!'" He put the notebook back in the drawer. "This way, at least I can show them that Wells Fargo agrees with me on the amounts."

Graham said. "Your anal auditor would have to accuse me too. We both do the count."

Nate smiled in a way that seemed both ancient and sad. "Yeah, but you'd get a pass. You're white and no tats." He stood up. "And married to the woman that makes this whole thing work. See you next week." He left Graham sitting at the table thinking about Renee Delgado, his daughter Alison, Valerie and money laundering. After a bit, he took Nate's notebook from the drawer, opened it on the table and used his cell phone to take pictures of a half-dozen pages.

The Tour

They say that being both old and rich tends to make one more conservative, where 'conservative' is a euphemism for 'risk averse.' And Alden Acres sure as hell is risk aversion squared. Write the check for the five million entry fee, pay the very stiff monthly dues, and be assured that no matter what happens to you, Alden Acres will take care of you in fine style. From independent living 'for active adults,' to assisted living, to a skilled nursing facility and even an Alzheimer's unit if you are among the fifty percent of today's octogenarians who will experience the disease. Everything except the mortuary at the end of the cycle.

"There's nothing like it anywhere else."

How many times have I heard that line? And Graham actually began a purely internal cataloging of notable cases of outrageous hyperbole he had experienced, beginning with yesterday's call from his literary agent. She opened their conversation with, "You're the only person who can write this book." From there, it was a very short jump to the always-vivid memory of his editor saying, "A war is the best thing that could happen to a reporter!" *And he was right, although the several ounces of shrapnel may not be what he had in mind.*

"Graham!"

Both Valerie and Maurice Chevalier stood looking at him and he realized that the man had been talking while he'd been lost in his past and fallen ten feet behind the two of them. The man wasn't really Maurice Chevalier of course, but that's how Graham thought of him and – truth be told – the man would have been pleased by the comparison. Valerie was a different matter entirely. *Nothing that I can do will please Valerie any longer.*

Valerie's specialty was impressing people, especially self-important people like their pompous guide. The man's name was Henri Malraux and he stressed the French pronunciation when he introduced himself, even correcting Graham when he addressed him as "Henry." "Please ... the 'h' is silent. The accent is on the second syllable." He was wearing a dark business suit and a tie, a very rare sight in Northern California these days. He came to meet them at the security gate at the front entrance, saying, "This is the best place to get the whole picture" and "There's nothing like it anywhere else." He raised his arm and slowly swept it across the vista before them, like a symphony conductor asking the audience to acknowledge his musicians.

Graham still had not overcome the aura of unreality that hung over him. *Are we actually considering moving into this place? We are upper middle-class suburbanites, not at all the demographic for Alden Acres – too young, too liberal, too poor. And yet here we are.*

Malraux was right: It was impressive. Alden Acres was a broad white slash across a bright green landscape; a series of glass and steel structures that, despite their whiteness, seemed part of the coastal hills. Even the half-mile long road that ran uphill from where they stood to the center of the complex was hidden among the dense forest of magnificent oak trees.

"The low-rise structures to left and right are the residences. The common facilities are in the center. Zero carbon footprint, 100% renewable energy sources. Architectural awards from every authority that matters." Malraux recited the facts with a practiced passion that Graham objected to and he could not restrain himself.

"Where's the golf course?" Valerie glared at him and smiled at Malraux. To Graham, the expressions seemed simultaneous. She said, "It's truly beautiful, Dr. Malraux. We look forward to seeing it up close."

"Then let's do that. And please call me Henri. The "Dr." is reserved for my in-laws." He smiled to make sure they understood that it was a small joke.

Everything about Malraux was large. He had the barrel-like torso of an operatic tenor, with exceptionally broad hands extending from the precise one inch of white cuff at the end of the dark gray sleeve. As he walked between them, gesturing at the passing features of Alden Acres, he moved his arms in short arcs, somehow reminding Graham of a Bulgarian weightlifter walking across an Olympic stage. His head was a match for his body, a series of overlapping facial planes with deep-set eyes and thick lips, capped by a swept-back mane of very blond hair that added inches to his height. And his voice complemented the visuals; it was all deep tones and resonance.

Graham disliked him more and more as they progressed through the tour. *He could be a TV evangelist, one of those unctuous salesmen with his own mega-church and a foundation.* He finally broke into the patter. "I'm flattered that you've taken the time to meet us and personally show us around. Surely you have marketing people working for you who handle first inquiries like this?"

He beamed at the question. "Yes, I do. A whole team. Lots of attention. From all over. But you're special. Both of you." *That's six three-word sentences in a row. Who needs grammar or punctuation?*

"Special?"

"All of this?" Malraux waved his stubby arm to encompass the half-mile long series of gleaming white structures before them. "Nice to look at. And to live in, of course. But what really matters? It's the residents. People like you. Interesting people. People that make things happen."

"Like us?" *I'm beginning to talk like him.*

"Exactly!" He put a hand on Valerie's arm. "You are CEO of a major not-for-profit. Big part of the safety net. Very prominent." He put his other hand on Graham's shoulder. "Pulitzer-prize winner. New York Times best seller." He stood back and beamed even more broadly at the two of them.

So he's googled us. I'll bet he's also checked our credit rating and bank balance as well. No need to waste time on those 'special' people who can't afford the five-million-dollar entry fee.

"We have almost three hundred residents. Most of them are couples like you. From all over. Active achievers. The one-percenters."

Is that what we are? And what's the scale called where we're in the 99th percentile? I'm not sure I want to know the answer. "Dr. Malraux, who –"

"And here's a good example. Someone you should meet." They waited as a man and woman approached them along the walkway. To Graham, they looked like a perfectly ordinary country-club sort of couple; casually dressed, early-seventies maybe. The only novelty was that each was holding a leash, at the end of which was a small shaggy dog. The two dogs were identical and a breed that Graham could not identify. *Probably the dogs are one-percenters as well as the owners.*

"Good morning, Henri." The man stopped in front of them but the woman continued on for a few steps and then knelt to stroke her dog's back. It was a curious lapse in civility, given that Malraux obviously wanted to speak to them.

"A nice day for a walk," Malraux said to the man with a sideways glance at the kneeling woman. He raised his voice slightly so as to include her in the group. "I'd like to introduce you to Graham and Valerie Dodd. They're considering joining us at Alden Acres." The man extended his free hand and said, "It's a pleasure. I'm Frank Shanahan and this is my wife Melissa." The woman responded when she heard her name, standing with the dog in her arms and turning to face them with a smile that was obviously forced. Graham had the impression that she was frightened of them. She motioned with her chin at the dog, "This is Corky. He understands everything I say."

It was an odd way to open a conversation and it was obvious that both Malraux and Shanahan knew it. Perhaps that was why Malraux moved to position himself so as to isolate the three men from the two women and said, "Melissa, why don't you show Valerie our library? We'll join you in a moment." Melissa's smile became more real. She handed Corky to her husband and said to Valerie, "It's much more than a library. It has music tapes and jigsaw puzzles. Let me show you," and she led Valerie toward a nearby entrance. Graham watched Frank Shanahan, who had a concerned expression as he watched the two women walk away. But Malraux clearly had an agenda and began as soon as the women were ten feet away.

"Frank, I'm glad that we ran into you. Graham, the Shanahan's are a great example of the kind of residents at Alden Acres. I won't call them 'typical' because there's no such thing as a typical resident, but I know you'll have a lot in common. Frank here is a retired executive turned philanthropist and he and Melissa were among the first people to buy in. Founding members, as it were. He actually helped build the place."

Shanahan stood with a fixed smile in place as Malraux talked, looking slightly pained, and Graham wondered how many times Shanahan had heard the same little speech. He also kept glancing at the door where Valerie and his wife had disappeared and was showing small signs of apprehension. Graham felt a little sorry for him, so he asked, "What did you retire from?"

"I was a manager in a global construction company. Ran around the world giving advice to people about how to manage large projects. Very dull and technical stuff."

"And you helped to build *this?*" Graham gestured to indicate the buildings behind them.

"My company was a subcontractor. I had a very small part."

The self-deprecating description surprised Graham. *Given Malraux's introduction, I expected an ex-GE chairman or an ambassador.* Malraux perhaps felt the same way and launched into a two-minute monologue regarding the cumulative achievements of "the residents." He gave the impression that the place was overrun with famous professors, corporate titans, retired admirals and generals, and – of course – loyal wives who were every bit a match for their eminent husbands. *He's lucky Valerie's out of range; she'd be raging about sexist troglodytes and headed back to the car!*

Shanahan was clearly not listening and noticeably relieved when Valerie and Melissa rejoined them. Valerie was leaning in close, talking to the other woman but caught

Graham's eye as they came close and gave a very slight, barely perceptible shake of her head. She said, "Graham, you'll love the library. They have real books, not just downloadable digital files. And guess what? They've got your book right out front."

Sure. Just like we make sure to put the portrait of Aunt Lucy out every time she comes to visit. But he smiled politely at Malraux.

Frank Shanahan put Corky down and handed the leash to his wife, clearly eager to be gone. "Dr. Malraux is right. Alden Acres is an absolutely unique place. We look forward to seeing you here." And he took his wife's arm and started walking in their original direction, almost dragging the two dogs along the path in his haste.

It was a strange, uneasy encounter and the feeling hung over the rest of their tour, during which they in fact met a professor, an ambassador and a retired two-star general; also a world-class chef, two or three ex-CEO's and two moderately famous novelists. Malraux was extremely diligent about reciting credentials and he was careful to introduce two women, going on at length about their accomplishments. One of them was a scientist and the other apparently a filmer of documentaries. Neither was accompanied by a husband. At first, Graham suspected that the people they came across were plants, purposefully put in their path as shills for Alden Acres. But he eventually accepted that they were chance encounters and that the residents of Alden Acres were what Malraux claimed – high achievement senior citizens who also happened to be white and ungodly wealthy.

The physical setting spoke for itself. The gleaming structures were the only manmade objects in the entire mile-wide swathe of green that ran from the highway to the crest of the eastern slope of the coastal foothills. Their extreme modernism and stark white exteriors made the green even more prominent, as though to emphasize that the oaks, pines, cypress and eucalyptus had the superior claim to the space.

Malraux told them, "We're in the middle of a forest. We have deer, bobcats, and the occasional mountain lion. From where we're standing, you have access to a hundred miles of forest trails. Views of the Bay, from San Francisco to San Jose."

As usual, Graham was fixated on what was *not* said. "This is watershed land. Supposedly not for development of any sort. And certainly not without an Environmental Impact Report that would usually take about ten years. How did you overcome that?" He asked the question out of pure spite; he already knew the answer. Both he and Valerie had already done considerable research on their short list of possible new homes.

Two men were sitting on a bench about ten feet away and one of them spoke before Malraux could. "That's a really good question. Henri will tell you that we are a special-purpose not-for-profit organization dedicated to providing ecologically-sensitive life-cycle housing." He recited the phrases like one reading from the marketing brochure they had received. More than a brochure, it was a full-scale glossy magazine, the kind of thing that residents would put on their coffee table for their guests to stumble across. "All that happens to be true, but the real reason we're allowed to do what others are not allowed to do is that we've got a boatload of rich influential bastards that wanted to live in an enclave on a forest mountaintop and look down – literally -- on the less fortunate."

Malraux looked pained but smiled in a way that told Graham that he had heard this before. "Graham and Valerie, this is Butch Melendy and his partner Salvador Fender. They both had long and distinguished careers as trial lawyers, so – as you've just experienced – they tend toward melodrama."

Everybody nodded at everybody, but the two men stayed where they were on the bench, clearly interested in how the newbies would respond to the irreverence. Valerie, however, was right at home with their type and said, "I don't think I've ever met a lawyer named Butch."

The other man – Salvador Fender – smiled at her and said, "Actually, I know of two others, although they won't admit to it and neither of them is as flamingly gay as *our* Butch."

Malraux was looking decidedly uncomfortable, but Valerie had an outright grin and said, "Forgive the question, but how in hell did the two of you pass the entrance exam for this place?"

They looked at one another as though deciding who should answer. Finally, Fender said, "I suppose I *should* say, 'because Alden Acres values diversity,' but the reality is that we got in because we are just as rich, influential and bastard-like as the rest of these folks." Butch added, "It also helped that they wanted to be able to say they were fully subscribed."

Melendy stood up and held out his hand to Valerie. "Welcome to Alden Acres, Mrs. Dodd. If it matters, my given name is Melvin, so you can see why I prefer Butch.

And I do hope that *you* pass the entrance exam. We need more people like you."

"It's Valerie. And I know I qualify on the rich and bastard scales. I'm not so sure about influential."

"You'll do OK. You married well." He turned to Graham. "I've read your book. I thought it was very good. Could have used a little more passion though."

What the hell! Maybe there's a hidden camera and we're being evaluated for our cocktail party repartee. "I'm an old-fashioned reporter. I was taught that passion gets in the way of facts."

Fender had been listening to the exchange and also stood up. He said, "It does. But somebody said that insanity is the absence of every emotion except reason. I'm a great fan of balance. Passion *and* facts. Certainly in the courtroom, but also in relationships and journalism." He paused and then added, "And in politics, where – these days – passion and facts seem to be interchangeable."

Malraux cleared his throat quite loudly and they moved on, but both Valerie and Graham carried away the same uneasy question: *Where did the passion go?*

Welcome to Alden Acres

They'd been at Alden Acres for a week now and this was their first real community event. The cocktail party swirling around them was a weekly Friday night happening, but tonight it was also billed as a 'Meet the New Residents' event featuring the Dodd's and one other new couple, the retired president of one of the California state universities and his wife, a pair of decidedly old individuals who leaned heavily on their cane and stayed in one corner.

Valerie whispered, "We're younger, better looking and smarter than most of the people in this room. Why do I feel so inferior?"

Graham had asked himself the same question and had an answer ready. "Because you know that they're judging you, and not on any of the dimensions that you just listed. In their world, those are the lesser qualities." Valerie smiled, as Graham knew she would. One of the things she had always liked about him was his acute sense of irony.

"So what is it that's so important to them that we don't have enough of?"

"Subservience, for starters. And *earned* wealth, of course, not the crass kind that comes from selling your house. Then there's our lack of breeding – no titles, advanced degrees, famous ancestors or billion dollar IPO's. As they would put it, we move in different circles. But worst of all, we're latecomers. Half the people in this room are founding residents." *And God help us if they find out that we got a better deal than they did!*

They were still faintly surprised to be there. The decision had been easier than either of them had foreseen, so much so that each of them had to re-evaluate some of their self-perceptions. The first shock was when they realized that the luxurious life style promised by Alden Acres was highly appealing to them, that their prior disdain for such places was a comforting snobbery permitted to those who couldn't afford it. The contract with Alden Acres was three hundred pages long, but it came down to a simple exchange: 'I'll pay you a great deal of money if you'll promise to take good care of me until I die.' The implied codicil was 'And we'll make sure you're in very good company until you do die.'

They had spent an intensive ten days before the visit to Alden Acres looking at options, mostly at 'executive homes' for rent. Given the nature of the housing market, they had been able to look at everything on the market. So it was perhaps not surprising that the final decision was made so easily.

Graham didn't remember who asked the question. "What do you think about Alden Acres?" Nor did he remember the discussion of pros and cons that followed. But he did remember the clinching argument against it.

"We're not that old." The decision to buy into Alden Acres was a stark reminder of aging, although everything about the place was designed to disguise the reality that it was the equivalent of an elephant's graveyard for rich folks. Emptied of its inhabitants, the place would resemble a five-star hotel in Geneva or a very well-endowed 'institute' in Aspen. But there were no children, no families, and residents in wheelchairs or using walkers were common.

The other and related objection was, "It's too soon." It was particularly hard for them to accept the fact that this was one of those 'for the rest of my life' types of decisions, like getting married or deciding to major in molecular biology or have a child. And, of course, there was the other thing, the lurking sense that their marriage, this old but new venture, this fresh start brought about by a slightly drunk Russian with too much money to be sensible, might not work and that this was not a good time to be making long term commitments.

So, two days after the tour of Alden Acres, they called Malraux to tell him of their decision, explaining that they thought it was too soon. "We're at least ten years younger than most of your current residents. Valerie is still working and we're not sure we're a good fit."

They listened while Malraux essentially repeated his "There's no place like it" spiel once more. Graham finally interrupted. "And it's a big financial commitment. We're rich, but we're not used to commitments of this size. It makes us nervous."

"Graham, Valerie. We really want you at Alden Acres. Can I call you back within the hour? I want to see if we can find a way to lessen your concerns."

"Sure, but—"

"Thanks. I'll be back to you shortly." In fact, it was twenty minutes.

"I have a proposal. We think of it as a deferred admission program. Reserved for couples that we badly want to join us. You sign a three-year lease and have the *option* to become full residents at the end of that period and pay the entrance fee at the rate prevailing at that time."

They were on speakerphone, and Valerie spoke first. "You said 'option.' Does that mean that we can walk away after three years if we choose? Without any obligation or payment?"

"Absolutely."

Graham said, "Henri, can we put you on hold for a moment?"

He turned to Valerie. "Nice to be wanted, isn't it? It's funny he never mentioned this option during our tour."

"Maybe he consulted with his boss, whoever that is. Or maybe he's running a pyramid scheme and desperately needs our five million to pay off an earlier sucker?" But Graham could see her processing the possibilities.

Graham held the phone up. "So?"

"Three years is about right. Gets you almost to Medicare age and me to retirement time. And we have the option if we want it. I think I like it."

He toggled the 'on' button. "Henri, it's a deal. Can you send me the various legal documents to look over?"

He thought Henri's response was tinged with relief, "That's wonderful. I'll start drafting the documents immediately. There is one additional condition, but I'm sure you'll approve. This agreement is entirely between us. As far as our existing and any new residents are concerned, you are full-fledged and lifelong members of the Alden Acres community. I'm sure you understand how important that is."

Ten minutes later, another call was made. There were no "hellos" or "goodbyes," just two sentences. "Graham Dodd is going to be living at Alden Acres. You need to be careful around him."

Henri Malraux was a textbook cocktail party host. He made sure that the new residents got to meet everybody in the room. About an hour in, Graham did a very rough headcount and came up with about a hundred, less than half of the total number of residents. He mentioned that to Malraux, who seemed unbothered. "Many of our residents are travelling. Some have second homes. And some are just plain reclusive. Privacy is an important feature for many of our residents."

Once again, Salvador and Butch were close by and listening. Butch said, "For example, there is no comprehensive list of the residents' names or apartments. If you choose, you can remain anonymous ... Garbo-esque."

"Or," Salvador added, "you can – like Butch here – be distressingly conspicuous. Leave them alone, Butch."

Valerie said, "It's OK, Salvador. We don't need a list. I can only remember half-a-dozen proper names in any case." Just then, Malraux brought the McNeal's and Shanahan's to join them. "These are the first couples you met on your tour, so they are especially pleased to have you among us." There was a flurry of handshakes between the men and polite nods for the women. Strangely, conversation dwindled to almost nothing. Other than Butch and Salvador, each of the other three couples seemed to carry with them a husband-wife tension that was sufficiently apparent that it stifled the usual small talk. The awkwardness persisted until Melissa Shanahan simply walked away to stare out the window. Her husband smiled an apology and went to join her. At that, Helen McNeal handed her empty glass to her husband and said, "I need a drink" and headed for the bar,

When they were alone, Valerie said to Graham, "It's funny. The only ones that seem to actually like their partner are Butch and Salvador. And they're gay."

Graham said nothing, leaving Valerie to make the association with their own marriage.

The Tipping Point

It was a classic case of the straw that broke a camel's back, a moment of critical mass that is not recognized as such until much later, even though such incidents – all those preceding straws -- occur frequently throughout a lifetime.

Like Albert. It was a long time ago, early in Graham's newspaper career. He was a very young reporter sitting in a courtroom. The defendant, a sixty-eight year old retired carpenter named Albert Swenson, was on trial for murdering his wife of forty-seven years. He pleaded guilty, but the judge asked, "Why did you do it, after all that time together?" and the man said, "Because she wouldn't let me use cream on my cereal." Graham was too young at the time, without enough experience, so he wrote it as a light one-paragraph human-interest story, but the exchange stayed with him and, decades later, he felt that he understood the motive. It even had a place in popular culture. It was called the 'tipping point.'

It had happened a thousand times before, varying only in context.

"Why are you walking the dog now, for God's sake?"

The question, with its characteristically harsh tone and stress on the word 'now,' caused Graham to stop, his hand on the handle of the door while the chocolate Lab looked at him with her big brown eyes and the "I must have done something wrong" expression that was her standard response whenever Valerie used that tone. She was Alison's dog, so Graham allowed that she did not know them well enough to know that it wasn't her fault.

By Valerie's standards, it was an ordinary line, a throwaway comment totally without malice or even the slightest bit of irritability, a genuine question of little consequence rather than a criticism of his inability to do as he was told, and most certainly not in any way an excuse for him walking out of their life together, like a petulant child who didn't get his way.

In fairness, she had been talking in this peremptory fashion throughout her life, first to her younger brothers and sisters, then to her parents as they sank slowly into their second and final childhood. For Graham, however, the question embodied her entire worldview. She could just as well asked, "Why aren't you doing what I told you to do?" or, more declaratively, "You don't listen." Either form would convey the key notion: that he lacked judgment and needed guidance on matters both small and large.

As usual, he evaluated the alternatives. *Respond in kind? You know how well that works! Instant escalation. No hope of a dialogue. Maybe something more subtle? Along the lines of 'Are you OK? You sound stressed. Is something bothering you? Is there anything I can do?' I could try reason; explain that I was on a long call with Alison and the dog was sleeping. But that would quickly become a harangue about my inability to manage my life.*

I could leave the dog and just walk away. If I did that – really left – she'd see it as a vast overreaction to a trivial slight and her retelling of the incident with our common friends will be that of head-shaking puzzlement as to my capriciousness. She'd fail to see the cumulative effect, like someone driven insane by the social equivalent of the Chinese water torture or bleeding to death by ten-thousand pin pricks.

Valerie's recollection was different, of course. Later, she would tell her women friends, "I told him to walk the dog at two-thirty! But, as usual, he didn't listen. Looks at me with that blank stare, saying nothing, leaving me to guess whether he's even heard me or is processing the third-order consequences of actually scheduling something concrete. He calls it 'lateral thinking,' making it sound like some rarefied cognitive talent. What it *is* is pure obstinacy, a refusal to do anything I suggest. Goes whenever it's convenient for *him*! No thought about what's good for me. Or the dog either, for that matter!"

When Graham returned from the dog park, he stood for a while at the entrance to the building, recalling the long ago courtroom scene with Albert Swenson. *She said, 'I told you that cream is bad for you! Why won't you listen to me!' and he took an ordinary hammer out of a kitchen drawer and hit her once in the middle of her forehead. Then he called the police and ate a bowl of cereal – with cream -- while he waited for them.*

He tied the Lab to the bench and walked the hundred yards to the main building. He went to the front desk and said, "I'm Graham Dodd, a new tenant. I'd like to reserve one of the guest rooms for a few days."

Meeting in the Woods

The man in dark clothes was a thousand yards up the hill from Alden Acres, in a small clearing near the crest of the hill and leaning against the front of the small forest green pickup truck that he had rented earlier in the day. He was considering a world that made him exceedingly uncomfortable. His first problem was that he had become accustomed to harsh landscapes, all rock and sand, painted in dull colors and framed by far off mountains. This dense greenery with its muted sounds and lack of horizons did not feel right. It was claustrophobic and threatening. The other problem was by being here he was violating a rule, the one that said, "Never let the enemy pick the meeting place." He thought about moving further downhill but the uneven ground and steep slope made walking slightly tricky. He had only two toes on each foot and had learned the hard way about how that affected his balance.

He remembered Omar's tutorial on the day he lost the toes. It was the morning after the night that everything went wrong. He regained consciousness to find himself sitting on the ground with his back to the overturned forklift, looking at the still-smoking remains of the helicopter. His hands were tied and his legs were stretched out before him, his bare feet pasty white against the dark rocky surface. The man he came to know as Omar was sitting on the ground facing him and holding a small bolt cutter in one hand.

As soon as Vargas opened his eyes, Omar smiled at him and asked in heavily accented English, "Where is my money?"

When he answered, "I don't know," Omar leaned forward and put the little toe of Vargas' right foot between the blades of the bolt cutter. "I can ask this question twenty times before we move on to other parts." He paused to allow Vargas to figure out why the number "twenty" and seemed disappointed when he displayed no reaction. "So, again, where is my money?"

"I don't know." Omar did not seem disappointed by his answer; instead, he smiled and began his tutorial on torture. "I'm doing this to you for the pain it causes." He looked into Vargas' eyes and squeezed the handles together. *Snip!*

"Was that painful?" He moved the bolt cutter to the other foot. "I prefer to go back and forth. There is a word for it, in your language. But my English is poor."

"Symmetry," said Vargas, wondering at his own complicity in his torture. But Omar smiled at him. "Some say that cutting the toes off makes it hard for prisoners to run away, but that's only if you take all of the toes. And even then, special shoes can compensate. Where is my money?"

Snip!

"I can stop whenever you decide to tell me something I need to know. Like what happened to my money. Personally, I don't think the pain is that bad; it's more about the psychology of losing body parts. Tell me what you think."

He paused, but Vargas just looked at him.

Snip!

"Seventeen to go."

Omar's matter-of-fact monologue was the worst part, along with his need to explain exactly what he was going to do to him. It seemed to go for a long time, especially after he set the bolt cutter aside and started with other tools, although later he learned that it was only four hours, allowing for the intervals of unconsciousness. Omar was nothing but a pragmatist and once he accepted that the money was irrevocably gone and that the CIA would probably think he had stolen it, he shifted alliances yet another time and joined with the Taliban to fight the Americans and British. That same pragmatism led him to adopt Vargas as a key advisor.

"You know about weapons and tactics. You have trained hundreds of Afghan soldiers. You know how the Americans think. And I will pay you. You can afford special shoes!" And he laughed.

It was an easy decision for Vargas. He could accept the offer or he could be shot, so that it was easy for him to set patriotism and loyalty aside. He was already a mercenary of sorts and his last employer had just abandoned him. So Vargas stayed with Omar. And he did not regret his choice because Omar listened to his advice and enabled him to kill people. But he did not forget those first few hours or what Omar had done to him.

He became a Muslim, indistinguishable from the other fighters in the visible dimensions and fully accepted, first with the Taliban, then al Qaeda and finally ISIS, moving freely between Afghanistan, Iraq and Syria according to Omar's shifting allegiances. Over the years, he grew a bank account in Lebanon and waited. Every now and then, he would search the internet for a particular name. One morning, it was there.

On the day he left, he drove Omar to a crossing point from Turkey into Syria, telling him that they were meeting a half-dozen Islamic State recruits from Europe. They stood at the crest of a rocky hill and waited long enough that Omar became impatient. When he turned to Vargas to complain, he shot him twice in the abdomen and then – very gently – supported him as he slid to the ground, his back resting against the driver's door of the very old Mercedes. Then Vargas sat back on his heels and watched the comprehension seep into Omar's eyes.

Omar held his hands before his eyes and watched his blood as it dripped from his fingers. He began to tilt, sliding down to his right until his head rested against the curve of the fender. His eyes closed, but his voice was strong. "I knew you would not forget. I was foolish to trust you but it has been so long ..."

Vargas spoke gently. "You have been good for me, in your way. But it is time for me to go. Insh allah, you will die quickly. But I want you to experience this first ..." He took the very large knife that he always carried and cut away the laces on Omar's boots, pulling them off, slicing away the socks and leaving the two pale feet resting on the rocky ground.

"Tell me what you think of this. Is it painful?" He lifted the left foot by the heel and began to cut, starting with the small toe. Omar smiled at him.

That was three months ago. Since then, he had been in Turkey, Germany, England and Canada, shedding parts of his identity every time he crossed an international border. Each of those crossings used up more of his bank account and with each withdrawal he thought again of the pallet stacked with bundles of U.S. currency, remembering how massive it looked in the middle of the Huey's cargo area.

He remembered waiting at the rendezvous point and watching the helicopter materialize out of the dark sky. He remembered shooting the three men, but it ended there.

Omar told him the rest of the story as he reconstructed it from the scene.

"We were thirty minutes late. It took longer than I thought to break away from the fight. The truck was gone, but your helicopter was still there. It never got in the air. The rotor chewed up the ground for a hundred yards and the machine must have been spinning around at the same time. It was still burning when we got there, with the two pilots still strapped in their seats. The CIA was quite dead, but we found you halfway along the track. You must have been thrown out of the machine. Nobody else, no live people, no truck. And especially no money. My money."

The air was very still in the small clearing in Northern California, although the tips of the trees were moving, just catching the onshore breeze as it flowed over the crest. And it was quiet; the greenery absorbed the sounds of civilization only a mile down the hill from where the man stood leaning against his truck. His impatience grew by the minute, to the point where he cursed aloud and pushed himself away from the hood of the truck. It was only then that he saw the figure twenty feet away, standing at the edge of the clearing and watching him.

That's not him. Too young. Maybe a hiker? But then the newcomer said, "Cursing is OK. Very American. But cursing in Arabic, as you just did, that's careless. Especially these days."

They looked at each other and, although they had never met nor even talked, each of them recognized the other. Not who they were, but *what* they were. Perhaps it was the way they kept their hands in sight and watched one another. It greatly simplified the dialogue that followed.

Vargas said, "Archer was supposed to come, not send some one."

"That would have been as careless as cursing in Arabic. He has no reason to trust you. So he asked me to meet you. My name is Karnek."

"I don't care what your name is. But it's important that you know who I am ... what I want from him."

"I think I know what you want. A lot of money that doesn't belong to you."

"Then you know – and he knows – that I need him. That we have ... a shared interest ... one where cooperation benefits both sides. It should lead to a form of trust."

The other man nodded and smiled. "Yes. Cooperation based on the reality of mutually assured destruction." The smile went away. "But he thought that you might be more interested in getting even. So he sent me."

Vargas just looked at him, still trying to decide how to deal with him. *How many times have I thought about just that... getting even? But there's always that memory of that solid cube of money.* "I don't care about revenge. It all happened too long ago. And I would have done the same thing that he did. So, no hard feelings." *The mission was to get the bundle on the ground. The Huey was down and on fire with me in it and the Taliban was coming over the hill. No time to retrieve bodies even if the man wanted to.*

The man named Karnek broke into his thoughts. "Suppose I told you that ... what you want ... It's all gone ... It's been sixteen – almost seventeen – years after all."

Who is this person and why hasn't he already done for himself what I'm trying to do? Both of us are professionals of a sort, dealing with an amateur client. "I wouldn't believe you. I've checked. The man is rich, even though he has no source of income other than his retirement account." He gestured down the hill, in the direction of the white buildings that he could not see. "Gone? I don't think so. He lives well, far beyond his apparent means ... he lives like a person with a secret bundle of cash. "

Vargas went on. "I think we're done here. Tell him that I'll be here tomorrow at the same time and that he needs to be here. Alone." He got back into his truck and drove away. The other man watched him go, thinking. *This is not going to end well.*

Karnek

Before technology changed the world, physiology was an important determinant of occupation. Warriors were strong, basketball players tall, and fighter pilots had keen eyesight. A fat man did not win marathons, nor did a slightly built woman operate jackhammers. In such a world, stereotyping was a useful social bias. If a banker shook hands with a carpenter, the calluses – or lack of them – told each of the men something about the other.

Now, with computers, artificial intelligence, drones, robots and all of the 'let's substitute capital for labor" mentality that went with it, almost anybody could be almost anything. The anonymous person standing next to you in the elevator could be a crane operator, investment banker, ship captain or a schoolteacher. Stereotyping still occurred, but it was pure Hollywood-induced bias, so that a muscular black man with a shaved head and tattoos was probably an ex-con and that slightly shaggy man carrying a thick book, smoking a pipe and wearing a bow tie surely must be a professor of some sort.

In such a world, Karnek was nondescript to the point of being invisible. Almost everything about him was *average*. He was neither fat nor thin, neither tall nor short. His hair was wispy and brownish, his eye color a washed out greenish brown. He wore chinos, earth-colored V-necked sweaters and – when the temperature dropped – a baggy tan windbreaker. If he purchased clothing with a logo, he would use a razor blade to remove it. He had a pleasant voice, but spoke infrequently, avoiding controversy of all forms. He was one of those people that left no impression whatsoever on those that he encountered ... unless he wanted to.

Among other trades that he pursued from time to time, Karnek was an assassin, although he did not think of himself in that way, preferring to think of himself as "a facilitator of unusual transactions." He had few employers and long stretches of time would go by without any contact, but the old man was his longest association and he had done more for him than any of the other shadowy figures that enlisted him.

Karnek had always thought of him as 'the old man' in his client list, even before he became old in a chronolgocial sense. It was because the man lacked humor or any sense of wonder. Karnek had never met anyone who did so much harm to others while displaying so little anger, empathy, satisfaction or any of the other emotions that distinguish a man from the lesser animals.

It was thirty months ago. The call from the old man was typical. "A person will call you shortly. I want you to help him. It is important that he should not know that I referred you." Karnek said, "OK," and the line went dead.

The client was sitting with a woman, each of them drinking a plain black coffee at an outside table at the Starbucks they'd selected for a first meeting. The place was crowded with the usual mix of techies, students and retired men with nothing to do. The book – a Tom Clancy paperback – sat prominently on the table to mark them as the ones he was looking for. He watched them for ten minutes. *A married couple. For a long time. Very comfortable with one another. But she's the one to watch ... the decision maker. He will do what she tells him to do.*

Both the man and woman watched the other customers, thinking that it would be easy to identify the man they were meeting and they were surprised when the ordinary looking man pulled out the chair opposite them and sat down. They hadn't even seen him come in.

"I'm Karnek. You wanted to see me. About a job." The way he said it, it wasn't clear which of them was the jobseeker. But it quickly became apparent that the woman was the one that he would be speaking to. The man had his head down, paying attention only to his coffee. The woman sat erect, her eyes assessing him, as if meeting a blind date and finding him unpromising.

She was expecting more. *I told Robert that I needed somebody 'special,' and Robert said that he knew somebody that knew somebody.* "I'll call him, but the kind of person you want may not be interested. All I can do is start the process." *And then, when I thought we were done, he said,* "Are you sure you want me to make the call? Once you start, it's hard to reset."

Her first impression was a mixture of surprise and disappointment. The man sitting across the table could have been a bus driver or an actuary. There was no threat to him; no hint of suppressed violence or the barely concealed greed that she had envisioned as essential for transactions of this sort. He sat quietly with his hands folded on the metal table between them, waiting patiently to be acknowledged.

She spoke first. "Thank you for coming. I wasn't sure you would."

"It's a favor for a friend. His recommendation gets me here listening to you, but that's the only commitment." *They – she -- does not need to know that I have already accepted the job. That would only complicate our relationship.*

"I understand, and I appreciate the chance." She hesitated, suddenly aware that she had no idea how to proceed. It was not that she was engaging in a criminal conspiracy; she had done that before, but always as an agent for her husband or broker for a corporation or government department where they had deniability and, if that was not enough, where serious people would watch their backs. This was new, being on her own, and it was not a pleasant feeling.

She began, "Nobody can know—" but the man stood up abruptly, looking instantly tired of the conversation. "You're wasting my time, about to tell me all the conditions that you're going to impose. I think this is a bad idea." He half-turned away to leave.

"Wait! Please." *My source said, "He's hard to deal with. He doesn't care about your motives or any of the "why" questions, just the "who, what, where, and when" of getting it done. He will do exactly what he says he will do. No more, no less. And he expects the same from you. He is not to be taken lightly."*

"We need help." But the man just stood there, waiting for more. She looked around, suddenly conscious of the space around them. "We have a very large amount of money – in the form of cash – that we need help with."

Karnek stared down at her, considering among other things why anybody at this stage of negotiation would voluntarily disclose that they have a lot of cash lying around. But finally he nodded and sat back down. "So what kind of help? Protection? Storage? Money laundering? Transport?"

The woman shook her head as Karnek ran though the list. "We've got the transport and storage taken care of. The rest we need help with. We will pay you well."

"How much cash are we talking about?"

The woman smiled at the absurdity of what she was about to say. "We don't really know. We've never counted it. But it's somewhere around a hundred million dollars."

It took him six months to get all the parts aligned. During that time, Karnek grew to appreciate the woman's instinctive grasp of what was required, of how much risk was tolerable. She was the one who found Jay Gould. "I met him at a small dinner party. He's smart, but greedy. Feels undervalued where he works. And where he works? It takes in large amounts of cash from several different sources that we could piggyback on."

He took it from there, and in the two years since then, he'd heard from the woman only a few times. The man was his main contact and it was quite clear to both of them that he was doing her bidding. Karnek continued to be impressed by the man's acceptance of that role. So when he got the call from her husband last week, he knew that something had changed.

"We have a different kind of problem that we need help with. There are some people that are difficult for us to deal with. Someone has turned up that knows what we've got and where we got it."

Karnek noted that the man said 'we' but didn't mention his wife. But all he said was, "Tell me about the people who are difficult."

"His name is Vargas, and he wants half of the money."

Breakdown in Negotiations

This time Vargas waited in his pickup, tucked out-of-sight among the trees bordering the clearing on the crest of the hill above Alden Acres. It was late in the day and the fog blowing in from the Pacific filtered through the trees, moving with surprising speed and lowering the temperature rapidly. The fog also enabled Karnek to get within ten yards of the truck before Vargas saw him. He was carrying a canvas duffel bag and wearing a tan windbreaker zipped to his chin. He stopped in front of the truck, put the duffel down on the grass, put his hands in his pockets, and simply stared until Vargas got out and confronted him.

"You again. I told you I wanted to talk to the person you work for."

"What you want and what you get are different."

He spoke in a mild, matter-of-fact tone, in sharp contrast to the content of his insult. Vargas seemed to consider the statement, then brought his right hand out from behind his back. It was holding a large handgun and he let it hang loosely at his side.

Karnek nodded at the weapon. "I'm just the messenger, but if you shoot me, you lose the contact and let the man know that you're a lousy negotiator. Why don't you put the gun away?"

"So. This is a negotiation?" The gun stayed at his side.

"Not quite. But I have an offer. From him to you."

"Let me see your hands." Vargas lifted his arm, so that the muzzle pointed approximately at the man's midsection. "Slowly."

Karnek brought both hands out very slowly. They were empty. "Why not be completely sure? So there are no mistakes." And he took the few steps to the truck, leaned against the hood with his arms extended and his feet spread wide. Vargas put the handgun in his waistband and patted Vargas down, moving his hands down from his shoulders to his ankles. Then he moved back and he and Karnek faced one another again, separated by four or five feet. Vargas still held the handgun but pointed at the ground between them.

"OK. So now we know that nobody gets shot," Vargas said. "So tell me about this offer."

"Two million dollars in hundred-dollar bills." He nudged the canvas bag with his left foot. "It's in there."

"And what does he get in return? Other than to keep all the rest for himself?"

"You go away and leave him alone."

"Is that… this offer … is that what you advised him to do?"

"I don't give advice. I just do what the man asks me to do."

"Well, I'll tell you what –"

Karnek interrupted, still thinking about the conversation with the man when he picked up the duffel bag. "But if he had asked for my advice, I would not have recommended paying you *any* money. In my experience, blackmail is an addiction. You would come back." He shook his head. "But he feels that you have something coming. I think he feels bad about leaving you behind. Even though he thought you were dead."

The woman would have agreed with me. But she wasn't there.

"Suppose I want more than two million?"

"Not to be. This is a one-time offer. Take it or leave it."

Vargas raised the gun slightly. "What if I shoot you, take the bag, and reopen the negotiations with the man himself?"

Karnek looked away, seeming to look for something within the fog. *He's decided. I suppose sixteen years of brooding about what happened requires an outlet; something more dramatic than walking away with a duffel bag filled with cash.* He sighed and asked, "So. Will you accept the man's offer?"

Vargas was staring at Karnek but not seeing him. *He's trying to decide whether he's better off shooting me and dealing directly with the man, or whether to counter-offer with me as the broker.*

Vargas chose the latter option. "I'll keep the two million as a good-faith deposit. Tell the man I want another –"

The gun was in the right-hand sleeve of Karnek's jacket. He had designed it and the sling that held it in place himself after testing several varieties of derringers. It was a three-shot twenty-two caliber device in a plastic frame, weighing less than a pound and accurate up to no more than ten feet. When Karnek made a slight motion with his wrist and raised his arm, the bullet had only two feet to travel.

They met at the same Starbucks. It had added an outdoor seating area in the more than two years that had elapsed and they sat in a remote corner, removed from other customers. As before, when Karnek arrived, both the man and the woman were waiting, but the relationship between them had clearly changed. This time, it was the woman who kept her eyes down and her chair turned away from the two men. And it was the man who took the lead.

"Is it done? Did he take the money?"

Karnek sat down and looked from one to the other. The woman would not meet his eyes and the man was making little twitchy motions to keep her attention. "He wanted to take the money, but only as a deposit. He wanted more."

The man started to speak, but Karnek cut him off. "But to answer your first question, it is done. I killed him."

The woman looked up sharply, seeing him for the first time. But the man did the opposite, looking away and shaking his head. "Was that necessary? You could have –"

"It was necessary," said Karnek. The woman spoke simultaneously, "It was the right thing to do. He would keep coming back." She looked surprised at her own outburst, but then said with some vehemence. "He was supposed to be dead anyway. For sixteen years now." Then she sank back into herself as though exhausted by her display of emotion.

The man tried once more. "Did you have to –"

Karnek stood up. "You can cancel our arrangement at any time. Do you want me to quit?"

"No," the woman spoke softly. "We need someone just like you." She reached out to lay her hand on her husband's arm. After a slight pause, "Tell him, Griffin."

The man spoke the words but he was looking at his wife. "Yes, she's right, Karnek. We need you. More than ever."

CEO at Work

"My time is up, Ms. Dodd, but I want to close by stating for the record that I think you and your organization are prototypes for the society that we need to become. Keep up the good work."

So much for the softball questions and self-congratulations. Now the hard part.

Valerie sat stoically while the Democratic representative passed the microphone to his Republican colleague, reminding herself not to grimace. It wasn't hard. She'd played this game many times, usually in Sacramento but every now and then on the big stage in DC.

The legislator leaned forward, fumbling with some papers in front of him. She waited patiently, knowing it was all an act. The man was from an all-white rural district in the far northern corner of California and was quite open about his views of people like her. "Ms. Dodd, I want to say up front that I'm a real admirer of yours – *"She smiled to herself. Remember: Rule One: When politicians speak, ignore the first phrase. It is a lie designed to set up the real message that begins in the next phrase "* – but I can't help but worry about your budget. You're spending ..." he fumbled with his notes ... "$140 million of taxpayer money every year."

Actually, it's $132 million, but – Rule Two – never correct a politician while the TV cameras are on. "Approximately, yes sir. And I appreciate that's a big number. And we're also raising another $50 million from private sources. We are the largest provider of essential safety net services to your constituents and citizens."

"Well, they're not all *citizens* now, are they?"

Congratulations, senator. You got your sound bite out there for all your bigoted followers! "They are people in need. That's all that we require to offer our services."

The man didn't even pretend to be listening. "And this $50 million that you raise. Much of that seems to come from Bingo games, selling raffle tickets – I'd call that gambling -- and running a whole slew of companies that compete with legitimate small businesses – a moving company, thrift shops, ..."

"Those are also job-training programs, sir. And as I've laid out in my written submission to this committee ...."

It went on for another hour, long enough that her face felt frozen into a permanent expression of intense interest, as though she was hearing the questions for the first time and found them fascinating. As she left the hearing room, Jay Gould joined her. "Nice job, Valerie. You really should be sitting on the other side of the table."

Gould was her Chief Financial Officer and had been for several years, but he still didn't understand her. She stopped and looked at him. "Me? A politician? I don't think so." They walked on a few steps and then she added, "How about you? We probably pay you about half of what you could make in the corporate sector."

"Nope. I like my job. And the two of us work well together."

Yes we do. The City Magazine called us "Ms. Outside and Mr. Inside." Jay manages the contracts, operations and finance and I deal with the people and the politicians. Between us, we do a lot of good.

Gould was thinking along the same lines as they walked back to the parking lot where their company car was parked, although his view of where the credit was due was slightly different. *She is good.* *But the place would go to hell in the proverbial hand-basket if I walked away.*

He was probably right. NEW SF was one of the largest and most complex social service complexes in the country, serving a population of addicts, homeless, immigrants, mentally ill and other developmentally disabled citizens of the Bay Area. The $132 million of public funds came from over 300 separate contracts – federal, state and local – each with its unique and Byzantine compliance requirements. The fifty million of other funds generated by their own enterprises, on the other hand, came without strings and minimal reporting requirements. Among other things, it meant that they could pay decent salaries, particularly for the executive team. It also meant that they needed each other.

The complexity was important to Gould, because he was the only one who could visualize all the interconnected parts and the adjustments required to operate in an environment where cause and effect relationships were so murky. It meant that any manager within the organization who needed resources had to ask him, "Can I do that? Where can we find the money so that I can ...?" The sentence "You need to see Jay about that" was the catchphrase that ended many management meetings. This gave him tremendous status, both within the agency and its primary client – the City of San Francisco. But the real value of the complexity was that it enabled him to run a sophisticated and highly profitable criminal enterprise on the side.

It had been running for eighteen months now; long enough and smoothly enough that he wondered why he'd waited so long to launch the business. It was typical of Gould that he conveniently forgot that neither the business nor its methods were of his doing.

The man had approached him in the gay bar in Oakland that he visited every Friday night. There were other and better choices much closer to home, but he was convinced that his career was dependent on him staying in the closet, even in San Francisco. The fact that he ordinary looking man who slid into the booth opposite him knew him and was seeking him out was slightly alarming. As was his directness ...

"My name is Karnek, and I have a business proposition for you."

Gould looked at him closely but could see nothing to help him assess the man. "I don't think I'm interested."

"Your salary at NEW SF is one hundred and forty-five thousand. With my deal, it could be three times that."

Gould's look of surprise and the slight hesitation in his response told Karnek that the deal was done, although Gould didn't know it yet. He asked, "Is it legal?"

Karnek said, "No," and was unsurprised by Gould's complete lack of any reaction.

Karnek's tutorial on the finer points of money laundering ran for the next month. Gould was an apt student. He already was good at finance and his natural greed provided all the motivation needed. They ran with small amounts at first but quickly scaled up to the point where their system could handle several hundred thousand dollars a month. Karnek was pleased with the fast start, but knew that Gould would eventually be troublesome.

Valerie sat staring at the phone on her desk. She'd just listened to Alison's voice message that closed with the question that Valerie realized she'd been avoiding for the past two weeks ... "What's going on with you and Dad?" She listened to it three times, trying to decide if the question and the tone in which it was asked signaled merely a child's plaintive and inalienable claim on her parents' full attention or whether it was a genuine concern for their marriage, grounded in the unquestioning belief that it was worth preserving.

She's like him. The same way of thinking, generating scenarios, options and alternatives. Analyzing forever, always seeing both sides, putting off decisions until the last minute. Missing the obvious, especially if it involves 'soft' stuff – feelings instead of facts. They're smarter and funnier than everybody around them so that when you put them together, they automatically play off one another, in their own little bubble, even if I'm with them. It's a lonely feeling, worse now that we see each other so little.

So when Alison asked, "What's going on with you and Dad?" she didn't tell her about their slow tilt toward divorce. Instead, she brushed it off, saying something about "...him being in one of his huffs. He'll get over it."

The reality is that the idea of life without Graham somehow seems to have gone from possible to plausible. Maybe because those words – I want a divorce – are about to be out in the open, hanging there non recallable and ominous. I can visualize ... even look forward to ... how much easier it would be for me if he wasn't around.

"Valerie?" Jay Gould was standing in the doorway, looking at her with a trace of concern and she realized that he'd said her name three times before it got through to her. "Sorry Jay. I was daydreaming. What's up?"

He came in and sat down in the chair alongside her desk. "Good news for a change. The Mission Street bingo game is up by a solid twenty-percent over last year. I thought at first it was a fluke, but it's real and it's not going away."

"That is good." Valerie ran the numbers in her head. *We got fifty million in business income last year and bingo was the largest piece of that, about thirty-five million. And the Mission Street game is the largest single bingo site, maybe fifty percent of the bingo revenues. So twenty percent ...* "That's like a couple of million bucks more? How come? I thought those games were maxed out."

Gould's expression didn't change, but inwardly he reminded himself that Valerie Dodd was good. *Maybe she doesn't like the business side of the organization, but don't pretend that you can feed her bullshit without her knowing it.* "They are, in terms of the attendance figures. But the Mission District demographics have changed. The millennials have moved in in droves and rediscovered bingo of all things. We're getting a lot of the young professionals that have decided they're willing to pay a lot for a studio apartment in the Mission just to say that they live in San Francisco. They've got a lot more money and a higher tolerance for risk than our traditional players."

Gould was quite proud of this story. *It's both plausible and untestable. The bingo players are as anonymous as they can be. The two million or so extra dollars are just thrown into the canvas bag labeled "Cash Receipts: Mission Street" before it goes into the safe, a little bit every game.*

"That's great news Jay. God knows we can use the money. The city and county of San Francisco is talking about serious cuts because of the idiots in Washington –"

He broke in, sliding a sheaf of papers onto her desk. "There's a little more to it. But it's all good. We've got an anonymous donor who's promised us two hundred thousand dollars to renovate the bingo hall. We can knock out a wall, add some space, and spruce up the place to get another thirty-forty seats. Juice up the revenues even more."

"Better and better. So what's this?" She indicated the papers he'd put on her desk.

"The standard Capital Appropriation Request. As you know, our financial policies and bylaws require both our signatures on any expenditure over fifty thousand bucks. This is all the detail on how we'll spend the two hundred thousand. The specifics are on page six, but we're using vendors we've worked with before, so there's nothing out-of-the ordinary for you to review."

She turned to page six. It was an Excel spreadsheet with six rows, each describing the purchase of either goods or services from a specific vendor for a specific amount. The total came to exactly two-hundred thousand dollars. She flipped back to the cover page and signed her name alongside the signature block with her name and title.

"What's the timeline for getting this done? And who's the anonymous donor?"

"Timeline? One month. The donor? I truly don't know. The approach to me came through a law firm. All I know is that the money is coming from ... to quote the lawyer ... people who have recently come into a lot of money and want to share it with us." *And it will appear in the form of cash donations totaling two hundred thousand, no single donation greater than five thousand. We will provide the appropriate IRS form to enable somebody somewhere to take a charitable deduction for their donation. That makes them better off by about eighty thou. And those vendors? They're all stooges for our supposed benefactor, doing sham work where it will cost them maybe twenty thousand in return for the two-hundred thousand that we'll pay them. So the man gives us two hundred and gets back eighty in tax benefits and another one-eighty in profits … minus my 'commission.' It's charity, but in reverse.*

He picked up the signed form and stood up to leave, but she stopped him with another question, one that was highly troubling. "Jay, would you get me a report on the Mission Street bingo games – a graph of nightly revenues, attendance and payouts? Say, for the last two years? I need to have some better background in case the board presses me on this." She said "thanks" without waiting for a response and stood up, ending the meeting. Gould went back to his office at the other end of the hall. He closed the door behind him and used his cell phone.

"It's done. Dodd signed the CAR, no questions asked. You can start funneling the two-hundred thousand whenever you're ready."

No need to tell the man about Dodd's closing questions. That would just make him nervous for no reason.

Advisory Services

The message in Graham's voice mail was quite businesslike. "This is Renee Delgado from the U.S. Treasury. I'd like to meet again, as soon as convenient. Please call me."

He debated his options. The most appealing one was to simply not return her call, but such an action did not sit well with his journalistic instincts. *Some of my best stories came from sources that I didn't want to talk to very much. And she was afraid of something.*

She picked up on the second ring. "Renee Delgado." It was very brusque, the voice of a busy woman.

"This is Graham Dodd. I'm returning your call, but I see no reason why we should meet. As I said before, I'm not going to help you in your investigation of NEW SF."

The brusqueness disappeared. "Mr. Dodd. Thanks for calling. And what I want to talk to you about has nothing to do with your wife, NEW SF or my current investigation. I promise."

"You do know that I'm retired? So if you're looking to leak some juicy tidbits for the morning edition, you're talking to the wrong person." *That's not strictly true and we both know it. And I don't think she's interested in that particular kind of politics in any case.*

"I do not intend to use you in that way. And, by the way, I don't play those games. Never have, never will. What I would like from you is advice."

"About ...?"

There was a long pause. "I know a lot about criminals; the kind that operate outside the law, hack into bank accounts, run pyramid schemes, hurt people ... I can find them and put them away because I have this huge sledgehammer called the federal government that I can use against them. I'm good at it and still naïve enough to believe that I do some good. But..."

Graham thought he knew where she was headed, but he waited, needing to hear it from her. "But where I need help … your advice … is how to take down the institution itself. The one I work for. No, not take it down, but expose some of its problems."

"Pogo said it best: 'We have met the enemy and he is us.'"

"Who the hell is Pogo?"

"A furry swamp creature; the product of the imagination of a cartoonist named Walt Kelly."

"The only Pogo I know is the Project On Government Oversight. But your fuzzy cartoon critter knew what he was talking about. And that's where I need your help."

"OK. There's a small Italian restaurant called Fidelio's on Bryant in Palo Alto. I'll meet you there at seven. You can buy dinner in exchange for the invaluable advice."

"Great … and thanks."

"Ms. Delgado? One word about NEW SF or my wife and I walk out. I mean it."

She was already there when he got to the restaurant. To his surprise, she was dressed in blue jeans and a baggy sweater, sitting at a corner table and typing with both thumbs on the iPhone held before her. Other than being twenty years too old, she could have passed for one of Palo Alto's many hopeful entrepreneurs waiting to make her pitch to a VC. She stood and they shook hands.

He gestured at her outfit. "I gather you're not coming here straight from the office?"

"You'd be wrong. My office these days is the front seat of a rental car. But thanks for coming. I really do appreciate it. I've ordered a cheap bottle of Chianti …"

"Perfect. Now, back to Pogo --" He stopped when the waiter appeared with the wine and menus. After they ordered, she talked without interruption for twenty minutes, letting her pasta get cold and taking occasional sips of the Chianti. At first, it was merely a fascinating but familiar story about the new Trump administration's unfamiliarity with governing, with anecdotes about overzealous deputies, ham-handed personnel decisions and the demoralization of career Treasury officials. It was one of those first-person "I was there" kind of stories that make good reading and she told it with skill.

When she finally paused to taste her food, he said, "You're a good story teller, but it's old news. Every halfway decent columnist has their own insider … leaker … in the White House or one of the major cabinet departments. It's blogosphere journalism at its best …or worst, depending on which side you're on."

She shook her head. "If I wanted advice on that stuff, I'd be having dinner with a gossip columnist. Where I need your help is with the next bit."

For the next twenty minutes, she talked of more sinister maneuverings; using terms like subversion of due process, collusion, obstruction of justice, cronyism, self-dealing, the abuse of power, and conflicts of interest. The stories were darker, more tentative and she lowered her voice to a near whisper in keeping with the content.

When she paused, he said, "You have first hand evidence of corruption at high levels of government –"

She was shaking her head before he finished the sentence. "Not evidence. Suspicions, even smoking guns, but not evidence. Not yet. That's where I'm hoping you'll have some advice. I've read your articles, your book. You were a lone wolf, ferreting out corruption in some of our major institutions, particularly the military. You had the same problems ... not knowing who to trust ... viewed as a traitor to the cause. How do I think about this?"

"That's easy. Like an investigative journalist. Think Woodward and Bernstein. Your weapons are transparency and sunlight, not the sledgehammer ..."

They talked another two hours, finishing the Chianti along the way. When they left the restaurant, they were on a first name basis and she had not once mentioned NEW SF or Valerie.

Graham walked with her to her car. "Two last thoughts," he said. "First, on the DC issues, you and I want the same thing and I'll do whatever I can to help you with that." She nodded, waiting. "The second thing ... more advice, if you like ... is that I need to warn you. The sledgehammer is real and there are a goodly number of people that will not like the sunlight. You need to be very careful."

She smiled at him. "No sweat. I'll just quote Pogo to them."

Conversation with an Ex-General

Graham explored Alden Acres thoroughly. He had more incentive than most of the residents, given that he had moved out – or, in his view, been forced out – of the luxury apartment that he and Valerie had just purchased. The guest quarters where he was living for the moment was the equivalent of a suite in an upscale hotel, not the sort of place that one wanted to spend a lot of time in. So he ate meals in one of the two on-site restaurants and frequented the various other rooms, the features that Alden Acres liked to refer to as 'amenities.'

At the moment, he was in "the billiards room." Although not labeled as such, it was clearly the equivalent of the men's locker room in an elite private country club, right down to the brands of whiskey at the bar, the big screen TV and the array of black and white photos of African big game. Women were not expressly prohibited, but there was a quite clear albeit tacit standard that this room was for the boys. He wasn't sure but thought that the "card room" in the opposite wing served as the women's equivalent.

He was at the billiards table, playing an idle game of rotation, trying to sink the fifteen balls in their numerical order. He wasn't very good at it or much interested, so he had only eliminated the number one and number two balls when a second man wandered in and stood watching him for about thirty seconds before approaching him.

"How about a game?" He held out his hand. "I'm Thad McNeal. We met briefly when you were doing the tour with Malraux, and again at the cocktail party. No reason for you to remember me."

Graham shook his hand. "Graham Dodd. And I do remember you and ..."

"Helen," said McNeal. "How about that game?"

"I'm not very good," said Graham.

"That's a good sign. Anybody proficient at pool either comes from a sorry childhood or spent a lot of time in the military. Sometimes both."

He's one of the ex-generals. Two stars, I recall. Retired out of the Pentagon into the boardroom of an aerospace company. Helen wanted to be in the Bay Area because the grandchildren are all in Silicon Valley.

McNeal racked the balls and gestured for Graham to break. He got lucky, scattering the triangle nicely and actually sinking two balls, the four and the twelve. McNeal said, "Nice start. Maybe you should have bet." He used his cue to move the sliding tabs to show a score of sixteen.

Graham scratched on the next shot and McNeal made the one, two and three balls before missing. The score was sixteen to six. Ten minutes later, the last ball was in and the game was over. Graham still had his original sixteen points; McNeal had one-hundred-four.

"How about a drink?" Graham asked. "I'll buy."

They sat at the bar. The large-screen television had an English soccer game with the sound off.

"How do you like Alden Acres?" Graham asked.

McNeal grimaced. "I feel like I'm on a grounded luxury cruise ship. It's OK, I guess, but the idea that I'll be tended to as I steadily deteriorate for the next twenty or thirty years is not attractive. In fact, it's hard to accept."

"Maybe that's what MacArthur meant when he said –"

"Old soldiers never die. They just fade away." McNeal said it for him, and Graham detected a faint note of wistfulness in it. "His farewell speech to Congress. 1951."

"I guess soldiers need wars, don't they? You get to Vietnam?"

McNeal looked closely at Graham as if he was suspicious of hostile intent. "Shavetail lieutenant, fresh out of the Academy. Lucky to get out alive. And gung ho enough to make it a career." He stared into the glass of smoky whiskey and Graham wondered what he was seeing. Then he sat up. "What about you? They say you're a writer."

"That's what my agent calls me. My wife calls me a journalist and I still think of myself as a reporter. The nomenclature is confusing. But what I am *not* is a soldier ... nor a pool player, apparently."

McNeal stood up. "Well, I can teach you to be a better pool player, but it looks like you've missed the opportunity to go to war."

"I didn't actually. Just not with a gun. I spent some quality time with the lst Marine Expeditionary Force in Fallujah. I was an embedded reporter. Left there in 2004 with some leftover shrapnel in my knee and a strong distaste for politicians talking about how we were winning. I decided to write a book about it."

McNeal sat back down. "I know. I read your book. At one time, it was required reading at the War College. I was there in 2004. Not in Fallujah, but in Iraq. Winning over hearts and minds." He said the last phrase with more bitterness than Graham thought possible. *Maybe that's his problem with*

Alden Acres and the long slow slide into senility. He thinks he should have done more?

"We're still in there, and Afghanistan," Graham said. "The longest-running war in our history. And still no light at the end of the tunnel ... to coin a phrase from your Vietnam days."

"And there won't be. It's a black hole, sucking up money and lives." *Again, that bitterness.* "We'd bring in AR-16s for Iraqi soldiers and their commanders would sell them to the Taliban. We'd ship medical supplies to an orphanage and the staff would sell them on the black market while the kids died. We'd build a water distribution system for a rural village and the mayor would hand it over to his relatives. Secure a road and the local militia starts collecting tolls from farmers taking their crops to market. Start a school for girls and ---"

Graham put his hand on McNeal's arm to stop the rising tone, feeling the rigidity and the anger. "I get the picture, Thad. It's a different culture –"

But McNeal was in his own world of memories. "It wasn't just the Iraqis. We did it too. We ran the whole bloody war with for-profit contractors. Your marines were there to do the dying. All the rear echelon stuff ... the "civilian interface" was the term they used ... that was all done by corporations. And they were just as corrupt as the Iraqis or the Afghans. Maybe twenty percent of what was authorized actually got to where it was intended. Especially in the early days. We scattered cash around wherever we went. Hell, I personally carried a million dollars in cash around with me for a month. To hand out to 'the influencers.'"

Graham watched McNeal and knew that he was seeing replays in his head; that he was talking mostly to himself at the moment. "Our soldiers, the ones that did the fighting, they were kids. Mostly poor kids. Nineteen year olds from Omaha and Charlotte and Fresno. They're watching me hand out thick wads of hundred dollar bills to illiterate farmers who sell opium when they're not selling their twelve-year-old daughters. And those kids are wondering why they can't get some of those wads of money. It's hard not to feel entitled to a share of all that cash."

Graham broke in, startling McNeal back into the present. "Some of them tried. There were lots of stories floating around about guys who were suddenly rich when they rotated home."

McNeal asked, "Remember the bank in Baghdad?"

"Yeah, I do." *But which one? There was Dar es Salaam, a private institution. Employees showed up one morning and found the vaults empty. $282 million gone, all in US dollars. They say the guards took it. Then there was the Central Bank. Saddam and his sons drove away in three trucks loaded with cash and securities – they think maybe a billion dollars.*

"It was easier for the Iraqi's," McNeal said. "They could hide or spend what they stole. My kids? They had a cot and a foot locker in a barracks with a hundred other people. No way they could stash more than a few thousand bucks! Some of them tried … got themselves to Leavenworth real fast."

McNeal fell silent for a few seconds, then looked at Graham for the first time since he began his angry reminiscence. "Sorry. I need to break the habit of telling people what I think."

"It's OK. Remember, I'm a reporter. I like people that talk about bad things that happen to them."

McNeal took the bill from the bar top, signed it and said, "I'll buy. Partial atonement for the harangue." He walked away, ramrod straight.

Graham barely heard him. He was still grappling with what the man had said, "It's hard not to feel entitled to some of that cash." *You need a minimum net worth of five million plus to move into this place. I wonder where a two-star general gets that kind of money?*

Graham's War

Graham stayed at the bar, thinking about McNeal's bitterness and the way that it triggered so many memories of his own.

The first to come to mind was Graham's editor, waving his cigar in large arcs to emphasize the sarcasm. "One advantage of announcing a preemptive war is that it makes it a lot easier to plan your press coverage. Not like the old-fashioned way, where reporters have to sort through a lot of canned bullshit handed out at press conferences and then go out and actually talk to real people." It was March 2003 and he had just assigned Graham to be the paper's chief 'embedded journalist' with the First Marine Division in the opening days of Bush's invasion of Iraq in search of Saddam Hussein's mythical weapons of mass destruction. "You're one of several hundred approved embedded journalists. The military views you as just another weapon to help them win the *real* war, the one for the hearts and minds of the *American* people. Never mind the Iraqis. You're cheerleaders ... flacks ... a battalion of propaganda experts!"

Graham was unperturbed. "I've been at this reporting game for almost a quarter-of-a-century now. It's a huge opportunity to be up front with major breaking news. I think I'm smart enough to separate the wheat from the chaff."

"Yeah, but then they'll insist that you print the chaff!"

Graham spent thirteen months with the troops, more than almost every other embedded journalist. He filed stories on house-to-house combat, village pacification programs, up-armoring programs for Humvees, Iraqi prisoners, life in the Green Zone and whatever else he encountered. He made it a particular point to cultivate close relationships with the troops. Not the press officers and 'information officers,' but the corporals and sergeants and lieutenants that actually did the fighting. He also spent a lot of time learning some basic Arabic and developing Iraqi sources, both civilian and military. His stories were edgy, shaded with a not-so-subtle critique of the war and the way it was waged, but he stayed just barely within the parameters imposed on embedded journalists by the Pentagon.

He didn't know it, but his press credentials were about to be revoked. Both the Iraqis and a few high level officers within the coalition forces were disturbed by his recent interest in digging into the corruption that had plagued the war from its very first day. Graham figured his current project would be the last story he filed from the war zone, but he never got the chance to be sent home by the military. The IED achieved the same effect without any political blowback about "censorship of the press."

But a month before the IED, Hamid found him sitting in the shade of an Abrams tank. He was one of the Iraqi NCOs paired with an American training officer and he and Graham had developed some rapport after spending five days under fire with a Marine platoon that was assigned to "aggressive patrolling" in Fallujah. The platoon lost three eighteen-year-old PFC's to sniper fire in those five days.

Hamid said, "I saw the press release about the new Iraqi unit that's about to be deployed in Fallujah. It was very positive."

Graham glanced at him, mostly to verify that the irony was deliberate. "Just because it used phrases like 'turning point,' or 'Iraqi's taking ownership of their war,' or 'elite combat-ready troops?' It's called spin, Hamid ... and it's a press release. Nobody pays any attention anymore."

"You should." When Graham looked at him closely, Hamid went on, "You Americans are paying the wages for the soldiers, and you've equipped every one of them with the same arms and personal equipment that your marines have."

"Iraq is broke, Hamid. America is rich. It's called a redistribution of income, and all for a good cause."

"But who is the income being redistributed to?"

So that's the purpose of this little visit. The word's out, I guess. 'Graham Dodd is interested in the underbelly; the dirty little truths about how the war really gets fought ... or not.' With that thought came a bone-deep fatigue, a wanting to be somewhere else writing about something with a happy ending or at least a storyline that reaffirmed good intentions. The sensation didn't last long because Hamid was watching him closely, knowing that his question would inevitably have its intended effect. And it did. *Hamid knows where the money is going. And he wants to tell me. So that I can tell the world.*

The story was front-page, above the fold for three days in the *Times* and got major play on prime-time news. It was as embarrassing to the Pentagon as it was career enhancing for Graham. Unlike most of the 'he said, she said' allegations of fraud and abuse that the anti-war crowd trumpeted, this one had hard facts – interviews, pictures, copies of made-up invoices and – the crowning touch – an on-camera interview with Ahmad, an ex-governor of the province where the new Iraqi contingent was supposedly being trained.

On paper and in Pentagon press releases, the new Iraqi battalion was the face of the coalition's new war fighting strategy. It featured a thousand highly mobile Iraqi soldiers equipped with the latest light infantry gear, armored vehicles and helicopters for close air support. They were trained by the U.S. but would operate independently. As the Pentagon put it, "This new battalion demonstrates that the Iraqi's have skin in the game. It's their war and they're the ones who are going to fight it."

The truth that Graham documented mercilessly in the world press was that there were only three hundred and twelve actual soldiers. And they were poorly trained and demoralized. The other six hundred and eighty eight existed only as names on a payroll ledger, having either deserted or – more likely – never existed in the first place. And even those soldiers that could be counted were equipped with out-of-date weapons and vehicles, wearing uniforms that didn't even match. It seems that their officers had sold the good stuff on the black market, which was basically a conduit to the Taliban and other splinter groups.

Graham found Ahmad, the ex-provincial governor, living in a seaside villa in Egypt. He was openly amused. "Your country wants … needs … to say you have a strategy for getting out of this never-ending war that you should never have gotten into in the first place. So you spend money like an ugly rich woman buying cosmetic surgery, knowing in your heart that it's not going to work no matter how much you spend. And us? We're glad to be paid twice; first by the Americans and then by the insurgents, who like all the shiny new American-made toys."

Graham knew that his readers would want him to ask Ahmad the key question; the one he already knew the answer to. He changed it to a declarative sentence. "You were a senior Iraqi government official…. But you were helping to destroy Iraq, your own country."

The amusement went away, replaced by a flash of anger. "It was my country at one time. But you have destroyed it. Handed it on a platter to the Shia and the Iranians. I am Sunni. And the Americans have made me rich so that I and my extended family can live where we like."

Graham's editor made him leave out a part of the story. Ahmad told stories about others that benefitted from the arrangement. "Americans. Corporations. The ones that sold us weapons and then sold us more when we 'lost' them; the ones that got paid for training sessions for phantom soldiers; that got a commission for processing payroll for those same non-existent soldiers." For all such exposes, Ahmad was a reliable source; he was the one who met with the companies, took bags of cash from them.

"You can't use that stuff," the editor said. "All you've got are allegations from a corrupt Iraqi who's on the lam from his own judicial system. We'd have lawyers swarming all over us. Not to mention the DC crowd and half of their donor base."

The story broke the day before the improvised explosive device ended Graham's Iraqi tour. It was sheer paranoia, but Graham could not shake the thought: *I wonder if that IED was arranged by a disgruntled military contractor?*

A Walk in the Woods

"Can we talk?"

Valerie stood in the doorway of the guest room. She was dressed for her Saturday morning hike – sweatshirt, shorts and pink tennis shoes. Graham could not remember her ever missing the ritual; nor could he picture her in any other outfit on Saturday morning. *That's another one of our differences. She loves ritual and predictability in all its forms. And exercise.*

"I'm not sure there's much to talk about. Nothing new, anyway."

"Actually, I think there's quite a lot to talk about. But walk with me. A half-hour up the hill. Good for your knee and I promise not to be disagreeable." It was a promise that she had no intention of honoring.

He thought about it, then shrugged. "OK, let me change shoes." Sixty seconds later, they were at the point on the property where the manicured grass ended and a dirt trail disappeared into a dense grove of Douglas fir trees.

He asked, "Do you know where you're going? I seem to remember something Malraux said about 'a hundred miles of trails.'"

"No. But it's uphill, so we'll always be able to see the Bay and this place. It does kind of stand out, after all."

They walked in silence for a while, due in part to the uphill track, but also because it seemed in keeping with the silence all around them. The path narrowed and divided several times, but they kept to their uphill bias and Valerie seemed to know where she was going. As she had predicted, the bright white buildings of Alden Acres were easy to find from their uphill elevation, although often obscured by the dense greenery.

Graham judged them to be fairly close to the crest of the hill. The trees were closer together and there were frequent course changes to avoid dense patches of prickly brush. "I think our trail has become a deer path," he said. "Let's stop for a bit."

"Another minute or so. I think we're almost there."

There? So she has a destination in mind?

Three minutes later, they emerged in a small clearing that had a dirt track running alongside it, a parallel set of ruts made by tires, not deer. Valerie said, "Butch comes up here. He said that the state forestry and fire service people come through here every now and then; hence the road. Nice, don't you think?"

He looked around. The clearing was sunlit and ringed by majestic old-growth redwood trees. Their needles were thick on the ground, such that it was like walking on a sponge pad. Somebody had gone to the trouble of dragging a major log out of the trees and Valerie headed for them, seating herself with the clear expectation that he would join her.

He didn't. Instead, he stood and glared at her. "The staging is pretty obvious. You didn't have to drag me into the woods for marriage counseling."

"I want a divorce."

Later, he would think back and admire her choreography. The seemingly random hike, 'finding' the intimate little clearing in dappled sunlight, even the upsetting suddenness of her 'I want a divorce.' But right then, at that exact moment, a fox came out of the brush about ten feet to her right and walked across the clearing. He – she? – was a lovely red color with a magnificent bushy tail and an absolute indifference to their presence.

And the fox was carrying a naked human foot in his or her jaws.

The rest of the body was twenty feet from where Valerie was sitting on the log. It took a few minutes to find it because of the dense underbrush. What gave it away was the trail of broken limbs where it had been dragged through the brush that paralleled the two ruts that defined the so-called 'road.'

Graham stood looking at it. *I hoped that I would never see another decomposing body again. Although this one is more intact than some.* He had to put both hands on Valerie's shoulders to turn her around and point her back toward the clearing.

"You have your phone?"

"Yes."

"Call 911. Tell them where we are, on the trail uphill from Alden Acres, that there's a fire service road along the crest, that we've found a body."

"But, he's ... he's been ... we should get the foot from that animal ..."

"Just call 911. And stay on the line. So they can find us."

"Yes."

It would be a while before either of them would remember why they had walked up the hill.

First Investigation

"Henri won't like this at all."

Graham, Butch Melendy and Salvador Fender were sitting in the library drinking coffee. It was mid-morning and the third time they'd met in that particular space, not by prearrangement but because each of them was attracted to the closed-off seating arrangement with four deep chairs placed in front of a floor-to-ceiling window with a 180° view of the Bay. Graham used the time and space to read the New York Times. Butch just sat and looked out the window, while Salvador played endless games of Sudoku on his iPad.

Graham looked where Butch pointed. An unmarked but very obvious police car had pulled into the circular drive outside the main building and a man and a woman were standing looking at the imposing building before them.

Butch said, "To us ex-defense attorneys, they look like cops. Henri, on the other hand, will probably introduce them as potential residents. Don't want to give the impression that just anybody can walk around the place. Or that any of our exalted residents would be sought by the police."

"Won't work," said Salvador. "Finding a half-eaten body on the premises leads one to expect cops to come calling. Henri's only regret will be that they didn't come from Scotland Yard."

"Not those two," Butch objected. "Even from here, the guy looks like Danny Divito. He's four feet tall and about that wide."

Salvador put down his iPad and leaned forward for a better look. "More like five feet four, I think, adjusting for the foreshortening that goes with our overhead view. But the woman's another matter entirely. She looks like Hollywood's version of an LA homicide detective."

"She's my daughter," Graham said. "And if you weren't gay, I'd suspect you of lechery."

Both of them looked at Graham with equal parts surprise and pleasure. It made him wonder what it would take to embarrass them. "Her name's Alison. She's a detective sergeant in the County Sheriff's office. The Danny Divito lookalike is Mark Manning. He's five-feet five inches and as smart as she is pretty."

Graham hadn't seen Alison for three weeks, but he wasn't surprised when she knocked on his door two hours later. She looked tired.

"Hi kid. Am I a suspect?"

The lopsided smile made him want to hug her, but he knew she wouldn't like that under the circumstances. "Sure. Along with the two hundred or so other civilians living here. But this is an official visit, since you – and Mom – were the ones who actually found the body."

"You've seen the statement we gave the deputies earlier?"

"Yes. Mom was pretty shook up. I think that may be a first for her."

"Any ID?"

"Usual ground rules?"

"Absolutely." Alison was a by-the-book detective. The main exception was her relationship with Graham. She used him as a sounding board, sharing information, hypotheses and doubts about cases she was working. Part of it was the strong father-daughter bond, but an even bigger piece was his background as an investigative reporter, giving him the same drive for closure and respect for confidential sources that is in the DNA of a good cop.

So she told him, "In fact, the killer has done his best to keep the victim's identity a secret. You saw the hands?"

He nodded. "You mean that there weren't any? And that they'd been severed with a sharp instrument, not gnawed off by the local wildlife."

He closed his eyes, envisioning the appalling object half-buried in the pine needles. "Not much left of his face. Did the killer do that?"

"We don't think so. After the mice, rats, birds, coyotes and foxes, there's not much to work with. We've got a police artist working on it, but ..."

"Teeth?"

"All there, but no sign of any dental work to trace."

"How did –"

"He die? Given the condition of the body, there are multiple possibilities at this stage. But he did have what looked like bullet holes in his skull. Three of them."

Graham sat thinking, running through what he knew of police procedures. "Clothing? Wallet? Jewelry? Missing person reports? Abandoned cars nearby? Anything?"

"White male, maybe Hispanic, approximately mid-fifties, apparently normal. Except for –"

Graham said, "He'd been tortured." *The fox stood there looking at me with the foot in his mouth. The foot with three toes missing and burn marks.*

"Quite a lot. The feet, more burn scars on his torso, several broken bones. But none of it was recent. And there were a couple of old bullet holes. I'm betting he's been in a war zone at one time. Pathology can make a guess as to how long ago."

Alison took a small notebook from her purse, signaling that the flow of information was about to reverse direction.

"Were you ever in that clearing before you found the body?"

"Not me, but –" He stopped, suddenly aware of the implications. Then he went on, even more aware of Alison's discomfort. "I had the impression – that's all – that your mom – Valerie – knew of the place and that it maybe was her destination for that day."

"Do you know why she would pick that place?" Her voice was very formal and she was looking down at her notebook.

"I don't know that she *picked* it, first of all. And, second, I don't know why she chose that particular place to sit down. All she said was that she wanted to go on a hike." *But I remember what she said when she sat down on that log. She said, 'I want a divorce.'*

"Do either of you have access to a handgun?"

"No."

By now, her tone was that of the faintly suspicious cop, one who was accustomed to being lied to. She used that same tone to ask the most difficult question of all.

"Why are you living in the guest room?"

The Billionaire and the Nurse

Graham sat in a congenial silence with Butch Melendy and Salvador Fender in 'their' alcove in the library. He was on his second cup of coffee and almost done with the Times crossword when Butch broke out, "My goodness! It's a sighting! Call People Magazine!"

"Have you met our local multi-billionaire?" He gestured out the floor-to-ceiling window, toward the circular drive where two relatively young men were helping a man out of a large and old Cadillac sedan and into a wheelchair. The man was obviously old and quite infirm, although he was wearing a pinstriped blue suit that made Graham think of a Swiss banker. He and the Cadillac went well together. That scene was helped by the two men, each holding an elbow in the transition from car to wheelchair. They were dressed in identical gray suits and club ties.

"Looks like a scene from a James Bond movie. He'd be the villain with a plot to conquer the world. Who is he?"

"His name is David McDavid," Salvador said. "He's one of those residents who *really* likes his privacy. His parents lacked the imagination to name him properly but they were smart enough to own about fifty thousand acres of prime timberland in the Pacific Northwest. He's ninety-three years old and they say he had this place built just for himself. The rest of us are just here to provide some local color."

I guess a multi-billionaire won't mind having to pay for three meals a day at Alden Acres even if he doesn't eat there. "What about his personal staff ... those people with him ... Do they live in?"

"That's Tom and Jerry." When Graham looked at him with suspicion, Salvador said, "Their real names. And they do live here, but they're the only ones allowed. Alden Acres allows residents to have personal aides, but they can't be residents. Except for Tom and Jerry."

"Even if it's medically indicated?"

"If they need that level of attention, they move to the assisted living wing. Otherwise, our resident medical staff is on call." He pointed to the woman holding the wheelchair as the aides lowered David McDavid gently into it. "That's her."

The woman – presumably the 'medical staff' that Butch was referring to – helped to support the transfer into the wheelchair and once he was secure, she pushed him into the main entrance of the building, accompanied by one of the Tom and Jerry duo. The other got back in the Cadillac and drove it into the underground parking entrance.

"I didn't know we had medical staff on site," Graham said. "Is she a doctor?"

"The next best thing; a nurse practitioner with a specialty in geriatrics, or is it gerontology? I get them confused," Salvador answered. "And she's very good."

"At lots of things," Butch murmured, just barely audible, but with a conspiratorial smile at Graham. When Salvador frowned at him and shook his head, he waved him off and said, "Salvador disapproves of what he calls my flippancy about other people. He mistakes it for a moral stance."

Salvador came back immediately, with the kind of bored tone that made it clear this was an old and ongoing debate. "It's neither moral nor a stance. You just like to gossip."

Graham stood up to leave, knowing that the back-and-forth would continue for as long as he was willing to serve as audience. *But it worked. I'm hooked. Have to find out more about our nurse practitioner.*

One more question occurred to him. "How come Tom and Jerry are exceptions to the residency rules?"

Salvador smirked. "David McDavid is a part owner of Alden Acres. His money and political connections are what enabled it to be built. And his so-called *apartment* is about ten thousand square feet with its own private entrance and half-a-dozen bedrooms. It's as self-sufficient as a nuclear submarine on a six-month patrol under the Arctic icepack. In fact, this is the first time I've seen him use the same entrance as the rest of us ordinary people."

"Why didn't he just buy his own island or a castle with a moat? Why move in with us common folk?"

Butch patted him on the arm. "That's the question we're been trying to answer since we moved in. Please let us know if you find out the answer."

His chance to meet the medical staff came ninety seconds later. He was crossing the main lobby when he encountered the woman. She was pushing an empty wheelchair and changed course slightly, clearly aiming to intercept him. She stopped and held out her hand. "Hi. I'm Martha Mendoza. We haven't met, but I'm the resident medical person. And I know that you're Graham, married to Valerie. Our newest residents."

Everything was wide about her. From the front, she was a blocky woman with wide shoulders and hips. Even her face: a wide forehead, a wide mouth and wide eyes accented by thick eyebrows. But when viewed from the side, she was thin, with only slight bulges where breasts and hips broke the linearity. Perhaps because of the proportionality,

Graham thought she was attractive. It also helped that she had a wonderful smile.

Graham took her extended hand, conscious of being appraised quite openly. Her eyes were a liquid brown and they went well with the smile. "Thank you. And don't take this the wrong way, but –"

"I hope that we don't meet very often." She completed his sentence for him and he realized that he was about to repeat one of the oldest jokes that doctors and nurses were subject to. He smiled apologetically. "Sorry, Ms. Mendoza. Originality is not my strong point. But I am glad to meet you." *She doesn't lack for self esteem. Interrupts the paying customers and makes fun of herself at the same time.* She held onto his hand for two or three seconds more than convention called for, saying, "Call me Mendoza. And don't be put off by the job title. I'm also the fitness counselor and I chair the in-house book group. I also live here, so I look forward to getting to know you and your wife much better."

"Does the medical side of things call for lots of your time?" *Butch said 'She's good at lots of other stuff,' and I don't think he meant anything to do with book groups. Maybe the go-to drug dealer? Takes bets for the local bookie?*

"It's the biggest part of my job. But it's pretty concentrated among just a few of the residents. Most of you are pretty healthy." The smile dimmed somewhat and she was looking closely at Graham, as if she was aware of the real purpose of his question, of his need to know about the 'other stuff.' She gestured at the empty wheelchair. "Mr. McDavid, for example. He likes me to go along when he visits his oncologist. Calls me 'his second opinion.' But all I do is tell him to trust his doctors."

Then she said, "You're a journalist." It wasn't a question, and Graham wondered if Malraux was in the habit of circulating a bio of all the new residents. "Are you still digging up stories?" Graham was surprised by how quickly she posed that particular query. He had heard variations on that question at countless cocktail parties, coffee breaks at conferences, from taxi drivers, hairdressers, CEOs, congressional aides and whistle-blowers of every type. *She's got a story that she thinks the world needs to hear and she wants me to do it for her. I wonder what her particular grievance is? It's always a grievance and who better than a journalist to give it the kind of weight it deserves?*

"I'm retired. Haven't you heard? Anyway, journalism is obsolete. Done in by the combination of technology, fake news and generalized illiteracy." *Christ! I sound like a crotchety old man. One of those chronic whiners camped out in a neighborhood bar at eleven in the morning to latch on any poor soul who doesn't know enough to stay away from him.*

The woman was unfazed. "Nobody really retires any more. They just get a lot more selective about what they do. Isn't there a story you always wanted to write but the editor or the publisher or the owner wouldn't let you do it? Something important, maybe? Something that the world needs to know about that Twitter or Buzzfeed can't or won't do?"

Knowing full well that he was being sucked in, he said, "You sound like you've got such a topic in mind."

"Me? No way. But I'll bet that anyone living in this place has such a story. Like Mr. McDavid," and she gestured at the empty wheel chair once more. "He tells me that he's been an advisor for three of our presidents. Think of the tales he could tell."

Melissa Shanahan

Melissa Shanahan was in the library staring fixedly at the surface of a large game table that was covered with a partially completed jigsaw puzzle, one of those 5,000 piece things 'for advanced solvers' with tiny pieces that all looked the same. From what Valerie could tell from the box cover propped on its stand, it looked like a picture of a Jackson Pollock painting. Or it would be when completed. Right now, all it was was a thin perimeter surrounding a vast open space. *Right out of the Jigsaws for Dummies book ... Get all those pieces with straight edges first!*

Valerie stood behind the woman and watched her. She was hunched over in the armchair with her arms wrapped around her ribs as if defending herself from cold that only she was aware of. She reached out, picked up a piece and tried to fit into a space that only she could see. When it was obvious that it didn't fit, she replaced it on the table and resumed hugging herself. Ten seconds later, she repeated the sequence of steps.

Valerie did not like jigsaw puzzles. She associated them with either two-year-olds or 'old people,' neither of whom she wanted to associate with. Puzzles required patience and visualization skills. *Not my strong points. That's for Graham.* She turned away, aiming for the bookshelves on the nearby wall, but stopped when the woman spoke to her.

"You're Valerie Dodd. The new resident."

Valerie turned back, remembering the woman even as she started speaking. "Yes. I am. And you're Melissa Shanahan. You and your husband were the very first couple that we met at Alden Acres. You showed me through this very room."

"Did I do a good job?"

It seemed an odd question and Valerie frowned slightly, causing the woman to flutter her hands and say, "I mean, did I explain everything clearly? Did I say the right things?" She looked away, into the far corner of the room, but she was clearly waiting for an answer.

"You were a perfect guide, Melissa. And look, here I am – using the library!"

Melissa seemed to relax for an instant, but her eyes darted away again and she asked, "Did your husband enjoy talking to Corky? He usually doesn't share very much of himself with strangers."

Corky was the dog. Her husband is Frank. Is the woman drunk?

Again, Melissa's hyper-vigilance kicked in. She rolled her eyes as if to say, "I'm so silly! Not Corky. He's a dog. Frank. Did your husband get along with Frank?"

"I think so. They were talking about Frank's career. At least, that's what I think I heard." She turned away again. "It was good to see you again, Melissa. And good luck with your puzzle."

"Oh, I hate puzzles! But Griff says that they'll be good for me. He wants me to spend an hour every day on them." She giggled, an action so out-of-context that it startled Valerie. "But I haven't found a single piece so far. I'm afraid my brain just doesn't work that way. But I was very clever once ... not so long ago, really. I was the one who thought of the coffins. That was my idea."

She smiled brightly at Valerie, seeming pleased with herself. Valerie was trying hard to hide her perplexity. *Coffins? I don't think I'll follow up on that. And who the hell is Griff?* She said the first thing that came to mind. "When I was little, I would finish a puzzle and my mother would coat it in plastic and hang it on the wall. It was embarrassing."

Melissa gripped her arm and pulled Valerie close to her. She whispered, "It's called decoupage." Then she giggled, "Décolletage. The French have such strange words." Her grip was tight enough to be uncomfortable, and she didn't release it until Valerie tugged her arm free.

OK! Like having a conversation with a random phrase generator. Time to go. Valerie turned to go once more and bumped into Frank Shanahan, who had come up behind her. He was looking concerned and Valerie thought she knew why. He seemed to confirm this by nodding at her in a way that she read as 'thanks for your help.' He bent to kiss his wife very lightly on the top of her head and whispered in her ear.

Whatever he said frightened her. She stood up abruptly and would not look at Valerie. Her husband took her arm and very gently guided her out of the room, talking the whole time. Valerie caught only a few phrases. "Corky is your dog, Melissa. Your dog. He loves you."

Update

"How are you doing with the handless corpse?"

Alison and Graham were having one of their occasional 'keep in touch' dinners, a practice that began when he and Valerie moved into Alden Acres. Alison said that she didn't like coming there; that she disliked having to be "admitted" into the high-security complex and that she badly missed being able to drop in at the house where she'd grown up. Graham sympathized with her; he had yet to adjust to the idea that he needed protection from the outside world.

"No ID yet. We've got a hotel desk clerk and a car rental agent that think it's possible, just maybe, that he was a customer. Approximately a month ago, which is consistent with the approximate time of death. The hotel guy may have rented him a room that he didn't come back to, and that room had one ordinary suitcase and clothes that were bought at the Target store in the local mall. The name on the hotel registration is Andrew Lofgren and the address is a place in Topeka, Kansas that doesn't exist. The car rental agency had the same data. The clerk remembered him because he insisted on a dark green pickup. He paid cash and the vehicle was returned on time the day after he rented it … left on the lot after closing time."

"Cause of death?"

"Three twenty-two caliber hollow-points, one in the center of his forehead and then two in the temple. Nice neat little holes. Shots fired from very close range, maybe a couple of feet."

"Sounds like a professional job. What about the signs of being tortured?"

"The scars were real. The coroner said that they were old, at least a decade. She also said that he lived a hard life, probably most of it outdoors."

"Anything from the scene?"

"Nada. We think he was shot near the road at the crest of the hill and then dragged into those dense bushes next to your clearing. But even that is just an educated guess. This all happened weeks ago, remember."

"His hands –"

"Were sawed off with a fine-toothed blade, probably a hacksaw. And no, we haven't found them."

They sat in silence for a moment while the waiter poured the wine and hovered until Graham had made a show of tasting it and nodding his approval. Alison fidgeted with her wine glass and was uncharacteristically tense. *She's trying to figure out how to deal with this mother and father split. She can't take sides and she doesn't even know that we're talking divorce. It's going to be hard for her.*

But Alison wasn't thinking about her parents. "Whoever killed him probably came from here."

That startled him. "Alden Acres?"

"Seems logical. The only way to access that clearing is by the forest service track or the trail up from here. The clearing where you found him is two miles from the entry gate and it just doesn't seem likely that a professional would choose to be discoverable for that long. Much easier to do the ten minute walk up from here."

Graham thought about it. "Y'know, Alison. I don't think you're going to solve this one. Your best – only? – hope is to get an ID on the victim and that seems unlikely. No fingerprints, not a local, no missing person reports, barely recognizable facial features due to the wildlife ... I think this one goes to the 'unsolved' category."

Alison nodded, but she was only halfway listening. "I tried to raise the NEW SF issue with mom –"

"And got thrown out of the room, I suspect."

"About right. But maybe with both of us expressing concern, she'll check it out for herself. Have you talked to her?"

"Not yet, but I will."

They sat in a comfortable silence until Graham – against his better judgment – asked the question. "Uh, Alison? How's the online dating world going? Any action?"

She tried her stern 'none of your business' glare, but it quickly dissolved into the classic 'I'm such a klutz' look that he knew so well. "I think I need to update my profile. Most of the responses I get come from firemen or policemen who like to hunt, work on cars and watch a lot of football. And here I thought I was attractive to the sensitive type. ... poets and philosophy majors."

Graham poked her arm. "What we need are a few more murders at Alden Acres. Then you'll be so busy that you won't have time to worry about a love life."

Graham would remember that line.

Conversation With Valerie

Graham was in "his" closet in their official residence trying to decide what clothes he should move into his temporary quarters in the visitor's apartment. The residences at Alden Acres featured a very large master bedroom, including two very spacious closets. Everything about the place was designed to appeal to a demographic that had a large wardrobe and was accustomed to having space.

His decision was complicated by his internal ambivalence. He had moved into the visitor's room as a spur-of-the-moment act of defiance, one of these 'the hell with you' gestures that every married man or woman envisions but rarely acts out. That was ten days ago and since then he and Valerie had not talked, even when they inevitably encountered one another in the public spaces of Alden Acres. The lone exception was their excursion into the forest with its two dramatic changes in routine. The first was the discovery of the body; the second one Valerie's declarative sentence: "I want a divorce."

"You won't need to move many clothes."

Her voice startled him. She was standing in the doorway to the closet watching him. He could read nothing from her expression.

"But –"

"You still live here. I'm gone most of the time. The fees are paid from a joint checking account. Come and go as you like. Except for that." She nodded her head to indicate the king-sized bed behind her. "That's off limits. We'll work out the other protocols as we go."

He looked at her, thinking, and then said, "I saw Alison yesterday." *Is that one of the protocols to be worked out: who has first claim on our daughter?*

"So did I. In her role as a detective. She asked me whether I had ever been to that clearing before."

"Had you?"

"Yes. I was scouting for a suitable place to talk to you."

I guess the sentence 'I want a divorce' warrants some forethought as to staging. How supremely ironic that that lovely red fox would pick that exact moment to wander out of the woods carrying a human foot!

"She asked me why I was living in the guest quarters," Graham said, without looking at her.

"And what did you say?"

Graham picked his words carefully, knowing that he was hedging his bets and wondering what that meant. "I said that it was a temporary arrangement." *Leaving open the possibility of either divorce or reconciliation.*

She looked into the distance, her mouth scrunched up in the way that it did when she was thinking. "I wonder if this was the right thing for us."

Right thing? What? Marriage? Divorce? Selling the house?

Maybe the perplexity showed, because she added, "Alden Acres. It's been almost a month and I'm not sure this was a very good idea."

"We thought it was." *You even made a list. Classic Valerie. A sheet of paper with two columns, one labeled "pro" and the other "con."* "What is it that bothers you?"

"You mean other than the once-inconceivable notion that we're talking about divorce? It's … what was that old movie about all those rich people living in the hotel in Berlin?"

"Grand Hotel. It had Greta Garbo, Joan Crawford and both John and Lionel Barrymore. It had two great lines. Garbo said, 'I want to be alone,' and another character says, 'People come. People go. Nothing ever happens.'"

"It's like that. You have a bunch of rich people, marking time until they die."

"That's a little extreme. First, some of us – including you – are still working, not marking time. Second, it's an interesting lot. For different reasons, I grant you, but –"

Valerie wasn't even listening. "Melissa Shanahan is showing signs of dementia. I saw her in the library yesterday and she confused her dog with her husband … talked about coffins and décolletage … acted very strange."

Is that what's bothering her? That she is reminded every day of what's coming?

"Classic signs of dementia, I think. Her husband seems to be very attentive," Graham said.

"He's scared to death. And trying very hard to cover up what's going on with her. I think he's afraid that they'll insist on her moving to the memory care unit."

"Uh, Valerie?"

Something in his voice alerted her. She crossed her arms across her body, the classic defensive posture for receiving unwelcome news.

"Is everything OK at NEW SF?"

She looked at him, clearly suspicious. "You mean other than not enough money, too many needy clients, underpaid and overworked staff, and mean-spirited politicians who don't like what we do, how we do it and how good we are at doing it?"

How far can I press this? "That's all business as usual. Anything out of the ordinary?"

"Graham, just say it. What is it that's bothering you? And no, there's nothing any more threatening than any other day in the life of NEW SF." She took a step toward him and said, "Have you heard something that I should know about?"

He reached for some of his shirts, picking three of them at random. "Nope. I just thought that you looked a little frazzled after that hearing in Sacramento." He turned and headed for the door.

She followed. "Typical Sacramento bullshit. You sure you're not trying to tell me something?"

I should have known better than to start this. She's got a very highly developed antenna system when it comes to self-preservation. "I'll see you at dinner. Like you said, we need to talk."

He hung the shirts in the guest room closet, noticing for the first time that he had selected three identical white dress shirts that he hadn't worn in years. *Nice work klutz!* He stood staring at the shirts, thinking about what Alison had told him and Valerie's reactions to his very tentative probe. *Two things are pretty clear. The authorities are suspicious of something, enough so to risk violating the privacy of citizens. And Valerie is operating in her 'business as usual' mode. That's not a happy combination.*

Time for some investigative journalism. Like Mendoza said, nobody really retires any more. They just get more selective about what they do.

Internal Monologue

Frank said I'm supposed to do something, but I can't remember what it is. It's to be done every day and for a certain amount of time. He said it's good for me, that it will help me to .... to ... to do something that's good for me. But what was it? Not bridge. He said we won't do that anymore after ... after ... something that happened that was my fault. But I can't remember what it was. It must have been bad because we both like bridge and we were good at it.

And he won't leave me alone. I like to be alone. I'm used to it. He was gone so much of the time. In places where it was hard for us to even talk for weeks at a time. Daddy told me that what he did was important and that it wouldn't last for long. Now he's around all the time. He goes everywhere I go.

Why am I dressed like this? I don't remember putting this on. It's not a good color for me. And these shoes aren't mine; they're not at all what I like. It must be the pills. So many of them with such strange names that I can't say. The woman – what's her name – Mendoza – she watches me take them. I don't like that. How does she get in and who is she?

He wants to get rid of me. I've heard him talking to the woman Mendoza ... about the dementia center and how it's time. Time for me to go there. But he needs me. He was worried about the bodies so I told him about the coffins and what Daddy wanted for me. I wish I could see Daddy. He smoked cigars. I remember how he would take me along some of those nights, before ... before Frank ... before the baby. What was the baby's name?

I wish I could remember things. Frank doesn't want me to go out, even to walk in the gardens or trees. Don't talk to people, he keeps telling me. I'm afraid to talk to people. They look at me like I'm crazy. What was the baby's name? And did he have a coffin too, a little white one with gold handles?

He's changed. He won't play bridge with me any more. He makes me eat things I don't like, take pills and he won't talk about the baby. Daddy would, but Frank says I can't see him either. He calls me Melissa but that's not my name. I can't remember what my name was. I don't like Melissa.

There's that bell ringing again. I'm supposed to do something when the bell rings. But I can't remember what I'm supposed to do. Maybe take a nap? That sounds good. I think I'll take a nap.

Marriage Therapy

Graham was alone in the library, drinking a cup of coffee while answering emails on his laptop. It had become an early-morning ritual with him, partly to escape from the hotel-like atmosphere in the guest room. It was designed for overnight stays for relatives and visitors of the residents and had all the ambience of a Holiday Inn located at a freeway exit ramp, so that he sought other venues during the day. Happily, Alden Acres was a large sprawling complex, almost a self-contained small city, so that he had lots of options. The library was one of his favorites.

He saw Henri Malraux walk by the archway and glance at him. When he stopped, clearly trying to make up his mind, and then headed straight for him, Graham had a pretty good idea what the agenda was. "Hello, Henri. Kind of early for you, isn't it?"

"Graham. Good to see you. Early? No, I like this part of the day. Very productive for me." Malraux nudged a chair closer and sat down. "I'm glad to catch you. How is everything?"

What you really want to know is when Valerie and I will stop quarreling with one another so that I can move back in the apartment and out of the guest room. It must be annoying when your uber-rich residents turn out to have the same tedious marital problems as the ordinary people at the bottom of the hill.

"Thanks for asking, Henri. Everything is fine, just fine. We're still adjusting to Alden Acres but it's clearly the right place for us." *I see no reason why I should make this easy for him. I wonder if he'll even bring up such a sensitive topic?*

But he did. After an awkward twenty-second silence, Malraux said, "Um, about the guest room, I was wondering —"

"I know, I know. I've tied it up for two weeks now. But I talked with your operations person ... Barbara, I think ... and I told her to let me know if one was needed. I can be out with two hours notice. *I also read the bylaws and policies. As you probably know, there is no clause that covers how long a resident can stay in one of the four guest rooms. I guess they assumed that no sensible person would be willing to spend two hundred bucks a night just to make a point with his wife.*

Malraux smiled politely but wriggled in his chair. "Yes, Barbara told me. That's good of you. But, still, it must seem strange. Living in what's basically a hotel room that's a two minute walk away from your wonderful apartment?"

"Actually, I've spent half my life in hotel rooms. This one is particularly nice." He smiled to make his words even more ambiguous than they sounded. *Why do I dislike this man so much that I can't even tell him what he wants to know?*

Just then, Butch Melendy and Salvador Fender wandered in, headed for their usual morning alcove overlooking the entry to the main building. Malraux stood up and Graham imagined that he welcomed the interruption. "Good morning, gentlemen. I'll leave you to enjoy your coffee." He walked out, pausing only to frown at the incomplete jigsaw puzzle occupying most of the center table.

"I think Henri displays a mild indisposition this morning," Butch said. "Perhaps he's detected a small tear in the social fabric of Alden Acres." Salvador just groaned slightly, saying only "Butch," but in a way that conveyed a lifetime's worth of reproach.

Graham closed his laptop and stood up. "Mind if I join you for coffee? And don't be so hard on Henri. He views marital discord as the equivalent of termites in the woodwork or antiquated elevators ... something to be patched up so that the five-star ratings don't suffer."

Once the three of them had moved to their usual corner and gotten their coffee, Salvador came back to the subject without any preliminaries. "So, how are you doing with Valerie? Are we still in the 'I'm not going to be the one to say I'm sorry' mode? Or have we moved on to the 'You're not meeting my needs' stage?"

Graham wondered for the hundredth time how it was that this pair of aging gays knew more about the state of his marriage than he did. At first, he made the usual denials, but quickly realized that they could sense the rift between Valerie and him, as clearly as though the two of them emitted subsonic pulses of anger, hurt or any of the other distress signals of a troubled relationship. He wondered if Valerie had opened up to them, remembering the instant rapport that was so evident between them when they first met. Now, he welcomed their awareness and actually looked forward to a daily status report. *This must be what marriage therapy would be like.*

Graham waved his hand in the air as though brushing away their characterizations of his marriage. "I'd call it the 'Can I live without this other person in my life?' phase. Marked mostly by daydreams of other women and a fear of being alone for the rest of my life. It's a pathetic and selfish form of introspection."

The two men stared at him, looking concerned. *Oops! I think that's what they call 'over-sharing.'* He tried for a quick retreat. "Sorry. What I should have said was that I am in the phase where any expression of genuine interest in my state of mind just makes me feel sorry for myself." When their concern seemed to deepen, he tried again. "You never practiced family law, did you?"

Salvador said, "We were criminal defense attorneys. But a few of our clients did murder their spouse." Butch immediately added, "You might call that the final phase of a broken relationship."

All three of them picked up their cup simultaneously, unsure of how they had gotten to this point. Graham finally broke the silence. "Frankly, I don't know what phase we're in. Hell, I don't even know what *I'm* thinking about the whole thing, let alone Valerie." *But she said, 'I want a divorce.' A simple declarative sentence. What is there that you don't understand about that?* He stood up. "Thanks for listening … and for chasing Malraux away."

Butch said, "You might ask him for advice. He's been married five times."

McNeal & Shanahan

Graham found Thad McNeal and Frank Shanahan sitting at one of the mahogany tables in the card room. He watched them from the doorway for thirty seconds or so and got the distinct impression that neither of them was comfortable. Each of them sat back in their chair with their arms crossed on their chest, not quite looking at the other man. An iPad was propped open in the middle of the table. He walked over to the table, noting that both of them seemed glad for a third party.

"Hi. Am I interrupting?"

"Not if you can tell me why this thing won't work!" Shanahan pointed at the iPad. "It won't connect to the internet."

"And I can't help him." McNeal said. "The only trick I know is to drop it on the floor once or twice."

Graham smiled. "I know a little bit, once the caffeine kicks in. They tell me there's a perpetual coffee pot somewhere around here."

McNeal pointed to an alcove at the side of the room. "In there. It's one of those fancy do-it-yourself gadgets. Choose from twenty different brews and push a button. Tastes OK, but it's not the same as picking up a coffee pot and pouring it into a mug."

The "gadget" turned out to be a top of the line industrial strength espresso machine with a gleaming stainless steel finish and a daunting number of levers. Arrayed next to it was a pyramid of ceramic mugs, each with a different photo of the California coastline. *No paper cups for the residents of Alden Acres. And they'll probably justify it as an environmentally friendly luxury … no clogged up landfills for them.*

He took his mug back to the table, sat down and pulled the iPad to him. "Lemme see what I can do." It took him twenty seconds and several finger taps before he slid it back to Shanahan. "It was locked on to some open access WiFi network nearby; too weak to connect for more than a few seconds. I signed on to the Alden Acres network; plenty of signal strength."

"Thanks." Shanahan held up the device and said, "They say these things have revolutionized business, but I'm glad I missed that particular revolution."

Graham doubted that. *The man retired from a global enterprise only a few years ago. I think he understands technology more than he likes to admit.* But he let it stand. "They certainly changed the newspaper business. Every piece of it." *When I started, I'd do the legwork, write the story, turn it in according to a deadline and read it a day later in an actual newspaper. Now I have a blog, a Twitter account and a website. The "newspaper" is in electronic format and there are no deadlines. It's all real time.*

McNeal startled him. "You don't sound real happy about that."

Who would be? Or am I just becoming one of those old fogies that remembers the good old days that never were? Both of the men were looking at him, clearly curious how he would respond, reminding him yet again that he was perceived as a fairly exotic creature. "It was a different world. A lot better in some ways, I think, but it's gone and it's not coming back."

"Adapt or die?" McNeal asked.

"There's a third option." Shanahan said, "You say 'the hell with it' and retire, like I did."

McNeal turned to Shanahan and something in his posture or the slight change in his tone of voice made his words take on a hostile tinge. "That's maybe an option for a corporate executive with a golden parachute. Or a lot of stock options. Or a really big severance package."

Shanahan gave McNeal a sharp look and was clearly evaluating alternative replies, but Graham intervened. "Anybody that's signed up for this place," and he waved his hand to take in everything around them, "managed the financial side of their retirement plan pretty well. But what is it that you retired from, Frank?"

It seemed to Graham to be a step back toward civility, but McNeal didn't let it go. "He *facilitated* transactions. Very important stuff. Made things happen." Again, the hostility came through clearly, enough so that Graham regretted his decision to joion them. *These two have some history together. I wonder what they were talking about when I came in?* He pushed his chair back from the table. "Good luck with the iPad, I think –"

"I retired from a global construction company. It's Dutch and I worked there for more than thirty years." Shanahan was talking to Graham, but looking at McNeal. "I don't think General McNeal approves of big corporations."

"Just certain ones. I was on the Board of a Fortune 100 company for five years, so I'm OK with the idea of big for-profit companies." McNeal was very matter-of-fact, but then his voice took on an edge. "What I'm not OK with is the idea of private armies disguised as everyday capitalist enterprises and that's what NRE was, by my book."

"Thanks for the help with the electronics," Shanahan said. He stood up abruptly and walked away. It was a fitting end to the increasingly tense exchange with McNeal.

Graham remembered McNeal's bitterness about military contractors and the corruption they brought with them from their earlier conversation. *But why lean on a retiree from a Dutch construction company?* "It's none of my business, but weren't you a little hard on him?"

"Do you know that we've spent over four trillion dollars on our wars in Afghanistan and Iraq?"

Graham answered, "Actually, I do –" But McNeal wasn't listening. "A lot of that – mostly wasted -- went to companies like his. They built things, then either we or the other side blew them up, so they built them again. And got paid twice, of course."

OK, so now we've established that wars are good for economic growth. This conversation is going nowhere real fast. Let's divert. "Shanahan said that he was involved in the construction of Alden Acres."

"Yeah. One of the environmental sticking points was about how the construction itself would damage the ecosystem and watershed. So NRE contracted to build the place without using any roads except the tree-lined and very narrow entry road that we all use every day. It meant that they brought in all the construction materials and heavy equipment by giant helicopters ... flying cranes, basically. That was Shanahan's company. Pretty impressive, actually."

"And the Shanahan's were one of the first residents to sign up?"

"That's what they say. But people – including us – were enrolling all during the almost-three years that the place was under construction. We all showed up on opening day. The only one that was acknowledged in any way was McDavid. He was the first. But he didn't show up at the ceremony."

"What's he like? I haven't met him yet."

"How would I know? I've seen him up close exactly once. He's got the entire wing to himself with his own private entrance and his assistants ... you've seen the Tom and Jerry duo? ... to maintain his personal space. Mendoza and Malraux are the only ones that deal with him and they're under orders not to talk about him."

"But you've talked to him, at least that one time. What's he like?"

"My so-called conversation lasted about ninety seconds. And most of that was him ranting about the goddamn liberals – his words – and how they're ruining our great country. Oh, yeah, and the confiscatory taxes and lily-livered foreign policies ..."

The memory of that ninety seconds is bothering him. "I gather your views are different."

McNeal shrugged. "I was a two-star general. Most people assume I'm as far right as one can be. Actually, I like to think of myself as apolitical, probably because I've seen firsthand what happens on the ground when politicians – Democrats and Republicans alike – start talking about abstract concepts like freedom, duty and 'surgical strikes' and 'boots on the ground.'"

"I wonder why McDavid chooses to live in a community like this, even with all the privacy that it offers. He could be in a walled villa on a Greek island or a remote castle in Northern Scotland. Why here?"

McNeal shook his head. "Good question, but I don't know the answer. There are rumors that he's a part owner. But even if that's true, he wouldn't have to live here."

Two minutes later, McNeal was gone, leaving Graham alone in the room to think about McDavid. Like most thoughts these days, they circled back to his own highly ambivalent situation. *He's like me ... living in a place where he doesn't need to be.*

The Book Club

"We should sit in on the book club. It starts in half-an-hour."

They'd just finished dinner together in the main dining room, part of Valerie's private plan to maintain appearances for what she called "the need to keep the rest of these people as unsure of what we're trying to do as we are." The syntax was tortured, but Graham understood it quite well. *We are engaged in muddling through. Neither of us knows where we're going or even where we want it to go.*

"We – I – haven't read the book. Don't even know what it is."

"There's no book. It's a 'meet-the-author' kind of session. It seems that Salvador Fender writes mysteries as a retirement sideline. I think maybe the genre is 'legal thrillers.' People tell me they're not bad. Kind of a cross between Erle Stanley Gardner and John Grisham. His main character is – surprise! – a gay Jewish defense attorney."

"That almost makes it an autobiography, doesn't it? It's funny: I've talked with Salvador almost every day. He's never mentioned that he was an author." *Mendoza said, 'Nobody retires. They just get more selective about what they do.'*

Valerie shrugged. "So, are you coming along?"

They met Salvador coming from the other direction just as they reached the entry to the library. He said, "I'm disappointed. I thought surely the two of you would have better literary taste than to attend readings by third-rate, self-published authors."

Valerie smiled at him and said, "It's either that or stay home and fight with each other. This seems the lesser of two evils." The rejoinder caused Graham to wonder whether she viewed their awkward estrangement as suitable for open sharing. *But, then again, it's exactly the kind of witty self-putdown that she's always been good at; the sort of comment that for many listeners hints at great affection between the two of them.* In any case, Salvador merely raised an eyebrow and then gestured for them to precede him into the room, saying, "I'll be there in about two minutes."

There were about twenty people standing around in small clusters. The only ones Graham knew for sure were Henri, the Shanahan's, the McNeal's and Butch Melendy. As he went toward Butch, the woman Mendoza brought 'the resident multi-billionaire' McDavid in his wheelchair, accompanied by the two aides. He found it hard to think of them as 'Tom and Jerry.' Graham could feel the change in the room's atmosphere when the quartet came into the room. The low hum of conversation changed slightly and the small groups standing around the room seemed to reorient themselves very slightly to better focus on McDavid. Valerie whispered to him, "They tell me he never attends any of our events, so this may be a first."

"Maybe it's that he's a billionaire and the rest of us mere millionaires." But Valerie had already turned away toward a self-serve bar that was set up in the corner with several bottles of wine and various soft drinks arranged along its surface. Two rows of chairs formed an arc facing a small table with a single chair. As soon as Salvador entered, a very frail and old woman clinked on a wine glass. "Our guest of honor is here. Shall we start?"

Thirty minutes later, Graham was impressed. *Obviously a well-read group. Good questions, and they've actually read his books, at least one of them. And Salvador knows how to play to the crowd.* He was presently engaged in an increasingly contentious dialogue with a man that seemed determined to get Salvador to admit that most "thrillers" – excepting his, of course – were far-fetched, lacking any connection to reality. "C'mon! A nuclear bomb is planted in New York City! How did it get there? How did the terrorist know enough to build it? Where'd the uranium come from? The author just makes up whatever suits his story!"

Salvador stood up and walked around the table to within a few feet of the man. He crossed his arms and stared at him with a thoughtful look. Graham thought, *I think we're about to see Salvador in his best courtroom cross-examination mode*, and confirmed it by looking at Butch. He was smiling, clearly anticipating what was coming.

"I don't write about nuclear weapons," said Salvador. "I kill my characters one at a time … just everyday murders that really aren't all that fictional. For example, I submit that most of us in this room could sit down at the breakfast table with a cup of coffee and a blank sheet of paper and dream up a completely plausible plan for a murder." He paused to let the hook firmly imbed itself in the minds of his listeners. "For example, for you men here," – he gestured to include the entire room – "suppose you wanted to kill your wife. How would you go about it?"

There was sudden stillness in the room and some tentative laughter. Graham was startled when Valerie spoke loudly from beside him. "Most husbands would just bore their wives to death. Leaves no visible marks. Technically, it's probably not even a crime." The laughter became more assured, coming mostly from the women in the room. Salvador bowed slightly to Valerie, but shook his head. "Doesn't count. That's social satire, not a viable plan for a murder."

Just then Melissa Shanahan stood up abruptly, clearly disturbed. She stood rigid, clenching and unclenching her fists, looking frantically around the room for someone or something. All eyes turned to her and the room went dead silent. Her husband moved next to her, putting his arm around her, leaning close and whispering. It was easy to see the instant that she realized that she was the center of attention. She turned into her husband and put her face against his chest. But everyone in the room heard her say, "We didn't kill them. It wasn't our fault. And they didn't need the coffins." And then, loudly, "I need to pee." Frank Shanahan paid no attention to the others; he walked her out of the room, leaning close to her and talking softly to her the entire way.

Even Salvador was at a loss as to restarting and the awkward silence dragged on. Nobody looked at anybody else. Then David McDavid cleared his throat and everyone in the room looked at him gratefully, glad to grasp at any alternative. He waited, as if to be sure of everyone's attention. "I would never murder my wife. But my in-laws, … that's another matter." It was a perfect transition and the mood in the room tilted back toward normal.

Then a man at the end of the first row spoke softly, as though still thinking through his words. "I wouldn't do it myself … kill my wife, that is. The husband is always the first and favorite suspect." Everyone turned to look at him. Graham had met him and knew that he was a biochemist of some sort. When they'd met, his wife was with him and Graham recalled a mousy overbearing woman who drank too much. She was not with him tonight. Apparently others were envisioning the couple as well because once again the silence took on an uncomfortable tension. Salvador clearly sensed the mood and moved to get back on more congenial ground. He said, "That's excellent, Matthew. Our hypothetical plot now has a hit man. That adds all kinds of interesting subplot possibilities. And that's one of my problems – subplots. How many and how complex ..."

The book discussion ran late. Salvador had compelling stories, rich in detail. Graham had the thought more than once that they were more real than fictional, dredged up from Salvador's own personal or professional life. Several of the people in attendance hung around to pester Salvador with more questions and others wandered off. Graham found himself in the bar with Butch.

"Salvador kind of went out on a limb with that 'How would you kill your wife?' line, don't you think?" Graham asked. "Not your usual hypothetical."

"Hypotheticals are always dangerous, especially in the courtroom," Butch said. "It can work well with a jury, though. Gets them thinking."

Shanahan came into the bar as he was talking and sat down next to them. Graham and Butch looked at one another, but Shanahan preempted any questions, saying, "I like hypotheticals. It worked a little too well in this case though. That guy ... Matthew ... clearly saw it as something more than a hypothetical. That was a little spooky."

No mention of the strange incident with Melissa. Seems to be a characteristic of the residents of Alden Acres. If you don't talk about it, it never happened!

To his own surprise, Graham found himself wanting to continue what Sal and Matthew had started. "People murder their spouses all the time. Almost all of them get caught, including the ones like Matthew who would hire someone else to do it for them."

Shanahan seemed intrigued and asked, "So how would you murder *your* wife? Hypothetically, of course." Graham looked closely at him and saw that he was serious, or at least curious about what he would say. "That's getting awfully specific, isn't it? I presume there's a point to it?" He noted that Butch was beaming, watching the two men prove his point about the lure of hypotheticals.

Shanahan shrugged. "Salvador says that we should be able to draft a plausible murder plan, one where we have a chance of success. Matthew got us started; I'm just being devil's advocate."

Graham sat up straighter. "OK. If we go with his hit man strategy ... Problem number one – maybe the biggest one – is finding the right person. The professionals don't advertise and probably wouldn't take on a new and unknown client even if I could find them." He thought for a bit. "So, an amateur then. But one with a predisposition to violence and motivated purely by money. A gang member, maybe."

In fact, I know just the person.

He hadn't thought of Amen Cartwright for a long time now. Ten years, probably. Cartwright was thirty-six when we met, in his tenth year at San Quentin. His real name was Joseph, but his street name was 'Amen,' because – according to the gang member that ratted him out – "You'd better pray if the man's after you." The word was that he was the enforcer for one of the major drug lords and had put a lot of people down. The state finally put him away when he slashed his girl friend for skimming from his cocaine stash. Graham had spent twenty hours interviewing him for a fifty-thousand word feature on prison rehab programs. He was pure evil. Beyond psychopathic even. If I asked him to kill somebody, he'd ask, "How much will you pay me?" and that would be the beginning and end of the negotiation.

Shanahan startled him out of his brief reverie. "You actually know someone, don't you?" The insight depressed him. *This is a little too real.* And once more, he wondered about Shanahan's real motives for this conversation.

He ignored the question. "So that brings us to problem number two– how to manage the contract?" Graham smiled at the thought, and immediately felt guilty. He tried to cover it up, probably making it worse by doing so. "Very quietly. No middlemen. Half the money up front, half when the deed is done. No face-to-face meetings. No documents. And he has to do it within a set time frame, so that I can arrange an ironclad alibi."

Shanahan was leaning forward, clearly following every word. *He looks like he wants to start taking notes! Maybe his wife should start worrying.* "Which leads to problem number three – How do you pay him?"

When the silence went on, Butch decided to take a part and said, "Surely, that's not a problem these days, what with computers. Just transfer money to one of those famous Swiss bank accounts. At the speed of light. Ah, but there would be digital traces. Account numbers that could be accessed. And your hit man probably wouldn't even be on the financial grid. Hard to wire money to somebody that doesn't have a bank account."

Graham shrugged. "So, we do it the old-fashioned way. Bundles of used ten and twenty-dollar bills." Shanahan remained silent, staring at Graham to emphasize that he was missing a key point. Graham frowned. "But where would I get that much cash without triggering some attention... leaving a trail?"

"So," Shanahan said, "problem number four -- You need to have access to an existing and secret stash of cash." After a pause, he added, "I suppose that means that it's easier for rich people to get away with murder."

Graham suddenly grew tired of the game. He stood up abruptly and said, "That was sort of interesting. Not your usual conversation at Alden Acres. But I don't think Valerie would approve of such speculation." He turned to leave and was halfway to the door when Shanahan said, "Who said we were talking about Valerie?"

An Alternative to Alzheimer's

Henri Malraux had a difficult job. He viewed it as walking a tightrope. Alden Acres promised a serene existence, one where the slightly unpleasant realities of daily life were kept out-of-sight, a place where everything was always in order and the days proceeded according to a rigid class code. On the other hand, the place was populated by individuals who were unaccustomed to being told what to do or how to do it, strong personalities with a long history of living life as they saw fit. For them, group norms were understood, not something to be codified in a written handbook. So there was no written rule that prohibited sleeping in the common areas; it was simply 'just not done.'

So early that morning, when Henri Malraux saw Melissa Shanahan in one of the leather recliners in the library, with the footrest up, a book turned face down in her lap, and her eyes closed, he watched her for a long minute to be sure that she wasn't just resting her eyes. Then he went to the librarian's desk and opened and closed a drawer quite loudly. When that didn't work, he stood to the side of her chair and said very softly, "Melissa?" By now, he was feeling slightly irritated and so he tapped on her shoulder more forcefully than he normally would. There was still no response.

Thirty seconds later, his sense of irritation had changed to outright alarm. Melissa Shanahan was dead. And she had died in one of the public rooms at Alden Acres, a clear violation of the group norms.

Henri was in fact very good at crisis management of this sort. He closed the library, called Mendoza and 911 in that order, and went to find Frank Shanahan. Two hours later, all was back to normal except for the closed library and the discreet note posted on the community board, with the kind of phrasing that left the reader unsure as to whether Melissa Shanahan had died or merely gone on a very long and unexpected trip to an exotic location. The black cloth edging around the notecard was the giveaway.

Graham read the announcement at mid-morning in a state of disbelief. *Twelve hours ago, Shanahan and I were talking – hypothetically – about killing our respective wives. And now she's dead?* He headed for Mendoza's office and caught her as she was leaving.

"Mendoza, what happened? Melissa Shanahan seemed fine last night." But even while he was speaking, he was picturing Melissa standing up distraught and being escorted out of the book club session by her husband. *But that's what they would call slight cognitive impairment, not a life-threatening disease.*

Mendoza seemed slightly amused by the notion that Melissa Shanahan couldn't be dead because 'she seemed fine last night,' but quickly slipped back into her professional mode. "Melissa Shanahan was old and increasingly frail. She has not been sleeping well and she went out to the library somewhere after midnight to look for something to read. She died quite peacefully while reading a book." When he seemed unsatisfied, she added, "Graham. It happens. Especially when you're old and displaying early Alzheimer's symptoms."

He called Alison, wondering about his motives even as he did so. He almost disconnected when she didn't answer on the first two rings. As it turned out, she was the first one to bring up the subject.

"Sorry about Melissa Shanahan. She was one of the few people you knew there, wasn't she?"

"Alison, how do you know about her? It happened only a few hours ago."

"No mystery. I look at the 911 call log every morning."

He tried to sound as bland as possible. "How does it work from here? Will there be any inquiry? An autopsy?"

She was silent briefly and he knew why. *The answers to my questions are easy. What she's wondering is why I'm asking them.* She responded, "It's up to the coroner. She'll review the woman's medical history and if she has any doubts about cause of death, she'll do the autopsy." She paused to make it clear that what she said next was not just a routine question. "Why are you asking?"

"It's a little weird ..." He went on to describe the book club incident and the later conversation with Frank Shanahan in the bar. He quoted Shanahan's parting comment verbatim: "What makes you think we're talking about Valerie?"

"I'll pass it on to the coroner. Given the little bit you've told me, I'd bet on an autopsy ... and a good long talk with Mr. Shanahan."

She called back two hours later. "The assistant coroner was already doing the autopsy when I called. They are treating the death as a likely homicide. Melissa Shanahan had some visible petechiae – tiny hemorrhages – in her eyes and scalp. They're a pretty clear sign of strangulation and more than enough to raise red flags. The autopsy is pretty clear; she was suffocated, probably by somebody holding a heavy duty plastic bag over her head."

"Any suspects?"

"The obvious one: her husband. Especially given what you told me about that conversation in the bar. Manning has him in an interrogation room as we speak. He declined to have his lawyer with him, which was interesting. His alibi – completely unverifiable – is that he was asleep, that she woke him up to say she was going to get a book, that he went back to sleep and knew nothing until Mendoza woke him up at six-thirty this morning."

"Motive? He seemed very devoted."

"There's what he said to you. That would seem to indicate intent. I looked in on him in the interview room and he looked terrible. He's either a world-class actor or experiencing extreme grief. And maybe, just maybe, he viewed it as a mercy killing because of the Alzheimer's. Quick and relatively pain free exit versus a long and undignified loss of self. We're seeing more and more of that these days."

"Any witnesses?"

"None so far. The coroner says that she was killed at about three AM and probably not in the library. We're still canvassing the residents but as you undoubtedly know, there's not much activity around Alden Acres after ten PM. And no interior cameras. As Malraux put it, 'Our residents expect complete privacy, and they get it.' All doors to the exterior have cameras, so we do know that there were no non-residents on site after that time. Unless they scaled a fence and had the entry code to one of the doors."

"So what's your professional opinion?"

Her reply was instant. "Shanahan murdered his wife. And we're not going to be able to prove it. He walks."

Graham Does Research

Shanahan said that he retired from a Dutch construction company. Let's see what Google has to say about that. Graham typed "Dutch construction company" into the Google search rectangle and, as always, was amused to get 6,450,000 'hits' in less than a second. *Makes a so-called investigative journalist about as relevant as Sanskrit scrolls.* He quickly narrowed his search to the top ten companies by size. *Shanahan said it was a 'very large' company. And McNeal referred to it as 'NRE,' so ...* His screen listed a company called Nationale Hulpbronnen Enterprise as the second largest company in Holland and quickly translated that into English as National Resources Enterprise, listed as NRE on the European stock exchanges.

That's why it sounded familiar. According to Yahoo Finance, it was a Dutch corporation that was the European half of a tax inversion merger with the Ross Sea Group three years ago. And Graham knew a lot about the Ross Sea Group. More specifically, he knew a lot about the founder of the Group.

Barry Wilder was an Alaskan wildcatter that got lucky while exploring for natural gas deposits in an unlikely spot on the Kenai Peninsula in 1965. Ten years later, he swapped his gas reserves for an oil services company that he renamed the Ross Sea Group and grew to the point that it was a rival to Halliburton in remote spots of the world. If the story stopped there, it would be a corporate 'Horatio Alger' case study and a paean to capitalism. However, both the company and Barry Wilder became notorious for their sponsorship of populist politicians and programs that trafficked in racism and xenophobia.

Graham found another corporate monogram that was even more familiar to him. The primary subsidiary of the Ross

Sea Group was a company called Advanced Base Logistics. ABL specialized in what they called "large scale project and facilities management in harsh environments," at first in the Arctic and then expanding to any remote or hostile part of the world where other contractors wouldn't go. ABL's primary clients were military forces, major defense contractors, and construction, mining, and oil exploration and production facilities. Among other services, ABL built and operated dozens of dining facilities and served meals to thousands of U.S. and other Coalition service members every day of the Iraq War.

I remember them in Fallujah. Their people wore one-piece light tan coveralls with 'ABL' stencils on the left shoulder and above the front pocket. Most of them looked like ex-military types and they provided their own security force. They mostly hired locals for the grunt work. Stayed to themselves for the most part, and the Marine officers in the field didn't trust them very much. Bartlett said, "They hang out with the spooks and the private military contractors. Pretty much do what they want and go where they like. Treat the civilians like shit."

He told me a story. His Marines were taking fire day after day from a three-thousand foot hill that dominated their area of operation. The higher-ups wouldn't let them go after it because it was the site of a small village that was the home of a local warlord of ambiguous loyalties and it had an important mosque. "Then one day, an SUV with ABL logos on its doors drove up the hill, spent two hours and came back down. The next day, a convoy of ABL vehicles towing bulldozers and a lot of equipment went up the hill. Two weeks later, they'd leveled the village. The mosque was still there, along with what looked like a prefab palace. They said it was for the warlord, who was now on our side."

Google had many line items concerning ABL. The company operated very close to the line between legal and illegal and was in the news quite a lot until a few years ago when it all came unraveled. It began with a 2015 incident in Afghanistan where six ABL sub-contractors were killed. The subsequent inquiry uncovered a massive over-billing scheme in ABL's Middle Eastern contracts. That in turn led to a flurry of stories alleging that ABL was awarded half-a-billion dollars in UN procurement contracts in West Africa with the help of a corrupt U.N. official. Allegedly, ABL executives bribed an official on the UN's Committee for Administrative and Budgetary Issues to give them access to all of the bids to support several UN peacekeeping missions. ABL's underbid its competitors in virtually every service category. The UN official, but not ABL, pleaded guilty to charges of corruption, wire fraud and money laundering and the losing bidders initiated multiple lawsuits. Shortly after that, Barry Wilder was subpoenaed by the Congressional Committee on Oversight and Government Reform concerning questionable billings for various logistics and construction services to coalition forces and major defense contractors at desert bases in Kuwait, Iraq and Afghanistan.

Wilder never appeared, and the congressional investigators found the ABL offices deserted, file cabinets empty, computers gone. The company simply ceased to exist as an operating entity. All the assets that could be found were liquidated to pay debtors and the employees scattered. The Ross Sea Group lived on, on paper, as a shell company until the Dutch transaction.

I begin to see why Shanahan didn't say anything about the Ross Sea Group or ABL. That would be like a banker saying 'Oh, me?

I'm a payday lender.' And I think I know why our ex-General McNeal is hostile to him. The marines didn't like the contractors. They didn't trust them and resented the way they operated outside the boundaries.

He tried but could find no record of an executive named Frank Shanahan working for any of the three companies in the last ten years, based on the few publicly available documents. Both the Ross Sea Group and ABL were clearly paranoid about press coverage and as private companies were able to stay beneath the media radar. He did note that the Dutch firm called NRE paid zero U.S. taxes and that Barry Wilder was still completely disappeared from public view. One industry analyst speculated that Wilder had died.

One more search. He typed in 'General Thaddeus McNeal' and immediately got a screen full of sites. He went to the "Department of Defense – Biographies' website and was amazed as always at the amount of detail that was available with a couple of keystrokes.

The general had indeed had a distinguished military career, starting in Vietnam and winding up in Iraq. But two biographical features stood out. The first was that he was a full Colonel in the Army's special forces on September 11, 2001 and one of the first officers to see combat service in Afghanistan against the Taliban. The other slight surprise was that Helen was his third wife.

New Horizons

It was their third hike together. Valerie and Thad McNeal were both fitness fanatics and spent from six to seven AM three days a week working out in the Alden Acres Fitness Center. They were usually the only people there at that hour. When he learned of her Saturday morning habit of exploring the trails in the surrounding forest, he'd asked if he could join. They quickly learned that they both preferred the harder trails and that they shared an obsession with metrics. They measured every aspect of their hikes – steps taken, elevation gained, calories consumed, pulse rate, respiration and whatever else the new technologies offered. Last time, they had gone further than Valerie had been so far, well past Skyline Drive and partway down the long slope to the ocean.

They were doing stretching drills at the head of the trail when she noticed the black holster at the small of his back as he leaned forward to stretch his calf muscles. He saw her startled look and pulled the holster loose from the Velcro holding it to his belt and put it into the backpack sitting on the ground near him.

"Thad? A gun? Is that legal?"

He was unabashed. "In my apartment, yes. Out here, no. But it goes where I go. Old habits die hard. OK with you? I promise not to shoot you."

"I grew up with guns. Once upon a time, I organized and ran a gun safety class in our town for teenagers. Got the local 4H club to sponsor it."

"Ever hunt?"

"Never. The idea of killing birds or animals seemed all wrong. What about you?"

He looked away from her, fiddling with the straps on his backpack. "Hunting birds or animals? No. But I've killed some *people*." There was no drama in his admission. He spoke as if telling someone the time of day.

Valerie mentally kicked herself. *The man was a career military officer. Multiple tours in Afghanistan, Iraq and god knows where else. Time to change the subject.* She pointed at the backpack. "What all are you bringing along? Other than a gun."

He hefted the pack in his right hand. "This? Extra fluids. A snack. We ran low last time, remember? Ready?"

They turned to start up the trail, but he stopped. "You work in the Mission District ... hang out with some pretty disturbed types. The Chronicle had an article last week ...a 911 call that almost went postal ... a guy in your office with a shotgun?"

Valerie was still having flashbacks about the incident. For an instant, she had thought she was going to die. "He's a client. A very confused one. My staff talked him down before the cops got there. Nothing happened." *He was raving about needing painkillers ... that our clinic wouldn't give him the right kind ... that they kept telling him, 'Take your meds!'*

McNeal was watching her closely and – she thought – seeing through her 'nothing happened' story line. He said, "Whatever. But I think you should have a handgun close by, even carry one; Legal or not. If you like, I can help you get one."

She laughed. "Thanks. I'll continue to reply on my martial arts training. And it would slow me down on these hikes. I'll probably have to wait for you, what with all the hardware you're lugging. Let's go."

They got to the clearing where she'd said, "I want a divorce" and the fox walked out of the brush with the foot in its mouth. They sat on that same log for their first short break and planned the rest of their route, using a very detailed topographical map that he pulled out of the backpack.

She teased him. "I thought you military types didn't trust plans ... how they never survive the first encounter with the enemy?"

"On the contrary, we rely on them for most of what we do. But we know they're going to be wrong, so we stay loose. What we don't like are the *plans* that the politicians draw up and then can't change because they'd lose face. Those so-called plans kill people."

Like the "Charge of the Light Brigade? Theirs not to reason why, theirs but to do or die?"

He nodded. "Lord Tennyson's poem. But it was also a real battle. One hundred and twenty-two men were killed needlessly. But that's nothing. The Battle of the Somme in our First World War killed a million men ... for a total of six miles gained. And then – my personal favorite – we have the invasion of Iraq ... a sixteen-year long 'preemptive war' in pursuit of non-existent weapons of mass destruction!"

His voice was clipped, angry; disproportionately so, she thought. *I wonder what else is going on with him?* Valerie stood up. "Ready? Since you're a general, you get to go last." And she moved off, uphill and at a fast pace, hoping that the route she was on was not the one he'd planned for.

They stopped after two hours. The sun was well up and both of them were sweating and thirsty. Part of it was the unacknowledged competitiveness that caused them to go faster and longer than they otherwise would. McNeal picked the route, occasionally consulting his map. Once over the crest, most of it was downhill or lateral, but the last twenty minutes was a steady climb and Valerie's calves were protesting enough that she was glad for the break.

"This is a special place." McNeal was already sitting, undoing the flap on his backpack. She looked around and saw that he was right, and at the same time realized that this had been his destination all along. "Yes it is," she said. They were on the crest of one of the many ridges between Skyline Drive and the Pacific, in a hollow enclosed on three sides by wind-shaped cypress trees and dense manzanita undergrowth. The open and downhill side faced the still-distant ocean, with nothing but undisturbed green between them and the beach.

"You've been here before?" By way of an answer, he showed her the map and she noticed for the first time a small inked-in 'x' near its center.

He handed her a granola bar and a plastic water bottle. "Malraux brags about the hundred miles of trails. I've actually hiked them. It turns out to be only ninety-seven miles, but most of that is open space, reserved for deer, hikers and the occasional mountain lion." He looked at her closely. "You like it?"

She didn't answer for long enough that he wasn't sure she heard him, but then she said, "Every now and then, I daydream about dying. In those daydreams, I have some hopeless wasting disease, but always something tasteful. I visualize walking into the forest and finding a spot like this and just lying down, going to sleep and not waking up. Now I've got an image to go with my daydream. This is perfect."

I've never told anybody anything like this. But the setting seemed right for such intimate disclosures. One felt enclosed, safe, unobserved ... and the distant view seemed to require the extraordinary disclosures that go with summits and secret places. *Sanctuary,* she thought.

He said, "Daydreaming about dying? It sounds like a person who doesn't like her life very much ..." At the same time, a slight breeze chilled her and that, coupled with his insight, changed the mood. She brought her feet under her, ready to stand up. "We need to start back, we've been gone –"

"Not yet," he said softly and put his hand on her knee to keep her sitting. "Neither of us has any particular incentive to get back."

His voice was neutral and he didn't look at her, but the words clearly conveyed his need to stay, perhaps to talk about his own daydreams. His voice also made her suddenly aware that for the first time in a very long time, she was conscious of being alone with a man in a private space. *He's planned this. Not just the destination, but the agenda as well.* He confirmed it when he started talking again, looking out at the faraway ocean. "Graham is living in one of the guest rooms. The two of you are like strangers who happen to be in the same elevator. I've watched: you don't like each other any more. You're going through the motions but there's nothing there."

"Thad. This is not – Graham and I -- "

"I know what that's like. Helen is a drunk. Always has been."

She tried once more, knowing that it would do no good; that his plan required him to get certain things said. "Thad, this is not the time nor place." *But you're wrong, at least about the place. You said it yourself – sanctuary – a safe place.*

He went on, for the first time turning to face her. "I've watched you. We're alike, you and I. Even the daydreams, and probably other fantasies as well. We both want ... need ... more than we've got ... more than what's possible if we don't change the script. There's too much to do and too little time. And neither of them ... Graham or Helen ... can help us be where we want to be."

Even as she was thinking *this is crazy!* she was seeing him as if for the first time. *He's years older than me ... wrinkles around his eyes that look like they're more about worry than aging ... a four-inch scar on his neck ... kind of a Gary Cooper look about him ... nice hands.*

What are you thinking? You need to stop this stuff. Right now. But instead she said, "Thanks for bringing me here. It really is a special place, and I'd like to come back here with you. But I need to work some things out –"

He put two fingers on her lips, very gently. "This is a good time and place to start. I was hoping you'd let me help." He moved his hand to enclose the entire right side of her face, turning her head to face him.

She shook herself and stood up. "Thad, this is way too fast." *But you didn't say 'this is wrong' or ''please don't do that' or 'I have no interest in you' or ... any of those other things that you should have said.* And it was obvious to her that he had heard all the things that she *didn't* say as clearly as if she had handed him a list. He stood up and said, "Not fast enough for me." He smiled in a mischievous way. "Or for my plan. But you're the boss."

"C'mon. I'll race you back to the geriatric ward." Valerie picked up the backpack and handed it to him. It was surprisingly heavy. "Must be some hefty snacks that you brought. What's in there?"

"A gun, a bottle of wine and a very soft blanket." He looked straight at her, unembarrassed by his admission. "But as I said, us generals always know that the plan never quite works like it was drawn up. Ready to go?" And he started down the trail at a very fast pace.

Six days later, they encountered each other at the regular Friday night cocktail party that Henri hosted for all the residents. She was standing with Graham trying to think of something … anything … to say to him so that people could see them talking together contentedly like an ordinary married couple, so that the antagonism would be less visible to those around them, although she wondered why that still mattered to her.

Thad McNeal and his wife Helen were across the room, standing with another couple whose names Valerie couldn't remember. She studied the two of them, wondering if there would be visible signs of what was obviously a troubled marriage. Helen was quite animated and gesturing, spilling wine on her shoes and dress. Her husband stood quietly, but then, as Valerie watched, he looked across the room and their eyes met. He put his glass down and walked directly over to them.

"Hello Graham. Excuse me, but I wanted to ask Valerie if we're on for our usual Saturday morning hike."

Graham said, "You'll have to ask her," in a way that left little doubt about the frostiness between Valerie and him.

Valerie smiled and said, "I'm looking forward to it, Thad. I'll see you at sunrise at the trailhead."

He nodded. "It's a date." He turned away to return to the trio on the other side of the room. He was about three steps away when Valerie called out to him, "Oh, and bring your backpack, will you? We'll need all that stuff."

Barry Wilder

Barry Wilder was very much alive. He was ninety years old and deployed his considerable wealth to enable him to live exactly as he wanted to live. Given his age and the disabilities that came with it – at least those that were impervious to money – he had most of what he wanted: extreme privacy, a sumptuous place to live, personal attendants, and – best of all – the power and influence that came with the money.

He was a fugitive, of course. But that was supremely ironic because his pathological need for isolation and privacy was perfectly suited to living below the radar and off of the so-called grid. What he missed most were the women. Not because they were inaccessible to him; they could be bought, of course, like any other commodity, but he no longer derived pleasure from them, no matter how creative they became.

He knew that according to the official norms of psychiatry that he would be labeled insane, with all sorts of scientific modifiers. He was amused to read the speculations in the supermarket tabloids about his condition and whereabouts, fueled by the "sightings" and blurry photographs from a long time ago. Every now and then, he allowed the flow of funds into his causes to become visible to a very select few. He had long ago learned that the *prospect* of money was at least as motivating as the actual *receipt* and he used that knowledge for maximum leverage among the many petitioners. But *real* influence – the kind where the politicians did precisely what they were told without any pretentious moralizing – required total secrecy. That had become much easier after the Supreme Court declared that corporations have the same free speech rights as individuals, so that political donations were effectively unlimited in dollar amount and their sources invisible.

Karnek disliked him. That was not unusual since he despised most of his clients. They were uniformly rich and felt entitled to the power that came with money, as though it conferred a moral authority over others. For them, the hiring of Karnek to break the leg of a man with overdue gambling debts was more about teaching him prudence than it was about the collection of an overdue sum of money. And by hiring him, they absolved themselves of the consequences, as though Karnek was an act of god rather than their agent. He took their money and did what they asked, but he fantasized about going back after the job and asking, "Do you know what you are?"

But the old man was special even within that set. He was more evil, even surer that his needs came before any moral or legal code. He was the purest example of a sociopath that Karnek had ever encountered. Nevertheless, he came when he called.

As usual, there was no small talk. "Tell me about the man called Vargas. The one who came back from the dead. Why did he wait so long?"

"I can guess, but I don't know for certain. We talked only twice ... briefly and nothing about his history."

Wilder waved his hand. "Guess." He knew that Karnek's guesses were usually quite accurate. Part of his value to him was the man's understanding of other people, cynical in the extreme. It contrasted dramatically with the apparent passiveness with which he carried out his tasks. Wilder was perhaps the only one that perceived the underlying contempt that Karnek had for his employers, and he wondered when Karnek would finally not only say "no" to the job, but would allow that contempt to show itself.

Karnek leaned back in the soft chair and crossed his legs. He ran the video of those two meetings in the forest through his mind. "He was speaking fluent Arabic ... instinctively, so it was effectively his first language. He has been in a place where money is unimportant, either because there's nothing to buy or the culture devalues it."

Wilder broke in. "Maybe it's just that money is a lot less important than revenge."

Karnek shook his head. "No, he didn't blame his partner for running off. He understood the context. He even told me, 'I would have done the same thing.' He just wanted more money. I think his goal was an even split. It was more about entitlement than revenge."

"But where has he been all this time?"

"I think he switched sides and went with the Taliban. It would have been either that or be killed on the spot. And once in, it's hard to get out, even if you wanted to. But I also think he liked war, especially wars without rules."

"And why did he show up now, after sixteen years?"

"I think ... my bet is that Vargas thought that one of you had the money. You – your firm – hired him for that one transaction ... to help with the receipt and distribution of the funds, along with the CIA, and their man was dead. You sent him and Archer to make sure it got done. He couldn't find you, so I suspect that Vargas watched Archer to see if the man was rich and found out that he wasn't ... until sixteen years later."

He said, "And sixteen years living with the Taliban will take its toll, even for the war-lovers. Maybe he just wanted to leave and viewed the money as the means to make it work for him."

Wilder nodded. He'd thought exactly that same way, so he'd been watching as well. *Archer lived on his salary. A big number, but he stayed within his means. Until he retired. Then he's suddenly filthy rich. The change could be detected if one has a long memory and is halfway good with a Google search.*

So he did steal the shipment. And then he stashed it for fourteen years ... like a very large 401k plan!

Karnek used the pause in their conversation to worry about what he did not yet understand. *I'm sure that Wilder did view it as his money and that he was monitoring the man's life style for the same reason as Vargas. So why is he letting him keep it? Hell, he's even helping him keep it!*

"How much did he offer Vargas?" Wilder asked.

"Two million. A one-time deal ... take it or leave it."

"Any progress on the part of the police?"

"No. And there won't be."

Wilder sat quietly for a moment. When he started speaking, Karnek had the distinct impression that he was unsure of himself. Not just about asking the question, but that he might be afraid of the answer. "His wife ... Is she ...?"

"When we met a couple of years ago, she ran the show. But that's changed and the man was calling the shots when Vargas showed up. She is showing definite signs of dementia. Do you want me to find out more?"

"No. She's not important."

Karnek waited, but there was no more. The old man stood up, a clear sign that he was done. On his way out, Karnek thought back over the meeting and came away with one clear thought: *The man's wife somehow matters. Why is she important to him?*

Surveillance

Maybe she's a spy. Karnek had been following Renee Delgado for the last two days and could make no sense of her behavior. He picked her up when she left her hotel and stayed with her until she returned twelve hours later. On both days, she rented a car from an Enterprise office in the next block and turned it in at the end of the day. One day it was a Honda Civic and the next a full-size Suburban. She spent most of those daytime hours sitting in her car and watching six different locations scattered from San Jose to San Francisco. As far as he could tell, she was also filming, using a small handheld video camera most of the time she was watching. To Karnek, it looked like a classic surveillance operation, what the cops would call a stakeout.

It was a very dull two days. The six locations were all in seedy neighborhoods. Four of them were storefronts in strip malls – a thrift store, a counseling center for women, tutoring services and what seemed to be a drop-in center for teens. Another one – according to the sign on the door -- was a construction company with a couple of dump trucks and a small bulldozer sitting inside the fence. The last one was a commercial office building with a directory that listed a dozen occupants, including lawyers, accountants and insurance agents. All that the six sites seemed to have in common was their lack of activity. None of the sites except for the office building had more than a few people going in or out while Delgado watched.

Delgado used her car as a mobile office. When she wasn't filming, she was on the cell phone much of the time and using a laptop the rest of the time. She didn't seem to be interested in any of the individuals going in or out of whatever she was watching at the time, nor did she try very hard to conceal what she was doing. She would park across the street or half a block from her target for the three or four hours of watching.

She also met Graham Dodd twice, once in the coffee shop of her hotel and then in a Palo Alto restaurant for a long dinner. She ate out alone other nights, at a Thai and then a Turkish restaurant within walking distance of her hotel. To Karnek, she behaved exactly as one would expect a busy female executive to behave on a business trip except for the daytime stakeouts, and that's what he reported to his patron. But after the two days, when he met with him and listed the addresses and names of the places she'd been filming, he got a startling reaction.

"She's too close. You're going to have to kill her."

Karnek didn't like it. He didn't like the lack of thought and even less the casual view of a life. Nor did he like the man's presumption that he was entitled to make such a decision and then snap his fingers as if Karnek was a waiter or a bellhop.

The man went on. "Ideally, she'd be raped and then brutally murdered by an illegal Latin type, preferably a thug who'd recently been released from the San Francisco jail system." The man maintained a straight face while he was talking and Karnek wondered briefly if he was serious, although the stacks of hundred dollar bills that he had pushed in front of Karnek indicated that he was. He guessed that it was a couple-hundred thousand bucks. *Not enough for what he's asking.*

He pushed the stacks back toward the man. "Here. Use it to hire a casting agency to do your killing … maybe someone who puts together Super Bowl commercials. Me? I'm old-fashioned; I just kill people. Very straightforward."

The man smiled, as though Karnek had just confirmed an obscure fact that was important to him. "I told him that you'd say no."

Karnek was startled. *So this isn't his idea. Somebody else ... somebody higher up on the food chain ... wants this woman dead. And unless this guy's being a smart ass for his own reasons, that person wants the killing to be blamed on an illegal Mexican immigrant. Wheels within wheels.* He shook his head, a gesture of such transparent disgust that the man's smile faded, replaced by a tightlipped grimace.

"OK, forget the elaborate stagecraft; just make it look like a mugging gone wrong." He pushed the money a couple of inches closer.

Karnek tried again. "She's a senior Treasury official. It will get a lot of attention. Feds and local. The first thing they'll look at will be whatever she's working on." Karnek guessed that the man wouldn't like the attention.

But he shook his head. "That's not a problem. She's the only one who knows what she's doing, at least for the moment. But that won't last long, so the timeline is very short on this one. She's here now. Mostly to talk with Graham Dodd, which is also not good. So she needs to be gone sooner rather than later."

Karnek pushed the money back across the table one more time. "It's a bad idea, for both of us. Give it another day and we'll discuss it then."

But then, a day later, he got the other call. This was from the old man, the one that he had worked for before and considered to be his largest and most profitable client.

"You've been following the Delgado woman."

Anybody else, I would ask how he knew that. But not him. "Yes. For the client you referred me too."

"What's she doing here ... in your opinion?"

"She's building a case against NEW SF. She suspects them of money laundering and she's getting first hand evidence by monitoring some of their storefront operations."

"Working alone. That's unusual, isn't it?"

It is. You'd expect to see a full team doing what she's doing. "Yes." He hesitated and then added, "I think she's operating off the reservation on this one. And I think I know why."

The man nodded. "I have a theory on that. But second opinions are always good. Why do you think that?"

"NEW SF is just a conduit, a pipeline where large amounts of cash go in at one end and slightly smaller amounts come out the other end. What she will inevitably find out is who is putting it in and who is taking it out."

"So? Isn't that in her job description? Once she knows that, she just calls in the Tactical Squad and they put everybody in jail. She gets some headlines and a promotion. What's her problem?"

The same one I have. She knows too much about people that don't like attention. But all he said was, "Remember Watergate? First, it was just a bungled robbery by some dimwitted hoodlums. Then it became political dirty tricks. By the time all the threads had been pulled, White House staffers were in jail and the President of the United States had resigned."

Wilder was silent, so Karnek went on. "I think Ms. Delgado has got the first thread between her fingers and is afraid of what will happen when she tugs on it."

A carjacking would be best. She's in the car all day, parked in questionable neighborhoods and flashing her cell phone and expensive laptop. She'd be a target of opportunity for any number of lowlifes that are in that habitat. So, on the morning of the third day, Karnek was waiting. He was wearing ragged clothes and carrying a frayed backpack that he had taken from a homeless man sleeping in a park opposite her hotel. The black hooded sweatshirt made him as anonymous as one can be in an urban environment.

The woman wants to make it easy for me. He followed her into the city, into the heart of the Tenderloin District, easily the most disreputable and dangerous few blocks in the entire city. Street crime was rampant, particularly against well-dressed and obviously well-off women by themselves. She parked outside a building that had no signage as to its purpose, but judging by the long line of ragged humanity along its front, it had to be a shelter of some sort. She was not in a good location for covert surveillance, but it was the only parking space on the entire block so he figured she didn't have much choice. He continued on for another two blocks before finding a space and hurried back. He walked past her car, but – as before – she was working on her laptop, her head down. Both she and her car were quite conspicuous and Karnek figured that the dozen or so men leaning against the wall were acutely aware of her.

So, we got witnesses. But not the type that will hang around to tell the cops what went down. Still, a distraction would be nice. A fire alarm, maybe? But as he scanned the immediate surroundings, he saw an easier solution. At the far end of the block, a very wild-looking man wearing nothing but sweat pants and a sleeveless vest was holding a crumpled cardboard sign, one that presumably asked for money. He wasn't helping his cause very much by his continuous shouting at passersby. *One of the city's resident paranoid schizophrenics. Just the thing.* He walked near enough to read the sign -- it said 'Iraq Veteran With PTSD. Please Help.' – and to pick up what he was shouting about ... the fucking civilians who sent their kids to Iraq and Afghanistan so that they, the fucking civilians, could keep going to the fucking mall. There was more about the fucking rich people who didn't pay taxes and the fucking doctors that wouldn't listen to him. *Raw, unfocused anger. All we need to do is to provide a suitable focus.*

He went up to him, holding his hands up in the classic "I surrender" pose. He could smell him even from ten feet away. "Hey man, I'm with you. The ones you wanna talk to are those dudes up the street. See that guy in the blue jacket, he was just telling me that anybody stupid enough to go to Iraq deserves whatever happens to him. He needs some reeducation."

The reaction was instantaneous. The man dropped his cardboard sign and walked fast – still ranting – toward the cluster of men opposite Delgado's car. Karnek followed about ten feet behind him, rehearsing his moves. *Let the man suck up all the attention, maybe even start a fight. Then move to the car, smash the window, drag her out. Get in, make sure the key's in ignition. Then shoot her and go. Classic carjacking. Woman chose to resist. A bad idea.* He moved the cheap six-shot revolver into the pocket of the hoodie.

The impromptu plan worked perfectly until the very end. He'd picked the guy in the blue jacket precisely because of his apparent belligerence and it paid off. As soon as the crazy got in his face and started yelling, he hit him with a roundhouse right hand and started screaming himself. The other men either started walking away or cheering him on. It was an instant madhouse.

It got even better. The woman had the car running, getting ready to leave. She was using her cell phone, apparently running a video because she was panning along the length of the building next to her. All of her attention was focused on the filming, so he was able to get alongside the driver's door before she was aware of his presence. *And the doors aren't locked!* He snatched the door open, grabbed the collar of the suit jacket she was wearing and dragged her out of the car by simply taking three steps back from the car. She was more concerned with hanging onto the phone than with trying to stay in the car. She sprawled backwards but from the expression on her face, he knew she was going to come at him. He got in the car, leaving the door open. He reached in his pocket with his left hand and got the gun out, bringing it to bear on the woman who was just getting to her feet with an expression of pure outrage.

Then it all went to hell. The car door slammed against his extended arm, pinning it between the door and the frame and causing the gun to fire. The round ricocheted off the pavement. There was a large black man leaning on the door and screaming at him. "Not on my block, asshole!" The pressure on his arm increased and he had no chance of pulling free. And the crowd on the sidewalk was now completely engaged in the new drama. He heard somebody shout, "Go Nate!"

Karnek swore to himself, wondering where the good Samaritan had come from. But his options were severely limited and he knew it. He used his right hand to slam the shift lever into 'drive' and jammed the accelerator to the floor. The car leaped forward, knocking two men to the ground and caroming off the car in front of him before he got it pointed down the middle of the street.

OK. Plan B. Ditch the car. Wipe it down. No prints. Take the purse and laptop so that it looks like a run-of-the-mill carjacking. Talk to the man. Find out how badly he wants the woman to be dead. Do it right next time. None of this extemporaneous bullshit.

Aftermath of a Carjacking

The cops were just leaving when Graham got to the shelter. He found Renee Delgado and Nate in the small room that passed for an employee lounge at the shelter. In practice, Nate tended to commandeer the space to take in another two or three people who otherwise would be sleeping on the sidewalk, so most of the volunteers brought their coffee from the nearby Starbucks. Renee was using the desk phone while Nate was hunched over and writing. He looked up when Graham came in and pushed the paper that he was writing on to the side.

Nate rolled his eyes. "These people want a *handwritten* statement. It'll take me twice as long and they won't be able to read more than the first three words. No wonder the cops are always complaining about the paperwork!"

"What happened? Why the cops?" He'd gotten the call from Renee twenty minutes ago, but all she said was, "There's been an incident. Can you come down to the NEW SF Tenderloin shelter? I'm with a friend of yours who says his name is Nate."

Renee replaced the phone in its cradle, using some force. "What happened is what the cops are calling a carjacking, or, as the sergeant put it, 'one of those things that happens a lot when ordinary civilians go into bad neighborhoods.' I'm halfway surprised that he didn't arrest *me* for something, maybe 'insufficient spatial awareness' or some other urban crime unique to victims." She was quite apparently angry and Graham looked at Nate for guidance, but he simply shrugged. He tried what he thought was a safe question.

"Are you OK?"

"I bruised my butt and my Armani jacket is badly torn. Skinned knees. Oh, yeah, and I've lost several hundred dollars in cash, all my credit cards, ID and a top-of-the-line laptop crammed with highly confidential government files."

Nate started, "Ms. Delgado –"

"It's Renee, Nate. Saving my life automatically confers the right to first names."

Graham was still trying to catch up. *Saving my life? She said 'there's been an incident.'* "Will one of you tell me what actually happened?"

Nate spoke first. "She was parked outside the shelter with the car running. Some white guy in a hoodie yanked her out of the car, threw her on the ground and took off with her car. I was outside trying to deal with a fistfight when I saw him go after Renee. Got there in time to chase him off … in her car, unfortunately."

"He was going to shoot me."

"You don't know that," Nate said.

"You didn't see his eyes. And he fired the damn gun at me!"

"No. It went off because I slammed the door on his arm."

Graham couldn't stand it any more. "Nate. Renee. Just tell me what happened? Please?"

Both of them looked at him as though they just now had become aware of his presence. She was obviously still upset, exhibiting definite residual effects of both fear and anger. Graham's instincts were to go to her and put his arms around her, a universal and asexual gesture on empathy, but he was pretty sure that such a move wouldn't go over well with her with Nate sitting there. *And maybe not so well even if he wasn't there. I don't think she's the type that wants or needs a strong man to lean on.*

"So, a carjacking?"

"Yes," Nate said. "No," Renee said. Graham sighed.

Twenty minutes later, he'd gotten most of the story out of the two of them. What was strange was that they agreed on all of the factual details, but disagreed entirely on the main point: Was it a simple opportunistic street crime – Nate's version -- or something far more targeted and sinister? When Nate left the room to deal with a sudden commotion in the outer room, Graham went and sat next to Renee.

"He did save my life," Renee said, "and he knows it too."

"Are you sure? The bastard had what he wanted. You were out-of-action, no threat, he was in the car with the motor running ..."

"I agree. So why would he take an extra few seconds to get a gun out of his pocket and aim it at me? Unless he didn't have everything he wanted?"

Graham had no good answer, but it didn't matter. She was saving her best argument for the last one.

"He planned it. This was not a spur-of-the-moment snatch and run job."

"And you think that because ...?"

"I saw the guy two days ago. He followed me for the entire day. He was harder to spot today because of the hoodie, but I saw him walk past me after I'd parked. He went down to the end of the block and talked to the psychotic vet, who then proceeded to come and start a fight next to me. It was a very clever diversion to give him cover."

I'd say this woman scores high on the urban spatial awareness scale. "You didn't tell that to Nate, did you?"

"No. And I didn't tell the cops either. That would get them thinking that this is something more than a hopped-up thug who's more lethal than your everyday purse snatcher. That's not what I want."

Two days ago she was staking out the NEW SF vendors. Today, she's watching the units that generate the large amounts of cash that are sloshing around in the agency.

"And Graham? I did see his eyes. I know this sounds melodramatic, but they were cold. There was no excitement, no nervousness from being in the middle of committing a crime ... just ... calculation ... maybe even boredom. And the gun was coming on line ..."

"Why would any one want to kill you?" But even as he asked, he was thinking to himself. *That has to be one of the dumbest questions ever asked.*

She didn't bother to answer.

Second Thoughts on Fidelity

"It's funny ... I used to think infidelity was a really big deal."

Renee looked at Graham with some obvious sympathy. "It's not your fault. You've been married to the same woman for a long time. Certain ways of thinking become automatic after a while. And comfortable." She poked him in the ribs with her bare foot. "Exactly when is it that you changed your mind? About infidelity?"

"About forty-two minutes ago. When you started to unbutton your blouse." He ran his fingertips along the patch of bare skin from her knee to the tips of her toes. He smiled at the memory. "Actually, thinking of all forms ended at about that same time."

Actually, it probably began when they got in his car at the shelter. She had trouble with the seat belt and I reached over to help her. We bumped our heads together and there was some incidental touching. It was awkward for a minute or so but seemed to go back to normal. She said that she needed a laptop, right now. I told her I'd take her to the Apple store. On the way, my phone rang and the Bluetooth ran it though the car's audio system so she heard what was going on. It was Valerie and she was in her best form as shrewish wife. It was a monologue, beginning with 'this is not working for me' and ending with 'this childish stunt of yours ... moving into the guest room ... I meant what I said about wanting a divorce.' I said 'hello' at the beginning and 'OK Valerie' at the end, nothing else. Renee said nothing during or after the call. When we parked at the mall, she said, "The laptop can wait. Let's go to my hotel." This time, I was the one who said nothing. When we got there, we both knew what was happening. As soon as the door closed behind us, she started unbuttoning the blouse.

They sat on the couch in their matching terrycloth robes with the elaborate hotel logo stitched on the front. She sat sideways with her legs stretched out across his lap. The bright sunlight streaming in the windows and the muted sounds from the lunchtime street scene added to the sense of unreality that each of them was experiencing at the moment.

She poked him again. "You were an international correspondent, semi-famous, often in faraway conflict zones where the usual rules of morality are suspended. You surely encountered many attractive women who wanted something from you. The thought of infidelity must have crossed your mind?"

"There were opportunities, but not as many as you think. And the complications were serious. Everybody had an agenda, and sex was usually more of a negotiating technique than it was an act of shared humanity." Renee watched him and saw the sadness settle on him and wondered about the mind-pictures that he was viewing. He sighed, "It was easier to be a prude ... or to pretend to believe that infidelity was a really big deal."

He sat up abruptly, looking startled. "Are *you* married? God, I know nothing about you!"

She laughed. "I was married at twenty, divorced at thirty. Since then, one very satisfying long-term relationship ... with a Republican congressman of all people, whom I shall not name. It ended two years ago, probably because he was a Republican. I have no family, play golf with a five handicap, read junk books, still like to look out the window on long plane flights, and I don't like to be touched while I'm sleeping. Anything else you need to know?"

He took her question seriously. "Yeah. Why me? Why this? Why now?" His gesture took in the room, their present intimacy and all of the wildness and irresponsibility of the last hour, the time that came after the instant that they both knew what was going to happen and were OK with it.

She thought about it, her head down and looking away from him. "I genuinely don't know. Some of it comes from what happened this morning … the guy with the gun … knowing that he wanted to shoot me … the reality that I was close to being dead … not here." She was quiet, still thinking, and Graham let her be. "And I think some of it comes from the two of us having these shared secrets … about what I'm chasing … listening in on that phone call from your wife … "

Again, a long pause, and then, in tones that were barely audible, "And some of it is … was … something I needed. I needed someone to be … close … really close to. And there you were … knowing all my secrets … and exhibiting some of those same needs … I think."

It was a long, disjointed answer; more of a plea than a reasoned response to his question. It exuded sadness, and he wanted to say something that would alleviate that feeling and convey his own muddled thinking about how they got to this point. Instead, it came out as surely the biggest cliché imaginable.

"So where does this go from here?"

The sadness became amusement. "Well, Mr. Dodd, I think that's entirely up to you. You're the one who's married with serious hang-ups about infidelity and mid-morning trysts. As for me, I like what just happened and intend to do my best to make sure it happens again."

Her expression darkened. "And since someone is trying to kill me, I should probably take advantage of every opportunity that comes my way."

It was a week after the carjacking attempt. They were in her hotel room, leaning back against the multitude of pillows that they'd retrieved from the floor around the bed. She had on a very faded T-shirt with a barely recognizable image of a surfer and was flicking through a series of documents on a laptop Graham was semi-reclining, staring at the ceiling and trying to decide if his pulse was back to approximately normal.

He nudged her knee. "When you were a kid, could you ever imagine your parents having sex?"

A quick glance at him, then she returned to flicking pages. "When I was a teenager, I couldn't imagine any one over thirty having sex. Except maybe Robert Redford or Jane Fonda. Why do you ask?"

"I was just thinking. If we'd met when I was, say, forty and you told me that I'd be in my sixties and doing … what we just did … feeling like that at this age, I would have laughed at you."

"Well, speak for yourself. I'm only in my fifties, so mind-blowing sex is pretty much the norm for me." She kept looking at the pages she was reading and Graham wasn't sure she was kidding until she turned her head and smiled at him. "And this was extra special. It's been a long time and I'd forgotten …"

She didn't finish the sentence. Graham said, "I've always had fantasies about a 'younger woman.' Probably because one of the editors that I worked for was always looking for what he called a 'bimbo story,' one of those tabloid specials where an old rich guy gets himself publicly humiliated by a nubile young thing."

"I'm not a bimbo."

"Of course not. You're –"

She recited, "The official definition of a bimbo is a woman who's less than half your age plus seven." She used a tone that made it sound like she was reading a statutory clause from a law book.

Half my age plus seven. He did the calculation. "So if you were less than thirty-eight –"

"I'd be a bimbo. Your bimbo. You'd be featured in the tabloids of our time as a dirty old man and I'd be a kept woman, one who wouldn't have to spend her days tracking illegal cash payments and fighting off assassins."

She closed the laptop. "Do you know who Barry Wilder is?"

Her question came out of the blue, leaving Graham startled by the sudden transition and with a multitude of questions. *Do I know who Barry Wilder is? This is getting spooky. Last week, I was digging up everything I could about the man. Now his name pops up in the middle of an unfolding story about fraud at Valerie's organization.*

"Why did you ask me if I knew who Barry Wilder was? What's he got to do with any of this?"

She didn't answer, but asked another question. "What *do* you know about him?" The way she asked it and the way she looked slightly away from and the way she became so still all signaled that it was an important question, one that she really cared about how he would answer. And she was looking at him as if assessing whether she could really trust him. Apparently satisfied, she moved into a sitting position, her feet tucked under her and facing Graham. "First, tell me what you know about him."

"OK, but it's not much. I've never met the man, so I know only what the rest of the world knows. And that's not a lot. He draws a lot of comparisons with Howard Hughes. Self-made, incredibly wealthy, friend and funder to a lot of wacky right wing fringe groups and political movements. Came from the Alaskan oil country and built the Ross Sea Group into a billion-dollar company, one of the largest privately held companies in the world. Ran the company the way he saw fit and that got him into trouble with authorities, particularly the U.S. Justice Department – that's your people, by the way – because of the Foreign Corrupt Practices Act. People say, but nobody has proved, that he funded some of the black ops that Reagan and Nixon and Bush ran in the Middle East and South America."

He paused. She said, "What about him personally?"

"There are some early profiles done by business magazines. Mostly puffery, saying he's brilliant, an entrepreneur, a new breed … that sort of stuff. Nothing about his childhood, hobbies, family or inner life. There's more than a hint that he's crazy, maybe schizophrenic and there's clearly a strong whiff of paranoia; he shuns any form of publicity. He's never given interviews, photo ops or made any public appearances. Then he dropped completely out of public view when his companies ran afoul of several of our laws. That's where the Howard Hughes comparisons come in. Nobody has seen him. He's probably dead; he'd be in his late eighties, maybe nineties, by now."

He stopped and looked at her. "But you know all this. The feds have been looking for him. Why are you asking me?"

"Remember that I said casinos were the only really large scale operations suitable for money laundering? A mostly cash business with anonymous customers?"

Graham nodded, and she went on. "Well, there's another organizational form that's even better – a political campaign. It takes in large and anonymous contributions and spends the money on things like consultants and ad agencies ... things that are easy to overpay for."

Graham said, "I'm getting the feeling that you've thought about this quite a bit."

She grimaced. "Only a thousand times or so. I've even given lectures on the possibilities to Treasury staff. But never in this outfit" – she daintily lifted the hem of her T-shirt – "and always with my Powerpoint slides."

Graham grinned. "I find the outfit does distract somewhat from your lecture. I think it's because your nipples are so clearly evident." And he reached out to brush the back of his hand across the front of her shirt. "So our villain has given away his cash, this time to a political campaign rather than an inner-city social service agency. How does that help him?"

She pushed his hand away. "Think about it."

Graham started talking to himself. "So if I'm a right wing crackpot with oodles of ill-begotten cash, I can use that to support my favorite causes and wash my money at the same time ..."

She said nothing but looked approvingly at him. Within a few seconds, however, that look became one of concern, as though his analysis confirmed some previously unacknowledged fear. And he knew what it was.

It's not a one-way deal. The money launderer is providing a real service to his counterparty. He expects something in return. Even if there are hundreds of laws and regulations aimed at making sure elected officials are not beholden to special interest groups ... or outright criminals. It could be quite hazardous to get in the middle of such an arrangement.

Suddenly, he remember their dinner in Palo Alto ... the Pogo reference.

"Trump. It's not Wilder you're afraid of ... it's Trump."

An Attempt at Proof

This isn't going to be easy. Graham was waiting for Valerie when she got home, still trying to think of ways to sugar coat the message. *She looks more frazzled than usual for a Friday night. I wonder how much of that is due to worrying about running a fraudulent organization.*

"Bad week?"

She seemed surprised by the question. "No. In fact, it was a very good week." *At work, anyway. The rest of my life is a colossal mess, but that's not something I'm going to discuss with him.* "We landed a major new contract with the Housing people. They'll pay for a big chunk of our beds in residential addiction programs." *But only because that lets them count the beds as an expansion of the city's affordable housing programs. Just as many people are homeless as before, of course. But the metrics look better. They should give the humanitarian awards to the bookkeepers rather than the politicians!*

He tried again. "That's nice, but you look like some one that needs a drink. Can I get you a glass of wine?"

"Graham, it's ..." She stopped, feeling overwhelmingly tired. She shook her head and sat down at the far end of the couch. "Graham, I can't do this small talk stuff any more. It's just pretending. Neither of us really cares very much any more."

She's right. It's either indifference or acceptance and I no longer care which of those is the appropriate description. Leave that to the marriage therapists who still have clients that are hopeful. But she does need to know about this.

"Valerie, have you heard of a man named Barry Wilder?"

She answered instantaneously, "No. Why?"

"I've heard more rumors ... about financial issues at –"

"Not this again!" She stood up, anger flooding through her. "You don't know anything about –"

He broke in, speaking quietly. "Your Tenderloin shelter – according to Nate's count – reported an average of one-hundred and ninety-seven dollars a night in cash donations over the last twelve months. That's seventy-one thousand nine hundred and five dollars in total. Here's the detail if you need it." He tossed his photos of Nate's notebook onto the coffee table in front of them. "Those are Nate's counts. And I can verify the Thursday night numbers because he and I do independent tallies and reconcile."

Valerie sat back down, looking at him like he was stranger who had wandered into their living room from off the street. He went on. "According to Wells Fargo Bank, the nightly deposits from the shelter during that twelve month period were three-hundred and thirteen thousand dollars."

It took fifteen seconds but then she asked the question that he knew that she would ask ... the one he couldn't answer. "And how do you have access to our bank records?" *I suppose I could tell her I'm sleeping with a very high-ranking Treasury Department executive who can subpoena almost anything she wants, but that would complicate things for everybody involved.* So he said, "That's not the right question. The right question is how did seventy thousand dollars of individual donations get magically transformed into almost five times that much cash while it was sitting in the night depository box at NEW SF?"

He put his finger on the additional column that he had added to Nate's notes: Selected from three-hundred and sixty-five entries, culled from a dozen multi-page bank statements and cross-matched by date and location. "Here's the detail. Nate's nightly numbers are being inflated by three to seven times the original amount." *The last entry was the one I verified with Nate last week. That two hundred and twenty dollars was up to nine hundred bucks by the time Wells got the cash.*

Valerie looked stunned, but she kept trying. "How did you —"

"Valerie. You may not like me very much at the moment, but you *know* me. You know that I'm very good at finding things out. And that I always – always – get the facts right. That's my job, and I'm very good at it."

She took the papers from the coffee table and stood up. "I need to look into this. Jay Gould will be able to explain it."

Graham said nothing, watched her walk away toward her bedroom. Later, he would second-guess his deliberate silence. *I could have ... should have ... warned her to be careful; that asking questions could be dangerous. Did I say nothing because she was no longer important to me, or because it was a small victory in an ongoing war and I didn't want to rub it in .... Or because I foresaw that by keeping silent I could help bring about what finally happened?*

The CFO

Jay Gould was beginning to suffer from an overwhelming sense of entitlement, a condition that often proved fatal for others in his line of business. But at this moment, that feeling was more than enough motivation for him to slip the three one hundred dollar bills that he had taken from the envelope into his pocket and feel justified in doing so. And even if some non-existent guardian angel or small voice of conscience would have said, "That's the third time this week you've skimmed. Twelve-hundred in total." he would have shrugged it off, thinking, "I deserve it. They couldn't do it without me."

The latter at least was true. Money laundering requires an insider and Gould served in that role. He was perfect, in that as CFO and the lone financially sophisticated executive in a complex enterprise, he had complete control over the accounting, reporting and auditing functions. He also had the advantage of being readily corruptible. He felt that he was undervalued and consequently felt little loyalty to the organization or its mission. He was greedy, in constant need of money and that may have been enough all by itself to tip him over the edge; but Karnek wanted an extra level of insurance.

They met at the usual place and the man brought the weekly bag of cash for laundering. Karnek took the bag and said, "Our insider at NEW SF is getting greedy ... beginning to think he's worth more. We need to find a way to keep him in line."

"You said that a two or three percent commission would do that."

You weren't listening. "No, what I said was that a two or three percent commission would be fair for what we're asking him to do. But we need something more than a financial incentive to make sure that he doesn't get squeamish on us."

"Squeamish? As in call-the-cops squeamish?"

"Yeah. That kind."

The man sat quietly, thinking. Karnek waited patiently, thinking his own thoughts. *He knows what I do, how I work. He's been in the middle of a hundred shady deals. But then there was Vargas. So he's also a guy that would rather spend two million dollars to keep his conscience clear than let me do what I do. He's what the shrinks would call 'conflicted.'*

"Can't you threaten him?"

"We tried that with Vargas, remember? You saw how well that worked. And this guy – his name is Gould – does not have any first-hand experience with people like me. It's hard for him to visualize the kind of pain that I can inflict. And if you can't visualize it, you're not afraid of it. We need some additional leverage."

The man smiled. "I can see his problem. You don't look very threatening. You're not very big and you look more like a shoe salesman than an assassin."

In the end, he agreed with Karnek. "OK. Leverage is always good. See what you can come up with about our Mr. Gould. We need him." He smiled. "Squeamish is bad. Leverage is good."

Based on his experience with other tightly wrapped executive types, Karnek began with the sex angle. He knew that Gould was gay, a fact that he did not particularly try to hide and that nobody would care about, particularly in gender-fluid San Francisco. In the end, it wasn't much of a challenge because he quickly discovered that Gould liked young boys, some of them very young indeed. It took less than a week for Karnek to build a compelling photo album dedicated to Gould's nocturnal habits. One of its side effects was that Karnek began to look forward to killing the man.

Karnek was right about Gould in some ways, but not all. He was right when he said that the man could not visualize the kind of pain that Karnek could cause him. But that left it to Gould's imagination to work out the possibilities. And he had a vivid if uninformed imagination.

In fact, Gould was afraid of Karnek. But the fear was less than the greed, so even though he truly believed that he was indispensible, he began to take steps to protect himself. He began by reasoning that the first and most important step was to make sure that the game would continue.

He and Valerie were just winding up a meeting in the conference room with the other department heads. The agenda was devoted entirely to a first pass at next year's operating budget, but unlike past years, the mood was upbeat. Not so surprising, given that Gould began the meeting with the announcement that they were planning on across-the-board salary increases of five to seven percent.

He followed Valerie into her office. His act of closing the door behind him served as an announcement that this would not be a casual meeting. NEW SF prided itself on its 'open door' policy for the senior managers and took it quite literally. Valerie did not go behind her desk, but instead stood alongside it, another non-verbal signal that this meeting – whatever Gould's agenda might be – was to be treated seriously. They stood facing each other.

"A good meeting," Gould began.

She nodded. "Yes, thanks to our cash position. I just hope it lasts."

Something in her tone was different, making the statement something more than a platitude. *Does she know something? Has she caught on to the games I'm playing?* But even as he posed the worried questions to himself, he was thinking how good his timing was for the conversation he was about to start.

But she did it for him. "Can you explain these for me?" She reached into the desk drawer, extracted a manila folder from which she took a single sheet. She handed it to him. "This is a comparison of the Mission Street Shelter's cash counts against the bank deposits. These are for last month, but I can show you more if you like."

He ignored the sheet of paper extended toward him. Instead, he sat down in one of the two chairs in front of her desk, leaning back to stretch his legs out. He said nothing until she went behind her desk and sat down. Neither of them acknowledged it, but they were both relieved to have the issue on the table.

"We have a benefactor," Gould began.

Her response was instantaneous. "Apparently. And an illegal one."

"One who gave us over a million dollars last year."

Again, she shot back, "In return for what?"

Gould sat up straighter, thinking about his options. *She's mad. But is that because she's been kept in the dark or because her beloved agency is operating in a criminal fashion?* He decided that it really didn't matter, that his message to her needed to be the same in either case. He also realized that he was enjoying himself, although what he did not appreciate was that he was acting out his idea of a Hollywood gangster.

"You don't need to know. And you don't want to know."

"You're wrong on both counts. I will not allow your scheme to threaten the mission ... the existence ... of NEW SF. And I won't hesitate to throw you under the bus to make sure of that."

He stood, placed both hands on her desk and leaned over it. "Two things, Valerie. Things that will happen if you blow the whistle on me. First, NEW SF will be severely harmed, probably shut down. Second, you'll be in jail."

She said, "I've done nothing wrong," but her denial had no force, telling Gould that she was beginning to anticipate where this conversation was headed.

"That's not what I'll say. In fact, you'll be the brains behind the operation, the one who set it up and arranged every little detail. I did what you told me to do. No more, no less. Remember that Capital Appropriation Request for the Mission Street Bingo operation? You signed it. And that's only one of a hundred in the last two years."

Valerie sat quietly, just looking at him, and he mistook her passivity for submission. But he was operating on a script and he had two more cards to play, the ones that he was looking forward to. "And you took your share off the top."

"My share?" Again, he was disappointed by her lack of anxiety.

He gestured at the credenza behind her. "Look in the drawer below your printer, the one labeled 'supplies.'" She swiveled her chair and slid the drawer open. He said, "The box of business envelopes."

She pulled the box out. The cover indicated that it held 500 letter-sized envelopes. When she opened the flap, however, it was half filled with currency. She slid a few of the bills out. They were all one-hundred dollar bills. Gould was disappointed that she did not seem surprised. "It's only a few thousand dollars," he said. "But there's more in other places. You might even find some of them if you go through your personal spaces really carefully. It's the ones you don't find that will be hard to explain."

She put the box on the desk in front of her. He said, "Oh, and there are some computer files that I've added to your drive. Very innocent looking files ... unless you're looking for evidence of financial fraud."

She nodded, but was only half listening, staring at the small box with its sheaf of hundred-dollar notes.

"Valerie?"

She looked up.

"One more thing." He pointed at the money. "The people who give us that money? They're not nice. If you go to the police ..." He tried to remember the words that Karnek had used to threaten him, but in the end just said, "You could get hurt. Badly."

She stared at him. *How could I be so wrong about him? How could I let such a pathetic person as this get to this point? Put me in this position?*

She asked, without caring about the answer, "If I keep quiet about what you're doing, will you stop? Shut down all your little schemes? You can resign with a good severance. I'll give you world-class references and you can start over somewhere else."

Her questions took him by surprise and, for a second or two, he considered it. Then he thought of Karnek. "No. There will be a short timeout. No more."

She nodded. It was the answer she had expected.

Valerie stood up. "OK then. I've got another meeting to get to. Downtown."

"Uh, Valerie? What about –"

"All those things I don't need or want to know about?"

"Yeah, those."

"I guess I'll have to learn to live with the consequences. So will you." And she walked out of her office, leaving the little box with its hundred-dollar bills sitting in the middle of her desk.

Death of an Insider

Crime, done right, is hard work. Even white-collar crime.

Jay Gould was a successful criminal up until now because he was careful, and that caution required long hours. Fraudulent invoices had to be fabricated, bank deposit slips faked, internal controls subverted; and most of those cautionary tactics had to be after hours, out-of-sight of other employees. And the effort had to be continuous. Any extended break by him – a short vacation or even a couple of days off to recuperate from the flu or a cold – would allow all of his slight 'adjustments' to the official records to become apparent.

The bitch is getting way too curious for anybody's good. That's the exact line he used earlier today on Karnek, who was waiting for him outside the entrance to the building when he returned from his lunch. He seemed at home among the panhandlers and winos, one of the benefits coming from his unthreatening demeanor. "She knows something's wrong. She's not sure what it is, but she's asking about the bingo numbers and for some historical reports on the other businesses that we run. She wants to see the daily cash donations record for the Mission shelter for the next week. She says 'I just want to get more involved in the day-to-day stuff,' but suddenly it's all about the numbers ... the *cash!*"

Karnek said, "So make up some numbers for her. You're good at that. And we'll play it straight for a week or two. Cash in equals cash out. All counts correct to the penny. All money laundering schemes on hold. She'll get bored and we can start up again."

Gould didn't like it, mostly because it meant an interruption in his stream of commissions. He'd become accustomed to that, especially when he started 'supplementing' it by skimming. He'd just picked up his new bright red Tesla this morning. And he was close to having enough for the lease on the new condo just south of Market Street. So his first reaction to Karnek's 'run it straight for a week or two' was to imagine all the little ways that he could avoid doing just that.

It was as if he was thinking out loud. Karnek gripped him by the upper arm, enough to hurt, leaned close and said, "Don't even think about it. You're going to be Mr. Straight Arrow until I tell you otherwise, a tight-ass compulsive bookkeeper whose books always balance. No games, no fudged numbers." He paused, released his arm and stroked the sleeve as if to erase any wrinkles he might have caused. "And if you deviate in the slightest from this arrangement … there will be consequences … severe unpleasantries."

Karnek watched him process what he was telling him. *He's scared, but not scared enough. He'll play along for two, maybe three days and then he'll think of ways to get cute.*

"Stay with the plan, Jay. Otherwise you're going to get hurt." He walked away, leaving Gould to work out the possibilities.

Then, two hours later, Valerie confronted him in her office with those columns of figures and talked about throwing him under the bus. It was not a good day for Jay Gould, although he felt good about the way he had handled Valerie Dodd; so good that he did not even consider confiding to Karnek that they had another co-conspirator.

Gould had spent the last hour before lunch reviewing and signing about forty invoices from various vendors. The way the SFO NOW accounting system worked – the one he had designed – once he'd authorized payment, checks would be written and mailed the next day. He was the only one that knew that six of those forty invoices were fictitious; the billings were for 'services' provided by Karnek's so-called vendors. They totaled just under fifteen thousand dollars. Even after two years of this, Gould was still amused by this particular scam. *All those felons living dangerously out there, holding up liquor stores and doing home invasions, and all I do is sign my name.*

However, Karnek's 'play-it-straight' strategy meant that those six invoices had to be pulled out, and that required the entire batch to be re-authorized because any missing invoice numbers would trigger inquiries by internal audit. So Gould was still in his office late that night, recopying and resigning the new batch. The last step was to access the accounting software – easy for the CFO to do – and change today's Accounts Payable entry.

It was after ten when he finished. The Tesla was the only car left in the agency's fenced-in parking lot, gleaming in the high intensity lights. The NEW SF office was adjacent to the elevated freeway, a hulking concrete structure that provided cavern-like shelter to hundreds of the tent-dwelling urban poor. Valerie actually liked the proximity. One of her favorite sound bites was, "These are the people we serve" and she sometimes would spend time in the encampment 'just walking around.' But the location and its population meant that security for office staff was a major concern.

Gould reset the security alarms on the main door to the building and then stood for a minute admiring the car sitting so prominently on the dark pavement under the bright lights. *It could be an ad,* he thought, *if it weren't for the ugly wire fence.* He could see dark shapes on the other side of the fence and he wondered what they thought about the automobile. Resentment and envy seemed about equally likely.

He opened the passenger side door and placed his briefcase on the seat. It contained the six fake invoices. The wastebaskets in the office had all been emptied and he did not want to call attention to them in any way, so the invoices were going home with him. The briefcase also had about a thousand dollars in small bills, this week's skim from the bingo receipts. *Karnek doesn't know about that so he won't know that I'm still doing it.* He was wrong about that, but it wouldn't matter much in any case. He walked in a wide circle around the front of the car, admiring it yet again. His circuit took him near the fence where a figure in deep shadow on the other side was clearly watching him and his circuit around the car.

"Nice car. I imagine it took a lot of bingo cards to afford that."

The voice, so familiar but so out of context that it took a second for him to realize the implications and then another second to finally become frightened. The bright flashes, the sound of the shots and the impact of the bullets all came in the third second, leaving him sprawled with his right arm outstretched as if pointing to the vehicle.

The photo that appeared on the front page of the Chronicle the next morning was taken from the elevated freeway, looking down into the parking lot. It made him look like an unfortunate pedestrian struck by the Tesla.

Graham had an early morning coffee meeting scheduled with Valerie, but she didn't show and she wasn't answering her cell. Such behaviors were so unlikely for her that he was getting alarmed. Then he saw the Chronicle headline "Executive Gunned Down in SF" and the stark photo, so he turned on the television and got the 'breaking news' version of a late night murder in San Francisco. He remembered Renee's four-part tutorial on money laundering with its requirement for an insider. *Jay Gould. That explains where Valerie is. I wonder if this is the start of unraveling all the other stuff?*

He was dialing his third attempt at reaching Alison when she knocked on his door, holding her buzzing phone in her hand. They sat down opposite one another at the maple island in the center of the kitchen. She looked like she hadn't slept much. He thought about their last visit. *That was about the corpse with no hands. We seem to meet in the course of murder investigations.* "I'm surprised to see you so soon. I thought you'd be busy," and he gestured at the newspaper spread out on the island between them.

He poured coffee into a mug and pushed it toward her.

"That's City of San Francisco jurisdiction. If they let them have it."

They? "Have you seen Mom?"

"No. She's been in the city … at the office … since midnight. I talked with her for about thirty seconds."

"What happened?" *She'll have called on Daniels by now.* Victoria Daniels was Alison's counterpart in the San Francisco Sheriff's Department and the two had become close friends. "Vic must be part of the investigating team at some level."

"She was one of the first detectives on the scene, but they chased her off."

"They? Who's 'they?'"

"The Feds.   Mostly FBI, but some others that are kinda vague about who they are or what they do. They've taken over the investigation … got the SF Homicide people doing traffic control."

I'll bet that one of those vague 'others' is named Renee Delgado.

"What did Vic say?"

She spoke rapidly, the verbal equivalent of a bullet-point presentation. "About ten last night. Gould was working late, not unusual apparently. Three shots from the fence line, a nice tight little group in the center of his chest. Dead instantly. No witnesses. Body found by security guard and called in."

"That parking lot has cameras –"

"One on every corner, looking inward. Two of them picked up the muzzle flashes. That's how we know the shooter was on the other side of the fence."

"Just the flashes? No look at the shooter?"

"To quote Vic: '… a dark shape. It could be a man, woman., a small child or an orangutan.' They'll try the usual photo enhancement techniques but she was not optimistic about the outcome. She did say that he, she or it said something to Gould before the shots. Apparently, he was looking toward the fence when he got it."

"Isn't that space under the freeway a pretty major camping spot for the homeless? Valerie mentioned it once … something about hundreds of people."

"It was basically a popup tent city. Until our benevolent city fathers authorized one of their periodic urban cleansing programs. Last night, there were maybe a few dozen people scattered across a couple of very dark acres, none of whom are likely to have seen anything or, if they did, to share it with the police. Unless maybe it actually was an orangutan."

Graham looked at the front page of the Chronicle, spread out on the counter. "Nice car. I'm surprised he could afford something like that."

Alison stood up to leave. "He couldn't, but he got a really good deal. The car is registered to a man named DeShaun Delavan. He apparently makes a living as a high-end pimp. I guess if you're running whores for techies living in the Mission District, driving a Tesla is good marketing. To make his most recent bail, he sold the car to Gould. For sixty thousand in cash. Which is strange because according to his bank records, Gould hasn't made any large withdrawals."

He stopped her halfway to the door. "Alison?" She waited, her back to him, the tiredness showing in her slumping shoulders. "This is going to be tough on Mom." She didn't turn around, but the words seemed to stiffen her.

"Why? She's got you to rely on, doesn't she?" And she walked out.

Subversion of Justice

Valerie's corner office on the fourth floor of the NEW SF building looked down onto the parking lot. The lot had been declared off-limits for the last three days, although the Crime Scene Unit declared that they were done with it two days ago. *It's an asphalt parking lot for god's sake! Do they think they're going to find footprints? Or maybe the name of the killer written in blood?*

She'd been in her office for most of the seventy-eight hours since the shooting. The first dozen or so of those hours was spent with an ever-changing parade of cops, starting with the local ones and moving up the spectrum from there. As far as she could tell, the murder investigation was now being managed by the FBI – a quite senior agent named Malone – with assistance from the Treasury Department, a woman named Delgado. The two of them worked out of Gould's office and, so far, had spent most of their time interviewing NEW SF staff, particularly the finance department.

In their single meeting, Malone had questioned her closely, and it surprised her when both his questions and the way he looked at her made her realize that he viewed her as a suspect. *Why not? Jay's been embezzling for a year or more, maybe something worse. I'm his ... was ... his boss. Surely I must have known what he was doing, maybe even been in on it. Maybe there was the classic falling out among thieves, or maybe I just wanted to shut him up. And what's my alibi? 'I was home.' Can my husband verify that? 'Well, no. You see, he's sleeping in the visitor's room in another building.'*

On the second morning after the shooting, the receptionist called. "Margaret just came in." Valerie was not surprised. Margaret Somers was the Board Chair and would obviously be concerned. She was also a major power broker in local political circles and a huge asset to NEW SF in fund raising. "I'm in my office. Tell her to come on up."

The receptionist's embarrassment came through quite clearly. "She came to meet with the woman named Delgado. They're in Jay's office."

It was ninety minutes later that Margaret appeared in Valerie's doorway. Valerie had spent most of that time making notes in the leather-bound journal that she used for meetings. It was open to two facing pages, one with a heading that read 'Gone,' the other 'Still Here.' Beneath those headings, both pages were filled with a list written in her precise penmanship. She took the book with her to the conference table in the corner of her office and when Margaret began, "NEW SF is going to need you more than ever in the next few months," she drew a large 'X' on the page labeled 'Gone' and focused on the other page labeled 'Still Here.' Until she actually marked the X on the page, she didn't know which alternative she preferred and she was struck by the sense of relief she experienced.

She took a deep breath and began, "It's a terrible tragedy, but I've been giving some thought to some actions that the Board and management should agree to as soon possible." She put a large checkmark alongside the first item on her list. "First, we need to hold an all-staff meeting ..."

She sat for a long time after Margaret was gone, staring at the journal with its list of 'to do' items, each with a neat checkmark in the left margin. *'Unexplained financial irregularities.' Margaret must have repeated it twenty times. Such an elegant and polite phrase; so much less jarring than 'Ms.*

Delgado thinks you're committing major financial crimes, but I've convinced her that we need you to keep things running while we work out what really happened and who's responsible.'

What Margaret did *not* say was what they both knew. *Appearances must be maintained. NEW SF and its mission are too important to be left to die. We have enemies who will use this against us.* In her few quiet moments since Gould's murder, Valerie was fatalistic. She had learned enough about Gould's criminality to convince her that if it continued, it would be only a matter of time before her agency was swept away by a tsunami of conservative righteousness. Now it would end and if all the stars aligned, both she and her agency would go on.

But there were other things that she did not know.

The old man's first call when he saw the TV news was to Karnek. When he appeared, there were no preliminaries. "What happened?"

"Gould couldn't go along with the program." *That's interesting. He didn't ask me if I was the one who killed him.*

"Had you stopped routing cash through NEW SF?"

"Yes. We did that two days ago. Gould didn't like it, of course. He would have gone along with it for a couple of days, but –"

"No matter. He's lost the option now. Your client has other avenues for getting his cash into circulation, I believe?"

"Several, but none as productive as NEW SF. It will be slower, probably riskier."

"How much is left to launder?"

Karnek did not let his curiosity show. *What kind of people steal a ton – literally, a ton – of cash and don't know how much they stole? Why is he asking me?*

"I don't know. I've never been given a number. *And I don't think he knows or even cares.* He just keeps handing me bags full of the stuff to run through the laundry."

The old man sat quietly, running through calculations that Karnek didn't even try to anticipate. Finally, he asked the question that was the reason for this meeting. "Should I worry? Remember your analogy about threads unraveling? Gould's murder will automatically start some very smart people looking into what the CFO was doing that got him killed. Because they're smart, they will undoubtedly learn that he was laundering money. But will they be able to connect it to me?"

Karnek said simply, "Yes."

"Yes, I should worry? Or yes, they'll connect the money laundering to me?"

Again, the one word, "Yes."

The old man smiled. It was one of the things he liked about Karnek, his absolute indifference to the opinions of others. "So what needs to happen?"

Not so long ago, Karnek would have responded with irony, something along the lines of, "Get your affairs in order. Your time has run out." But he had learned that this shrunken old man sitting opposite him could reach into and divert institutions and processes that the rest of the world viewed as implacable forces.

So he held up two fingers. "Two things. First, the Gould murder should seem to be an ordinary street crime, not something that calls for a major career-enhancing investigation by an FBI agent looking for connections to organized crime or massive political corruption."

"What's the name of the FBI agent in charge of the investigation?"

"Malone, out of DC."

The old man made a note on the pad in front of him. "What's the second thing?"

"The other side of the same coin. The Delgado woman was on the same track as Malone even before Gould was killed. She has to lose interest in NEW SF, or at least stop pulling on threads. She could justify that if she wanted to ... say that Gould was the main crook and there's no need to continue."

"She's federal, right? DOJ? And you already made a run at her."

So he knows about the screwed-up carjacking. No surprise there. "Treasury, not DOJ. The client that you referred me to ... that was his idea. I think it was the wrong thing to do. Luckily for her, a good Samaritan came along at the right time."

"What about a second try?"

Karnek shook his head. "No. Gould's murder changes everything. Four days ago, she was entirely on her own, chasing a rumor. She dies ... nobody pays much attention. Now, she's investigating an agency whose CFO was mysteriously murdered, automatically raising questions about the finances of that agency. If Delgado dies, every conspiracy theorist in the Western Hemisphere will jump on it and you'll be prime time news for a month."

The old man nodded. "So. Other methods then."

After Karnek left, the man went to his desk, extracted a large folio from the middle drawer and looked up a number which he then dialed.

"Arthur. It's been a while, but I know you've been busy ... Thanks ... Congratulations on the primary. That was one of the nastier contests I've seen ... Oh, I was just happy I could help ... Listen, are you still on that joint FBI Oversight task force? I was wondering if ...."

A Series of Conversations

"More cops," Butch said. As usual, he was monitoring the arrivals and departures in the circular drive in front of the main building. "But these are in uniforms. Henri will have a hard time passing them off as potential residents here for a tour."

Sal didn't even look up from his Sudoku puzzle. "That's not Henri's only problem. In addition to our murder spree, we had an ordinary robbery yesterday. That's why the uniforms, I imagine."

Both Butch and Graham looked at him until he put the puzzle down. "I ran into Mendoza on the way here. She said that our General McNeal had some valuables taken from his residence."

"Well it wasn't me," Butch said. "Thaddeus and I have different taste in valuables."

Graham mused, "Hard to imagine residents stealing from one another ... at least in this place."

Sal picked up his puzzle again. "Mendoza says that it was probably some outside workers in the building for the day. She also hinted that the McNeal's aren't getting along real well these days and I got a very strong impression that she halfway suspects Helen of staging the robbery."

Just then, Frank Shanahan came into the library and stood looking at the incomplete jigsaw puzzle. After a minute or so, he wandered to a far corner, picked up a newspaper and sat down in one of the armchairs. He did not read the paper, just sat staring.

"He looks old."

Salvador said, "He *is* old, Butch. We're all old. That's why we live in this place for old people."

Graham agreed with Butch. Shanahan looked about twenty years older overnight. *Easy to understand why. A double whammy. His wife of several decades is murdered and most of us, including the police, think he's the one who did it.*

The three of them were in their usual coffee venue. It had become a comfortable routine for Graham and the other two seemed to view him as a coequal, or at least as a useful foil for their stream of social satire. He had come to view them as a retired vaudeville team, or maybe a tag team of gossip columnists. But, in this case of Frank Shanahan, they had real expertise that Graham wanted to exploit.

"You were defense attorneys. Did you do murder cases?"

They looked at each other, knowing where this was going. It made them slightly more cautious than usual. Salvador responded for both of them. "Sixty-two cases between the two of us, over eighty years of combined practice." Butch added, "But we're retired, so if you're planning to do Valerie ..."

He ignored the comment. "So tell me, why isn't Frank Shanahan under arrest? He has to be the prime suspect."

"He is that," Salvador said, "but they need evidence ... probable cause ... before they can arrest a suspect. And that's harder than you think when you have a husband-wife homicide."

Butch picked up the thread. "With most murder cases, the cops try to establish a physical connection. An eyewitness saw them together; the killer leaves DNA or fingerprints or a business card at the scene. But none of that counts if the suspect and victim are living together. All of that evidence is irrelevant precisely because it's so plentiful and ordinary."

"Then there's motive," Salvador chimed in. "All of us watched the Shanahan's together. They were as close as two people can be. No hostilities of any sort ... totally dependent on each other." He nodded in Shanahan's direction. "Look at the man. He's a textbook case of grieving. He had no reason --"

Graham held up his hand to stop him. "There is a motive, but it's not the usual one. It's not hate, lust, greed, vengeance or any of our quintessentially human pathologies. It's exactly the opposite, in fact."

"A mercy killing," Salvador said softly. "She was disintegrating in front of us. The Alzheimer's ..."

Butch shook his head. "It was there, and getting worse. But it presented mostly as a mild confusion. She told stories about things that may or may not have happened a long time ago. She was still appropriate most of the time, especially in a place like this. And Frank covered for her quite well. You don't kill someone you love because they start to act a little bit loopy. Hell, I would have offed you a dozen times by now!"

Just then, Shanahan stood up and walked over to them. All three of them stood as he approached, an awkward formality that seemed somehow justified by his tragic circumstances. Sal waved at the fourth chair at the low table and said, "Join us for coffee, Frank?"

"No, thanks. Graham, can I talk to you for a moment? It's important. I'll be in my apartment. Please come by when it's convenient. Thanks." And he walked away, out of the library, leaving the three of them looking at one another.

Graham stopped at his apartment. For the last few weeks, he and Valerie had tacitly accepted an arrangement whereby it was 'his' when she was in the city and working and 'hers' on nights and weekends. In his mind, he likened it to life on a submarine, where there were two crews working alternative shifts but only one set of bunks. However, he was using it less and less, partly because he was spending significant amounts of time with Renee. Curiously, that clandestine affair caused him to view the Alden Acres residence as 'hers,' as though they had already worked out the community property arrangements associated with divorce. He still used his key but was careful to call out "Valerie?" in a loud voice to make sure that she was gone.

This time, he got a response. "She's not here." It was Alison, his daughter. She was sitting in the living room with a laptop computer in front of her on the coffee table. "There's a fresh pot of coffee. Come and join me." He filled a mug and sat down in the chair facing her. "Working?" he asked.

"Yes. On the Shanahan thing. Mom gave me a key to her apartment because she knew I'd be here a lot."

She said the key to ' her' apartment. So it's not just me that's dividing up community property. And Alison never had a key until now. I think maybe she's beginning to get ... accept? ... the idea that her parents are in a new phase.

Graham said, "I was just talking with Butch and Salvador, our resident defense attorneys. They say it's hard to find incriminating physical evidence when one spouse kills another."

She grimaced. "They should know. Even when we do, the defense gets it tossed out of court. But I thought we really had it this time. Melissa Shanahan was smothered by a plastic bag held over her head. Very nasty, very effective and – the good news for the victim – relatively quick. Forensics found traces of plastic on her teeth and – don't ask me how – tied it to a particular brand of kitchen products."

"And you found a box of precisely that product in the Shanahan apartment?"

"No, to our surprise. There were plastic bags ... Every kitchen has some of those ... but of a different brand. We did find the kind that was used to kill her in the Alden Acres supply cabinet. Pretty high-end stuff. Very pricey."

"So we're all equally likely to have done it? Us residents?"

"Or staff. Anybody with access to the kitchen supplies. It's a high-security building, so it's not going to be somebody wandering in from off the street."

Graham ran through the alternatives in his head. "Everybody's a suspect, which is like saying nobody's a suspect."

She nodded, "But there's one more odd bit. The spouse is the first one we think of, but we automatically look for outside possibilities as well – enemies, heirs, angry neighbors, swindled business partners, family feuds ... the kind of things that accumulate over a lifetime and can occasionally get you killed. Melissa Shanahan had no friends, no work history, no professional affiliations ... nothing. I've never come across a more anonymous person. She was Mrs. Frank Shanahan, period."

"So you're done?"

"We'll keep looking, but unless something new turns up ..."

Time to change the subject. Or maybe not. "Heard anything new from your grapevine on the Jay Gould killing?"

"Yeah. Talked to Vic. SFPD is running the case now and Vic's their lead. It's now being investigated as a street crime."

"But the Feds, the FBI –"

"Lost interest. Handed it back to SFPD with a strong suggestion to look at the homeless folks under the freeway or the pimp that sold Gould the Tesla. Vic can't find the former and the latter has a solid alibi."

A silence settled on them, each of them thinking the same thing. Finally, Graham brought it into the open. "NEW SF is ... was ... being used to launder money. Gould had to be in on that."

Alison nodded, looking at him very closely. "You and I both know that's what got him killed, probably for skimming. But that's still under Treasury jurisdiction. There's an investigator named Delgado out of DC that's handling it. Vic says she's very good, but the woman hasn't shared anything with her."

"Your mother –"

"Is working twelve hour days, mostly doing damage control. She *thinks* she'll survive as CEO once all the smoke has cleared."

"Actually, I was going to say something else."

"That the two of you are approaching a split? I know about that. She's been quite open about what's going on." Her tone was bland, but she was watching Graham quite closely and he wondered about her neutrality. *How do you explain to your adult child that the two people she's known for her entire life as 'Mom and Dad' – a singular proper noun – are two distinct individuals that no longer meet one another's needs? That longevity in relationships can be as deadly as it is comforting? That midlife crisis can occur past sixty?*

She went on, as though his thoughts were transparent to her. "It's OK, Dad. I don't understand what's going on and it upsets me to see the two of you on this trajectory. But it's your problem, not mine. I'll deal with it, no matter where it goes. I'm not losing either of you."

He reached out across the table, his palm up. She leaned forward and gripped his extended hand. It was a complete and wordless communication that affected him deeply.

She leaned back, closed her laptop and stood. "Alden Acres has not worked out very well, has it?"

Three murders – all unsolved -- close to us. And a disintegrating marriage since we moved in. Well, we were warned that 'geographic cures' didn't work.

Alison called ninety minutes after she had left. "Just got word from the higher ups. I know now why Melissa Shanahan had so little history. She just came into existence three years ago."

"Reincarnation?"

"Something much simpler. You know about the EB-5 Visa Program?"

"A foreigner pays a large sum of money and is granted permanent resident status?"

"Right. A million dollars invested in a new business that will employ at least ten American workers. Very popular with the Chinese and other millionaires that want a fast track into a capitalist haven. We now know that Melissa and Frank Shanahan entered the U.S. from Canada under the auspices of the EB-5 Immigrant Investor Visa Program. But that's all we know."

"I thought there was extensive vetting ... paperwork ..."

"There is. But Frank and Melissa Shanahan were apparently the names they assumed when they entered the U.S. As far as we can tell, the underlying records were expunged."

"Sounds like a Canadian version of our Witness Protection Program ... one that's reserved for millionaires?"

"We're talking to the State Department, Homeland Security and Immigration, but getting nowhere. The word we're getting is that the Trump administration has blocked any and all demands for access to the documentation."

He dialed Renee as soon as Alison had ended the call. "Where are you?"

"At NEW SF, untangling Gould's accounting system."

"What are you finding?"

"What I thought I would. He was adding outside cash to almost every daily inflow. When I get it all added up, I'm guessing it will amount to more than ten million bucks in the last year alone. It looks like about eight million was recycled back to the original source through a series of accounting tricks, but that's going to take some really detailed forensic accounting to pin down. From here on, my job is to try to identify who it is that gave Gould the cash and who he routed it to on its way out."

"But you know who it is. You've got those mom and pop operations that were invoicing for fake services or overbilling for cheap goods …" *The EB-5 program requires investment in new companies.* "Do you know when those companies were formed?"

"Yes. All of them were incorporated on the same day. Approximately three years ago."

"So, who owns them?" *I think I know the answer to this one.*

"An eight-layered hierarchy of Panamanian law firms, so far as I can tell," Renee barked at him. *The stress is beginning to show.* "I've got two large problems. First, it's going to be hard to identify the real owner. I'm finding legal structures that make your average drug cartel look like a bunch of amateurs. Second, I'm getting pressure to slow down, even some hints that I should cease and desist."

"The White House is worried about embarrassing major donors?"

"My goodness, no!" The sarcasm was thick. "I was told that we need to realign our scarce resources to match up with strategic initiative with high target values."

Sure.

There's no way to ask this delicately. "How are you doing with Valerie?"

"Well, I haven't mentioned that I'm sleeping with her current husband."

I think it's best not to respond to that. "What I meant was –"

"I know what you meant. We're fine. She's cooperating in every aspect and I'm fairly sure she was not involved in the mechanics of the fraud. The Board has asked her to stay on while the investigation runs and she's agreed. After that …"

She never finished the sentence, leaving Graham to wonder if it was a threat or a prediction.

Shanahan answered the doorbell within five seconds. "Thanks for coming."

He and Graham sat facing one another across the dining room table. Shanahan pushed aside papers that were scattered across the glossy surface to make a clear space between them. As far as Graham could tell, the papers were financial forms and legal documents.

"Frank, if there's anything I can do –"

"There is. A great deal. But it isn't anything you expect. I want to confess."

Graham had steeled himself for outpourings of grief, for the uncontained flow of recriminations and what-if's and if-only's and covert self-pity that inevitably follow the sudden death of someone that mattered. But he had no ready response for this. He sat stunned.

"Frank, I'm not –"

Shanahan smiled. "Not to Melissa's murder. Something else." He stared at Graham, waiting for his confusion to subside.

Something else? What have I gotten into?

"Why me? Confessions are for priests and policemen."

"Because I want you to write the story."

A Lot of Money

Shanahan talked for thirty minutes, interrupted by Graham only three times. He began with, "My real name is not Shanahan; it's Archer" and ended with "So that's what got Melissa killed." His story spanned the last sixteen years, but Graham knew that he was hearing the "teaser" version, a highly skeletal structure; that Shanahan was operating according to a script that only he had and that details would eventually be forthcoming.

Graham turned on the "record" app on his iPhone. Shanahan watched him do it and said nothing. *He's doesn't just want to tell the story; he wants other people to hear it.*

"You're not Canadian?"

"No. We were living in Toronto, but we had dual citizenship. The EB-5 Visa shuffle gave us a fresh start when ABL shut down." He smiled at the memory. "It's amazing how money can facilitate difficult transactions. Even create new identities."

"So how much cash was there on that helicopter?"

"A standard pallet is 48 inches by 40 inches. A US hundred dollar bill is 2.61 inches wide, 6.14 inches long, 0.0043 inches thick, and weighs one gram. Those are the official dimensions, as put out by the U.S. Treasury Department. If you do the arithmetic and allow for the inevitable tiny gaps, you can fit 98 hundred dollar bills on the surface of your standard pallet. A four-foot column would have approximately 11,160 bills or $1.116 million, so your pallet with 98 columns would be worth approximately $109 million."

He recited the cascade of numbers without any hesitation or fumbling, as though he had done it many times.

"I guess I'll trust your arithmetic, but – if it was me – I think I'd just count it."

He shrugged. "Suit yourself. It would take you a while. They're wrapped in bundles of 100 bills, $10,000 per bundle. So if you trust your source and the courier, you could just count the bundles. Of course, unless they're new bills fresh from the mint, there's a good chance that a bundle that size would be drug cartel money. Those folks are known to doctor the bundles. Dollar bills thrown in for filler, short counts. That sort of stuff."

"But an entire pallet of the stuff. That would be heavy ... Very hard to move around ... or to hide."

"1,093,680 grams, not counting the pallet itself. That translates to 2,411 pounds. More than a ton."

"$109 million is a lot of money. And a one-ton pallet ... You'd think it would have been noticed if it went missing."

"Oh, they knew it was gone. But they didn't know I had it. And in those times, right after nine-eleven, the rightful owners were focused on other things. This was one of those situations where the 'money is no object' rule was in force. Put it in perspective. I've heard estimates of $2.4 *trillion* for the wars in Iraq and Afghanistan. That's *trillion*, with a 't.' $109 million is like a grain of sand in the Sahara in that world."

"I still can't –"

"You've got to remember what it was like right after nine-eleven. We needed a target *right now* and Afghanistan was there, with bin Laden taunting us. All we had in the vicinity were some aging CIA sources and a few hundred special forces troops. We had the air, but the Taliban owned the ground. So we had to pay other people – the Northern Alliance – to fight the war for us. And wars are expensive. People lose their sense of proportion. Suppose an F15 or stealth bomber crashes. That's maybe a billion dollars. But it's OK. Those are *necessary* losses, the cost of doing business as global policeman. This isn't like a Brink's job, something audacious that captures the public imagination. This was collateral damage, one of those everyday horrible things that happen in wartime. A loss that must be seen in the context of regime change, the pursuit of Bin Laden, of a war being fought by others on our behalf. They were Tajiks, Hazara, Uzbeks and they all wanted to be paid. And they knew we had no other option."

It was a long monologue, without any 'ums' or 'uhs' or other verbal placeholders. *He's been thinking about this for sixteen years. Wanting to tell somebody.*

"But flying a ton of hundred dollar bills into a war zone? Doesn't that warrant an eyebrow being raised? Even if you didn't lose the whole damn shipment?"

"The CIA was fighting the war. And they didn't have any embedded reporters along. They came looking for the money, though. One man, two days later, asking questions and telling me the name of the dead man. Donavan, with a wife and two children somewhere in the Midwest."

Graham nodded. *CIA black money. Unappropriated funds, for use 'as needed,' sources unknown. Something that can't be missed because it never existed in the first place. A loss that can't be acknowledged because people would ask where it came from. It's like stealing from the mob ... they can't call the cops.*

Graham had yet to ask the obvious question: *Why are you telling me – confessing, as you put it – all this stuff now? It's long after the event. Or is it?* "You're right about it being a great story, and I will write it.   But I need an ending. What happened to the money?

Shanahan stood up. "Would you like to see it? It's only a thirty-minute drive."

Shanahan went through more of the story on the drive to Colma.   How the cargo was buried in Afghanistan for fourteen years and his one-man operation to dig it up and transport it back to the U.S. How Melissa set up the money-laundering operation and how everything was going so well until Vargas showed up.

"Vargas?"

"The decomposing body in the forest?   With no hands."

"Did you kill him?"

The question clearly bothered Shanahan. He averted his eyes and, for the first time, radiated a sense of guilt. "When this all started … November 2001 … I was pretty well running ABL. We were a tough company doing jobs other people wouldn't do in places they wouldn't go. Rules were for the other people. But I never cut any corners that got anybody killed.   I was in Afghanistan to build a police station. Then the man calls and I wind up with bodies all over the place and that pile of anonymous cash."

Graham waited, knowing that he would answer the question in his own way.

"I tried to pay him to go away, but he wouldn't." He was silent for a few seconds. "He killed three people that night in Afghanistan that didn't deserve to die, plus ... probably ... many others in his time with the Taliban and assorted other terrorists. I keep telling myself he earned it ... but ..."

I wonder how he feels about the deaths of Melissa and Jay Gould. I think this confession has a long way to go. Graham began to think of a way to steer the story back to the present, but he was preempted. "We're here," Shanahan said and he turned into the entrance to a self-storage complex. He entered a security code into the gate by punching four tabs on the numerical keypad and they drove to the rear of the complex, up to a garage-sized metal door with a small sign saying 'Interment Products Limited.' The signs on the units to the left and right read "LJS Luggage Wholesalers" and "City of San Francisco Medical Examiner Records."

Graham gestured at the sign on the door in front of them. "Deters thieves, I guess? Not much resale value in funeral goods." Shanahan smiled, clearly envisioning something visible only to him. "It was Melissa's idea. All of the clever ideas were hers." He slid the door upward and turned on a light switch just inside the unit. They were standing at the head of a narrow aisle running down the center of the unit. On one side was a wall of corrugated boxes of various sizes. The label on the nearest one to Graham read "Plastic Floral Arrangements." The other side of the aisle was formed by a virtual wall of stacked metallic-looking coffins. He counted them quickly ... ten columns, each with four coffins resting on metal shelves.

Shanahan went halfway down the aisle and stopped, placing his hand on the third coffin from ground level. "There were originally six. It took me two years to get rid of the money in the first one. This is the second one." With some obvious effort, he slid the coffin about two feet out into the aisle and lifted the cover so that Graham could see bundles of currency. To him, it looked about half-full. "Where are the others?"

"Right here." Shanahan slapped the surface of a coffin in the next column over. "These four." To Graham, the sound of his hand slapping against a metal box seemed wrong. He stood in front of the designated column and gripped the sides of the coffin and pulled. It was surprisingly light. He lifted the cover halfway, enough to see that the interior was empty. "Are you sure this was one of them?"

Shanahan was mute, staring into the interior of the metal box. He did the same with the other three coffins, pulling them free, lifting the covers to discover that they were empty. While he was doing that, Graham tested all the others by simply knocking with his knuckles and listening to the unmistakably hollow sound.

They stood looking at one another. The light from the single overhead bulb was quite dim, but it was enough that Graham could be surprised by Shanahan's apparent placid acceptance of a loss that approximated the better part of a hundred million dollars. *He knows what happened to his money. And he just doesn't care very much.*

"You know who took it, don't you?"

Shanahan didn't answer directly. "It was all here the day Melissa was killed. I picked up another batch that day, and I checked all four coffins."

He walked out and waited for Graham. He rolled the door down and locked it. As they got back into the car, Graham asked, "What now?"

"We have to finish the story. The ending is going to be spectacular."

"Are you done confessing?"

"Yes, but there are others who haven't yet begun."

Confrontation

They drove in silence back to Alden Acres. Graham tried to question him, but Shanahan just said, "Wait. You'll have all your answers after our next stop." They went to the bar where Shanahan poured drinks for each of them from a locker he kept behind the bar. Once they sat down, he took a napkin from the bar and wrote several lines. From where Graham was sitting, it looked like a grocery list. "I'll give this to you later, just in case some of the details slip my mind. Or if our meeting gets messy." He swallowed his drink in two quick gulps and said, "I'll be back in just a minute. I have to pick up one more thing." When he returned, he headed straight for the northern end of the Alden Acres complex, toward what Sal had dubbed 'the McDavid Enclave.'

When he saw where they were headed, Graham asked, "Why am I along for this part?" Shanahan stopped and turned to face him. "Your reporting for the Pulitzer? What was the clincher? The one element that made it stand out from all those other tell-all accounts of corruption in the Afghan and Iraqi wars that were filed by your professional colleagues?"

Graham told him, although he knew it was a rhetorical question. "The interview with Ahmad, the ex-provincial governor who actually ran most of the swindles."

"Exactly. So much more compelling for the reader than having to trust an author who merely quotes 'highly-placed, anonymous sources.'"

I guess that's an answer to why I'm being dragged along. His story has an Ahmad character. Shanahan had him hooked. He needed to hear the end of the story, the way an addict waits for the rush after inserting the needle in his arm. He checked his shirt pocket one more time to make sure his iPhone was set to record the audio side of whatever was about to happen.

As they approached the door to the McDavid complex, Shanahan handed Graham that napkin that he'd been writing on in the bar. He had folded it into a tight two-inch square. "Here. For later. Just in case." Shanahan rang the bell, looking directly into the security camera at the top of the door. A buzzer sounded and an accompanying voice said, "It's open. I'm in the living room." They walked down a dimly lit wide gallery lined with small tapestries and found McDavid in the middle of a vast room, sitting in an upholstered motorized wheelchair. A single table lamp alongside him was the only light, leaving most of the room in darkness. Shanahan stopped in the doorway, but after only a second or two went to the chair facing McDavid. Graham moved to the sofa, to the side of the two men.

McDavid nodded in Graham's direction. "Why did you bring him?" He sounded genuinely curious rather than unfriendly.

Shanahan ignored the question entirely. "You took the money." It was a simple declarative statement, a mere fact, not an accusation, delivered without any inflection whatsoever.

"Yes."

"Why now? After all this time."

"Because I needed it now. And you really didn't care about it. It was Melissa that cared. And she's gone, so I couldn't trust you … with your indifference and troubled conscience … to keep it safe." He paused and pointed to Graham.

"Your bringing *him* here ... and talking about the money in front of him ... proves that you are no longer reliable."

Graham watched and listened, struck by the familiarity between them, reminding him of two old men sitting on a park bench talking about growing up in the old country. Then, for the first time since this wild ride had started three hours ago when Shanahan said, "I want to confess," a ripple of apprehension ran through him. *They are openly talking about major crimes in front of me. I am a witness, yet they are unconcerned. Why is that?* He stole a glance around the room and the peripheral shadows suddenly seemed sinister. *Shanahan is harmless – he wants the world to know what he's done – and the old man is in a wheelchair. But who else is here?* But his attention was yanked back to the two principals.

Using the same dispassionate tone, Shanahan said, "You took the money. And you killed Melissa."

The old man looked away, toward the darkest corner of the room. When he turned back to them, he looked even older, sagging in his chair. "Yes. Not me personally. But I was responsible."

Shanahan asked the same question: "Why now? After all this time?"

McDavid leaned forward in his chair and said, "Suppose I told you that I was afraid that she would give away the whole thing. She was losing it, babbling, saying things she shouldn't. Eventually people would start asking questions and you and I would be found out. She needed to be silenced. She came to see me, you know? And I think she would have agreed ... that she should die now ... if we'd given her the chance." His posture and his voice formed an earnest plea, as though knowing his rationale would be rejected. And he was right.

"That's not good enough. Not for her. And not for me."

The silence lasted long enough that Shanahan spoke again, and this time in a sharper, accusing voice. "She was your daughter. You loved her."

"His daughter?" Graham's outburst was so spontaneous and loud that the other two men visibly jumped. "His *daughter*?" he said again, looking to Shanahan as though expecting him to retract what he had said.

Shanahan ignored him. He pulled his chair forward, so that he and McDavid were face-to-face, and very close. This time, he shouted the question, "Why?"

McDavid didn't flinch and Shanahan's anger seemed to infect him. The old man replied with the passion of a fire-and-brimstone evangelist. "Because you wouldn't do it! You didn't have the courage! You would have kept her alive, watching part of her disappear every day, until she became something she would have hated! Comforting yourself with the notion that love and compassion are the same thing!"

The words, laced with contempt and anger, seemed to strike Shanahan with a physical force, pushing him back into his chair and causing him to shake his head side-to-side, a non-verbal and unconvincing rebuttal of what he was hearing.

McDavid moved a switch on the upholstered arm of his chair to move himself even closer to Shanahan, speaking from a few inches away. "She came to see me that night. When she told you she was going to the library. She was crying, afraid of what she was becoming. Everything that she valued in herself was being taken away from her. She said, 'Tell me what my mother was like. I can't remember her! What was my real name, before I became Melissa?' She said, 'He makes me do puzzles. I hate puzzles.'"

"You had no right." Graham thought that perhaps Shanahan was crying now.

"You're a coward. I did what you should have done."

The room was silent, the two men momentarily drained and Graham was acutely aware that nothing could or should be said at this moment. Finally, the old man asked, "Do you have any more questions for me? About the money? Melissa? Or anything else? Maybe about what happens next?" Graham sensed a finality in the series of questions and his apprehension began to grow within him. He knew without the slightest doubt that whatever Shanahan said next would somehow determine whether either of them survived to walk out of the room.

Shanahan seemed unaware of the menace, or was past caring. McDavid waited for what seemed a long time and then leaned back in his wheelchair and said, "Karnek."

A man came out of the deep shadow in the corner, stopping at the edge of the lighted area and to the side, which put him directly opposite Graham. He said nothing, looking back and forth between the two men in their facing chairs as though waiting for direction. He looked familiar to Graham, someone he'd seen before but couldn't quite place, perhaps a gardener or a delivery man. He was dressed in dark khaki pants, a plaid shirt and a brownish jacket. He kept his hands in the pockets of the jacket, a spectator for the moment.

Shanahan did not react to the man's entrance other than to say, "Hello, Karnek" in a voice that was half greeting and half question. The man nodded but remained silent and watchful.

"So he works for you too," Shanahan said to McDavid.

"He does. I was the one who referred him to you."

"That means that Karnek here has a serious conflict of interest," Shanahan said with a wry smile. "Yesterday, I paid him a lot of money to kill you."

McDavid did not seem alarmed by the announcement. The old man turned slightly in his chair to look directly at Karnek. He said, halfway to himself, "You didn't mention that," but the man they called Karnek stood impassively, only half turning his head to look at Shanahan.

Shanahan was still smiling. "But I'm canceling that contract, so there's no conflict after all. And Karnek? You can keep the fee. I think those are your standard terms when the client calls off a job?"

Graham's sense of unreality was maxed out. He felt like an audience of one at a stage play put on solely for his benefit, a play where even the actors didn't know the ending. He didn't know it, but the ordinary-looking man across from him was suffering some of the same symptoms. Karnek had been thinking about the problem for the last twenty-four hours, ever since Shanahan had come up with what he called 'the last assignment.' *I should have known this wouldn't work. Two clients -- a father and his son-in-law that he doesn't think is doing right by his daughter. Now each of them wants me to kill the other one.* There was no code of professional ethics for people like him, but Karnek did not like ambiguity; he prized his reputation as the ultimate fixer and living up to his commitments. He could and did feel intellectually and morally superior to his clients, but he had always behaved so that he would never hear the words, "You didn't do what you said you would do." *Kill one of them? But which one?*

Kill both? And that means that the Dodd guy has to go as well. Why in the hell did Shanahan bring a journalist along to listen to him accuse his father-in-law of murder and theft?

The three men were all looking at Karnek, somehow sensing that he was conflicted and knowing that his working out of that conflict would be vital to each of them. The silence was so profound, the human tableau so frozen in time by the revelations and their possibilities, that the shot sounded far louder than it was. McDavid sat suddenly upright and then toppled over in his chair, jamming the lever that controlled the motorized chair so that it pivoted and ran against the sofa that Graham was sitting on, bringing the old man face-to-face with him. McDavid looked startled, his eyes open and unseeing. Blood was starting to seep through the front of his shirt, spreading even as Graham was trying to comprehend what had happened. The motor of the wheelchair continued to whir until Graham reached out and pulled McDavid's arm away from the control.

Shanahan had not moved, but his right hand now rested on the broad arm of his chair, and it held a gun, still pointed at the space where McDavid had been. Karnek was as before, standing with both hands in his jacket pockets and looking faintly surprised.

Graham thought back to their arrival. *He left me at the bar. Said 'I'll be back in just a minute. I have to pick up one more thing.' The gun. And he told me, "We have to finish the story. The ending is going to be spectacular." He was right about that. But it's not over yet.*

That last thought was confirmed when Karnek brought his right hand out of his pocket. It was also holding a gun, pointed in Shanahan's general direction. The two men looked at one another for a long time. Shanahan finally said,

"I'm sorry about changing our agreement without any notice, but I wanted to do it myself."

"That part is OK," Karnek said. "But I can't help wondering if you intended to include me in this grand finale of yours."

Shanahan looked at the gun in his hand as if he had just discovered it. "This is the second time I've used it. The first time was three years ago … in Afghanistan… he was a farmer … I think his name was Mohammed. He was young, relatively innocent. Not like him." He gestured with the gun toward McDavid. The casual motion with the weapon frightened Graham. *Maybe he intends to kill everybody in the room!* He noticed that Karnek now held his gun pointed directly at Shanahan.

Shanahan didn't seem to care. He placed the handgun on the broad arm of his chair and crossed his arms in front of him. He spoke to Karnek. "Were you the one that moved what's left of the money?" After a short pause, Karnek answered, "Yes. But not far. It's very close. In three very large trunks. You could find it if you wanted to."

Shanahan nodded. "From six coffins to three trunks … Still not very portable … I wonder how much is left?"

Karnek inclined his head toward the body in the wheelchair. "The man wanted to know, so I counted it. Seventy seven million, nine hundred and twenty thousand dollars. That's not counting the two million in the bag for Vargas. Remember that?"

"Of course, Vargas. Another person that I killed, one way or another. Along with Mohammed. And I tried to kill the Delgado woman but you screwed up. Thankfully. And one of us would have silenced Gould if she hadn't done it for us.

Now him," gesturing at the slumped-over McDavid. "And Melissa. That's too many deaths."

Graham remembered Renee talking about her carjacking assailant. "*A white guy in a hoodie ... his eyes ... they were cold. There was no excitement, no nervousness from being in the middle of committing a crime ... just ... calculation ... maybe even boredom.* He looked at the ordinary man opposite him and saw what Renee had seen. The fear pressing against his consciousness became even more intense and harder to suppress.

Shanahan actually smiled at Karnek. "Your contract with him" – he gestured at the slumped-over McDavid – "Is that still in force?"

"You mean, the contract where I agreed to kill you?" He seemed to think about it for a few seconds. "I suppose it is. The money's been paid. He never called it off. Like you did."

"So do it." And Shanahan spread his hands toward Karnek, as if to receive a gift.

Those three stunning words made the entire crazy few hours suddenly make sense to Graham. *That's the end that he's scripted for the story I'm supposed to write. He never intended to survive this meeting and he needed a witness.* His next thought was so out-of-context and yet so important and so obvious that for a few seconds he forgot about his present dangers. *He must have loved her very much.* The thought made him feel incredibly inferior to the man who was asking to be killed.

Karnek had not moved since he had come out of the shadow to stand at the edge of the light, other than to take the gun out of his pocket. Once again, he seemed to be evaluating his choices and Graham knew that there was no way he could influence the outcome. He was wrong about that, in an indirect way.

Shanahan uncrossed his arms and reached out to place his right hand on the gun, closing his fingers around the grip and extending his index finger alongside the trigger guard. With the same slight smile, he said to Karnek, "If you need some incentive, I can make it one of those 'It was either him or me' choices for you."

"If you do that, I'd have to kill him as well as you," and he gestured with the muzzle of the gun toward Graham. He sounded as disinterested as a bus driver announcing they'd arrived at their destination.

Shanahan nodded. "Of course. I hadn't thought about that." After thinking a bit, he asked, "What will you do? There's all that money –"

"I don't want it. I'll take the bag ... the Vargas payoff. And the fees ... from both of you. I can carry that with me. And it's plenty for my needs."

Shanahan was slipping away from them, into some inner reverie. "That was always the problem ... transport ... how to move all that cash around without people noticing. That was what Melissa liked ... the working out of puzzles ... being clever." He shook his head. "It's funny. I think of her as 'Melissa' now; I never thought that would happen."

Karnek put the gun back into his pocket and turned to leave, heading across the room toward the shadows where he'd first emerged from. He stopped but did not turn around. "For what it's worth, the man really did love his daughter."

"I know," Shanahan said softly, "but that didn't give him the right."

Karnek walked out, disappearing into the shadows. When Graham wrote the final story, he used that image over and over whenever the subject of 'Karnek' was touched on.

Graham looked at Shanahan, who was staring straight ahead, unseeing. He asked, very quietly, "Are we at the end of the story now?"

It seemed to require some effort for him to gather himself and answer. "No more narration from me. You'll have to fill in the details based on what you've learned. But – hey – you're a Pulitzer Prize winning journalist. That's what you're good at."

"Who's the hero? Every good story needs a hero ... or heroine?" Graham was stalling, hoping for some magical alternative to reveal itself as Shanahan's script wound to its inexorable closing scene. Anything but what Graham was imagining.

"No heroes. But you've got enough villains to make up for the deficit."

"Frank, this story starts sixteen years ago. I need –"

"Graham. Stop." He lifted the gun. Later, for his story, Graham would describe him as holding it in the way a Shakespearean actress playing Lady MacBeth would consider the fateful dagger. But in the moment, all Graham saw in him was sadness and resolution and all that he felt within himself was horror and helplessness.

"You have a choice," Shanahan said. "You can stay or go. I'll give you thirty seconds to decide."

Graham used twenty of those seconds in a state of horrific indecision. Then he stood up and walked back down the wide gallery lined with tapestries to the front door, walking faster with each step until he was almost running. He had his hand on the doorknob when the shot came.

Again, that same unbidden and humbling thought: *He must have loved her very much.* He opened the door and went out, closing the door behind him as gently as he could out of respect for the residents of Alden Acres.

Loose Ends

Henri Malraux was a wreck. Two murders and a suicide within a five-day stretch had reduced him to patrolling the public areas of Alden Acres and reassuring anyone he came across that all would be well, that their privacy would be restored and the institution's stellar reputation would be as before. The stress had even caused his French accent to slip a bit.

Mendoza found the bodies at eight in the morning when she went to give McDavid his daily shot. By eight-thirty, the place was swarming with police and any residents still on hand were on lockdown. Graham used the time for a serious conversation with himself. *So, will you tell them about your role in last night's events?*

There were more police and reporters in the halls than there were residents. As Butch put it, "One of the advantages of wealth is the ability to leave town on short notice." Butch and Salvador also agreed that the short and long run were still rosy, but that Malraux would not survive the medium term consequences. "In the short run, we're all committed. We've paid our five million and can't walk away. And in the long run, everybody will have forgotten about yesterday's news. But for a while –"

"As in one to two years," Sal broke in.

Butch continued, "Henri is going to have a hard time recruiting new residents –"

"And," Sal interrupted again, "since McDavid's majority ownership is now in the hands of a California probate court and –"

Butch's turn. "Nobody knows what the future will look like."

Graham laughed at them. "Talking with you two is like carrying on a conversation with Huey, Dewey and Louie Duck." *Not all of us are committed, however. I suppose I could tell them about our 'special arrangement' with Henri, but that would be problematical for Valerie. I can't imagine why, but she seems to want to live in this gilded cage.*

It was national news. At first, it was standard tabloid stuff -- a murder-suicide in a club for Silicon Valley millionaires. Then it was linked to an earlier murder – of Melissa – because the police discovered evidence from the McDavid residence that linked her killing to that apartment. Graham had inside information from Alison. "The plastic bag used to suffocate Melissa Shanahan was found in the McDavid apartment." Then the story went viral and global when it was discovered that McDavid was really Barry Wilder and that Melissa Shanahan was his daughter. The press was convinced that her murder was really a mercy killing sparked by her rapidly worsening dementia. The story was quite neat, all the loose ends nicely tucked in.

One of the ripple effects was a developing flap around the EB-5 Visa Program. It turned out that David McDavid and the Shanahan's were Canadian citizens whose actual names were Barry Wilder and Griffin and Gwen Archer. They were given green cards and an expedited path to citizenship by agreeing to invest a million dollars each in startup US companies that would in turn create at least ten jobs. Congress was threatening to hold hearings as to how three fugitives from the ABL debacle had managed to get the visas and new identities at the same time.

And so far there's been no mention of the fact that the companies that were created by the Shanahan's and Wilder were false fronts, sham companies that had no function other than as recipients of the laundered cash. That's another shoe waiting to drop.

So, will you tell them about your role in last night's events?

Why not? I'm an eyewitness and I'm not at risk of prosecution in any way. I was a pure spectator. There was no way I could have prevented either of the deaths.

But they don't need your testimony. It will be perfectly obvious what happened.

But they won't know the rest of the story – Afghanistan, the money, the toxic family relationship between the two of them, the money laundering ... And there's no way they'll be aware of the man called Karnek.

Most of that is irrelevant to what happened last night. And it's all going to come out anyway. It will just take a little longer.

Are you sure you're not just protecting Valerie by not coming forward?

Protecting from what? NEW SF will be investigated for financial fraud whether I tell my story or not. Anyway, I'm divorcing the woman. I have no obligation to her.

But you still care about her.

You're obviously trying to talk yourself into not telling them you were there. Are you sure it's not because you want some of that seventy-seven million, nine hundred and twenty thousand dollars for yourself? Nobody knows about it except you and a man that doesn't want it because it's too hard to carry around.

I want to deny that, but I keep thinking about those bundles of hundred-dollar bills in that coffin ...

You know what you really want … the real reason why you're not going to tell the police about your time listening to Shanahan and watching what played out in that room … You want to write the story, to see the whole of it in print rather than the sensational bits and pieces in newspapers.

Yes.

Graham's interview with the police was awkward. Partly because he was lying throughout most of the interview, but also because Alison was there, although relegated to an observer role. Her partner, Mark Manning, ran the session.

"Several residents saw you leave with Frank Shanahan on that night. We believe that you may have been the last person to see him before he went to the McDavid residence. So, anything you can tell us …"

"Not much, I'm afraid. He seemed quite distant, clearly distraught by the death of his wife."

"Butch Melendy and Salvador Fender have told us that he asked to talk to you, quite specifically. Just you. What was that about?"

"I'd helped him with a technical problem a while back… connecting his iPad to the local WiFi. He was having some other problems with it and he asked me to come by and look at it. He had one of the original models … quite old … and I suggested he should look at the new one. So we went to the Palo Alto Apple store to take a look."

"Anyone see you there?"

"Hundreds, I imagine but I doubt if anyone would remember. It was packed. They were releasing the new iPhone. We walked around a bit, window shopping some of the iPads, and went back home. Why are you asking?"

"Just trying to get a timeline. So you got back here at ..."

"Around ten. Pretty late for this place. We went to the bar, had a drink and went back to our respective apartments. At least I did. I can't speak for Shanahan."

"We think he went from the bar to the McDavid residence. Did he say anything? Was there anything unusual about his behavior?"

"No, other than that it was pretty obvious he was badly depressed. I tried to talk to him about his wife ... the usual kind of clichés ... "I know it must be tough ..." and, "If there's anything I can do ..." but that went nowhere fast."

"Any anger? Any talk of finding out who killed her?"

"No. And frankly, I thought that it was because he had done it himself. So I didn't press the issue and he didn't bring it up."

He asked Alison to stop by when she a chance, and she visited him an hour after the Manning interview. "The forensics are pretty clear. Shanahan shot McDavid at close range and then himself ... the classic gun under the chin technique. Very effective."

"Was there a note?"

"Not that we've discovered."

Does she know about the man in the shadows?" Be careful what questions you ask! And there was nobody else in the McDavid residence? Where was the Tom and Jerry duo?"

"Gone for the day. They've got ironclad alibis. But they are what we like to call 'persons of interest' for the Melissa killing. We know she was killed in McDavid's living room because of some rug fibers under her fingernails, and the bag that was used came from his kitchen. It's pretty clear that McDavid was physically incapable of the deed, so ..."

Just one more very delicate question: "Do you think there could be some connection to the body your mom and I found at the crest of the hill?" *Why would I want to plant such a thought? Do I care whether they connect Vargas, McDavid and Karnek? Do I want him to be caught?*

Alison looked at him closely and he did his best to look innocent. She shrugged. "We talked about the possibility. McDavid aka Wilder was not a nice person, and we know he played rough before he went underground. But there's nothing to go on."

A silence came over them and he noticed for the first time that she was tired. *For good reason. The bodies are stacking up. I hate to do this to her.*

But she forced his hand. "What did you want to see me about?"

He did not respond, casting about in his mind for an easy way out. But Alison was insistent, sensing that they hadn't gotten to the real purpose of the meeting yet. "You asked me to stop by. Remember?"

So he just said it: "I'm going to ask your mother for a divorce." *And I'm quite confident she'll agree to it.*

Alison turned to look out the window, as if seeking guidance from the hundred-year-old oak trees on the hillside. With an audible sigh, she said, "You telegraphed that a long time ago. I've gotten used to the idea." He thought she was trying to make his confession easier for him, but her next question changed that view.

"Is there another woman?" And before he could answer, she said, "There's always another woman ..."

He looked away, knowing he was going to lie once more. "No. We've just lost interest in one another. There's too much baggage and too little incentive to work on it." *That's true, and a sufficient explanation. Much better than saying 'Yes, there is another woman, but that's irrelevant to why I want a divorce.'* And then he was struck by a different thought: *I wonder if she'll ask her mother 'Is there another man?'* The thought made him glad that he had lied.

"Where will you –"

"I'm moving to Washington DC. I've got a story – a book -- that I need to write and that's where I need to be if I'm going to do it right."

"What's it about? Your book?"

A political thriller? Murder mystery? Police procedural? Expose of corruption at the highest levels of government? Maybe even a tragic love story? It could be any or all of those.

In the end, he just told her the truth as he knew it. "It's a story told to me one time by a man that was dying. I promised him that I would write it."

A Confession of Sorts

Graham took the plastic sleeve out of the leather portfolio that he was carrying. It contained an unfolded napkin, the one that Shanahan handed to him before he rang McDavid's doorbell, saying, "Here. For later. Just in case." He'd stuffed it into his pocket and forgotten it until the next day. Even in the protective clear plastic sleeve, it was wrinkled and the black ink had osmosed through the porous paper, making the five bullet points barely legible.

The first three items written on the napkin were autobiographical in nature. The first one was, "My name is Griffin Archer." The second, "I worked for Advanced Base Logistics for forty years." The third, "I was with a remarkable woman named Gwen Wilder for most of my adult life." At first, Graham was puzzled. Shanahan had already told him those facts during their ride to and from Colma, along with countless other far more dramatic events. *Why emphasize these three mundane historical elements?* He never came up with a really satisfactory answer, but since then had come to view them as Shanahan's obituary, how he wanted to be remembered. Not as a criminal mastermind, money launderer, exactor of vengeance, or ungodly rich, but as a simple man who had worked for a living and married a woman that he loved. And when Graham saw that, he knew that his book would have a hero. Not the comic book sort, nor even the damaged knight-errant or anti-hero of popular literature but a man that understood and regretted his flaws and – at the end – tried to make amends with a simple paper napkin.

The fourth item on the list was not about Shanahan at all. It read, "Your wife Valerie is having an affair with Thaddeus McNeal."

To his credit, Graham was sufficiently self-aware and objective that he charted the explicit emotional phases that washed over him even as he experienced them. He had written his senior thesis in high school about the Kubler-Ross Theory and its five stages associated with death and dying and he still remembered them – denial, anger, bargaining, depression and acceptance. In the case of Shanahan's statement of Valerie's infidelity, he would substitute "surprise" for "bargaining" and "self-doubt" for "depression," but still found it a surprisingly accurate portrayal of his changing inner states. He transited all five states in about ten minutes and, at the end, not only achieved "acceptance" but was grateful because it balanced out his accumulated guilt brought on by his rapidly escalating affair with Renee.

He was waiting in the apartment when Valerie got home from San Francisco, sitting at the kitchen island with a bottle of Chardonnay and two glasses. It was their longstanding Friday night ritual, beginning the week she had been promoted to CEO of NEW SF.

She put her briefcase on the counter in front of her and sat down facing him. She accepted the glass of wine with raised eyebrows. They clinked the glasses together and she said, "But it's only Tuesday night."

"Still, it's a special occasion."

"Which is?"

"It's the last one." She sat straighter, knowing there was more. "Like you, I want a divorce. As soon as we can do the paperwork."

Her eyes narrowed and she regarded him closely as she took another sip of the wine. "Please don't take this to mean that

I'm going to resist, but why now? What happened to tip you over the edge?"

He thought of some of the possible responses he could make to such a question, envisioning where they would lead and how persuasive they would be. She waited patiently, both of them settled comfortably into the dynamic that had worked for them for more than three decades of marriage. Their momentary comfort with one another even as they discussed divorce was supremely ironic and it made her 'why now' question even more difficult for him to answer. *What's the adage? 'Familiarity breeds contentment?' Or is it contempt?*

"You asked me what happened? Let's just say that I recently spent some time with a man that loved his wife so much that he killed himself rather than live without her. I can't see myself doing that for you."

His answer irritated her ... another and more common dynamic of their relationship. "That's bullshit. And you know it."

He hadn't intended to say it but he couldn't help reacting to her scorn. "Then maybe it's because you're screwing McNeal."

Valerie stared, open-mouthed. He waved his hands quickly back and forth, like a nervous professor correcting himself. "Forget I said that. It has nothing to do with wanting a divorce. McNeal is a symptom, not a cause. And I truly don't care."

She sat rigidly, her hands folded together on the counter top, her mouth compressed into a narrow strip. Graham felt sorry for her when she began, "I want all the art, a monthly stipend of –"

"Valerie. Stop."

She plunged on. "I've already met with a lawyer and have drawn up a settlement proposal.   She started to open the briefcase in front of her. You won't like it, but –"

He held up his hand, a stop signal. "There's not going to be any bargaining. We split everything down the middle – bank accounts, investments, retirement accounts, all the liabilities. And that's it.   There will be no valuation of so-called intellectual property, no retroactive compensation for your foregone income while acting as housewife, no support payments, no claims on future income. You won't even need a lawyer."

He watched her anger increase with every word he spoke. When he stopped, she stood up and spoke in the manner of someone addressing a door-to-door salesman that would not go away. "It's Tuesday night. Our agreement is that it's my apartment on weeknights. I want you out of here. Now. I'll deliver *my* draft of *my* proposed settlement agreement to you tomorrow morning. If you don't sign it, then you'll have to get your own lawyer and we'll let them fight about it."

He spoke softly and if she'd listened, she would have heard the sadness. "Valerie, that isn't how it's going to work."

"Fuck you Graham!" And she turned around to walk away. He allowed her three steps, and then he said, "Jay Gould."

She stopped but didn't turn around. After a few seconds, looking back over her shoulder, she said, "What about Jay Gould?"

"You killed him."

That was the fifth line item on Shanahan's paper napkin, although phrased as a question. *Who killed Jay Gould?* And Shanahan had answered the question for him. Graham had played and replayed his iPhone audio file of their time in McDavid's living room, particularly the segment when Shanahan was reciting his litany of killings to Karnek.

"Of course, Vargas. Another person that I killed, one way or another. Along with Mohammed. And I tried to kill the Delgado woman but you screwed up. Thankfully. And one of us would have silenced Gould if she hadn't done it for us. Now him," gesturing at the slumped-over McDavid. *"And Melissa. That's too many deaths."*

And one of us would have silenced Gould if she hadn't done it for us. So it wasn't McDavid, Shanahan or Karnek. It was a woman.

Valerie still didn't turn around. "That's ridiculous!" And when he said nothing, she said with much less emphasis, "You don't know that."

She didn't say, 'I didn't kill him.'

"The gun that killed Gould was a nine millimeter."

"So?"

"Thad McNeal had a nine millimeter handgun, a Beretta Nano. It's very popular with the concealed carry crowd. He reported it stolen from a bedside table the day before Gould's killing. He was having some new carpeting put in and the cops figure it was one of the installers." *And we've just established that you have easy access to McNeal's bedroom.*

She turned to face him, but stayed in place, about fifteen feet away. "You think that I –"

"There's more. You told the cops that you were home alone when Gould was shot. But you weren't. I came by the apartment to pick up some files. You weren't there. I was sitting in the bar and saw you come in at eleven. You were wearing blue jeans and a sweatshirt."

"Why would I kill Gould?" She returned to her chair, but her harsh challenging tones did not quite disguise a real underlying curiosity.

"He knew that you were close to exposing him as a big-time money launderer. I think he threatened you. Said something like, "I'll tell them that you were in on it ... that you encouraged him ... got a cut." It would be a plausible threat. People would have a hard time believing that you could be unaware of millions of extra dollars flowing through your business. Or maybe he didn't threaten you but you just wanted to keep him from doing more damage."

And maybe she was in on it, or at least allowed it to continue once she became aware of it.

Valerie spoke slowly, as though trying out ideas, weighing the strength of his arguments, evaluating alternative explanations. "Gould being killed brought everything into the open. Damaged NEW SF critically. Almost cost me my job. Why would I do that?"

"You knew the scandal was going to break in the next few days no matter what you did. Getting rid of him wouldn't change that, but it would save your reputation."

They sat in silence, each with their own thoughts. Then Valerie sat straighter, as though she had come to a conclusion of sorts. "Very neat. You've clearly spent a lot of time thinking about this."

"I have."

"What are you going to do with this ... *theory?*"

He looked directly at her, marveling at how he and this woman had gotten to this point. "I'm going to use it as leverage ... to convince you to agree to my version of the divorce settlement."

She smiled. "That seems ... insufficient. Your story, if true, would be worth a lot more than that."

"I've thought about that. But I'm really not interested in vengeance. For what? Creeping incompatibility, for god's sake? And Gould was sleazy, not someone I should care about particularly. It's going to be an unsolved murder if I keep my mouth shut, so no hapless street dweller gets put away for something he didn't do. And then there's Alison. If I go to the police with what I know, it will destroy her relationship with both of us; and I value that relationship."

"Still, it's pretty compelling. The local news people would love it."

Graham noted the reversal in their positions. *She's testing. Will he or won't he? Is it a plausible enough story to put her in jail? Can she trust me?*

"You can trust me, Valerie. I know that's not very reassuring coming from a man trying to negotiate a divorce. I could ruin you, but I don't think you'd face a murder trial. Most of my accusations are speculative and the rest are circumstantial. I doubt if my *theory* would satisfy a DA that there's enough to prosecute you. Maybe if we found the gun?"

She sat, staring at him, but entirely within her own head at the moment. He recognized the telltales: the index finger tapping on the counter, the biting of her lower lip. Graham did not envy her. *A woman with no good options.* Then her eyes came back into focus and she nodded as though to confirm what she'd been thinking. She reached into the briefcase and pulled her hand out with an object wrapped in a colorful scarf. She unwrapped the scarf and showed him what was in it.

"You mean this gun?"

He stared at it in horror, not yet aware of all of the possibilities. She said, "It's a Beretta Nano. Nine millimeter. Very nice weapon. Holds eight rounds. More than enough to kill several people." For what seemed a very long time, she and Graham looked fixedly at the gun, not wanting to look into the other's eyes for fear of what they would see.

Valerie stood once more. She rewrapped the Beretta in the scarf and slid it back into the briefcase. "Send me the settlement agreement. I'll have it back to you within the hour." And she left.

Endings

It was the worst decision we ever made, living here. But I'll miss this part of it. Graham was sitting in what the official Alden Acres brochure called 'the Meditation Garden.' It was a small glade surrounded by magnificent California oak trees with thick branches that ran horizontally for incredible distances, some of them now supported by vertical struts. The only other concessions to modernity were the carefully tended grass, the flagstone path and the wooden benches scattered around the perimeter.

He had his iPhone with him. Technically, that was a violation as the Meditation Garden was supposed to be free from devices that rang, buzzed or intruded in any way on the natural serenity. The irony was that the very privacy encouraged residents to frequent the place for those conversations that would not be possible in the public spaces.

Like the telephone call he had just concluded.

"Hello Valerie."

"I've left the settlement agreement on the kitchen counter. I've made only one amendment. I want to keep the lease on the apartment."

She wants to stay here! How can I be so wrong about a person that I thought I knew so well? "No problem on my end. I'll file the papers later today." He hesitated but finally could not stop from asking. "You *want* to stay here?"

"Our lease contract obligates us for three years. We have to pay whether we're here or somewhere else." Neither of them commented that her answer was non-responsive.

An awkward silence set in, then she added. "I talked with Alison this morning ... told her what we were doing. She's OK with it, I think. Not what she wants or ever expected, but ..."

"Good. There's probably a self-help group she can join ... for Adult Children of Long-Married Divorcees, or something similar." Even as he was talking, Graham was thinking *that's a really insensitive thing to say.* The thought was followed immediately by a question he knew he would never be able to answer. *How would Alison feel about their divorce if she knew that Valerie had killed Jay Gould?*

Apparently Valerie was thinking along the same lines. Her voice became more tentative. "She told me that SFPD has put the Gould case in what she called the "open, but unless something new comes along" category. Their thinking is that either Shanahan or McDavid had him killed because he was getting cold feet, or maybe because he was skimming, but they have no way of proving any of it."

Graham tried to keep his voice perfectly bland. "That's too bad. I hope they eventually get whoever killed him."

More silence. *We seem finally to have reached that point where we have nothing left to say to one another.*

He said, "OK then." She said, "OK," and cut off the call.

The voice came from directly behind him. "Nice place. It reminds me of a place I want to get back to." Like everything about the man, his voice was ordinary, unthreatening. Graham did not react; he just waited until the man sat down next to him on the bench. He was dressed exactly as he had been that night in the McDavid residence.

Graham edged to the far end of the bench that they shared. "I thought you were gone. I would be, in your shoes. Is your name really Karnek?" And then he remembered. "You've come back for the money!"

"You weren't listening the other night. I don't want the money. And I am going. Just this one last thing." He put his hands into his jacket pockets and Graham suddenly remembered the way the gun had appeared. Once more, the unremarkable colorless man next to him became something sinister and threatening and he silently cursed himself for his willful blindness about the seriousness of the game he was playing.

The man took his right hand from his pocket. It was empty, and he placed it on Graham's knee as they sat side by side, a perfectly ordinary gesture intended to emphasize a parting word between good friends. "My sources tell me that you talked to a homicide detective. According to those sources, it was established that you were the last person to see Shanahan alive, except for McDavid, of course. Those sources tell me you told the detective that Shanahan left you in the bar and you went off to bed. You've never been inside the McDavid residence."

"Yes."

Karnek stood up. "I just wanted to be sure. And to remind you that I would be very upset if your recollections of that evening ever changed." He waited until Graham made eye contact and said, "I would have to come back and kill you."

"Yes ... no ... I mean ... My story won't change. For many reasons, not just because of you or what you might do to me."

"That's good." He reached into his pocket once more and brought out his hand, this time a closed fist. "Here, just to finish up what Shanahan started." Graham held out his hand and Karnek dropped two keys into his palm.

"That's it then." And he stood up and started to walk away. Graham would always wonder why he stopped him. "Karnek?" He stopped, but didn't turn around, causing Graham to visualize Valerie taking that same position when he said, "Jay Gould." *Do people always turn their backs when they expect bad news?*

"Karnek, I'm going to write Shanahan's story, probably a book. It will be about the money, and McDavid and Melissa. Can I include you in it?" *Or will that get me killed?*

Karnek turned to face him and looked intently into his eyes. He took a long time to answer the question. "Will I be a killer? In this book you're going to write?"

Graham thought about lying, but knew that it would only defer the consequences and that he would be looking over his shoulder for the rest of his life if he did. He spoke very carefully, enunciating each word. "I know nothing about your part in Shanahan's story that I can use to say that you committed any crimes." *True, but weasel words. The kind of legalistic talk that people use to excuse very real sins. And this man knows it.*

Karnek thought about it for what seemed a long time, then slowly nodded. "It's Karnek, spelled K-a-r-n-e-k. Write your book. It's a great story." He left, walking quickly through the oaks toward the main grounds. *He looks like he could be one of the gardeners, maybe a delivery man.*

Graham slumped against the backrest to the bench and took in huge breaths, once more aware of the slight breeze and the way the oaks enclosed the space. He thought back over his call from Valerie and the unexpected visit from Karnek and felt good about how they had gone. *Only one more thing to get through and then I'm truly done.*

He looked at his watch. *She's late.* But then she was there, hurrying up the path from the buildings into the forest; looking every bit a thoroughly professional woman in a business suit and heels on her way to an important meeting. For the hundredth time, he reminded himself that he had no claim on this woman; that his divorce had nothing to do with her; that the move to DC was for purely professional reasons; that shared nakedness and incredible intimacies created no continuing bonds or obligations. But then she was sitting beside him running her fingers along the back of his hand and smiling at him, and he was thinking, *OK, no strings, no expectations … but hope is permitted.*

"Thanks for coming. Nice to see you again."

She grinned in a wicked way. "You mean fully dressed and vertical?"

She's different. No more Miss Buttoned Down Senior Treasury Official. "Uh, Renee, I'm getting the sudden feeling that something's changed. What's going on?"

She sat back, her hands folded in her lap, suddenly prim. "You called this meeting, so you tell me your news first."

"Actually, there's quite a lot I have to tell you, but I'd rather hear about your world first."

"Sure. Pretty dull and ordinary stuff. High level cover-your-ass maneuvering at the highest levels of government, leaving us dedicated career bureaucrats bobbing in the wake." Her voice was dismissive, but her eyes and body language told him that she was angry.

"That's one too many metaphors for me. What's happened?"

"A lot. First, I've documented – in great detail – a fairly ordinary money-laundering operation at NEW SF. It relied extensively on Gould. Maybe twenty million ran through the system in the last two years. Your wife may have been in on it, but I don't think so and I don't have enough to put her in front of a jury."

"I expected all of that based on what you said a few days ago," Graham said. "Sounds like a good day's work to me."

"Yeah. But what you don't know is that I can now prove where the money came from and where it went. From Shanahan to Gould to McDavid, also known as Wilder. It became pretty obvious once your fellow residents staged their shootout at the old folks home and the real identities came out." She nodded in the downhill direction where the gleaming white structures could be seen through the oaks.

"I still don't know where Shanahan was getting all the cash. Something highly illegal, for sure. Probably a stash from when the Ross Sea Group cratered. A lot of the company's cash disappeared at the same time that Wilder and his son-in-law went missing."

He was getting it from a coffin in Colma, stored in a self-storage unit rented by a non-existent company. Was it obtained illegally? Given the American experience in the last sixteen years in Afghanistan and Iraq, and what we've learned about the CIA, some might argue that when Shanahan buried the money cube he was acting in the best interests of his country. And when he dug it up and started laundering it, one of the unknowing beneficiaries was NEW SF, a major do-gooder organization.

"Graham? Are you listening?"

"Sorry. What were you saying? Something about the Ross Sea Group?"

"I was trying to tell you about my problem –"

"What problem? You're done! The three villains are all dead – Shanahan, Wilder and Gould – and how they died is a matter for the local cops, not the Treasury Department. The money-laundering operation is shut down and you've recovered what you can. There's nothing left for you to do."

"Just one thing, actually. I have to write my report."

"So?"

"Can we walk a bit?" She stood up and took a few steps along the path that circled the glade. He followed her and they began to walk very slowly along the flagstone path. She walked with her head down and Graham began to wonder, and to worry, about what was troubling her and what it might have to do with his own agenda for this meeting.

She stopped and faced him. "I've been told not to write the report."

"But that –"

"That would mean that this whole thing never happened. There was no money laundering, no illegal cash, that the world will think that Melissa and Wilder and Shanahan died because of the run-of-the-mill passions that cause family members to kill one another. What's the point of writing a long, tedious report? As you said, all the wrong-doers are dead and there are no victims."

Her bitterness became more obvious with every bitten-off sentence. By the time she finished, she was tightlipped and standing with her fists clenched against her sides. But she wasn't done.

"But the bastards in their pinstriped suits and power ties will be able to do what they've always done. Screw the little people! It's Watergate one more time!"

Watergate?

She went on in the same angry tones. "Barry Wilder was a major Republican donor for twenty years, up until he disappeared. He gave tens of millions of dollars that we know of – and probably a lot more that we don't -- to crackpot causes, Tea Party candidates, climate deniers, fake research studies, industry lobbyists ... the famous Washington swamp. If I write my report and link him to money laundering, all of his past activities get opened up, including the way that he funneled money into political action committees – PAC's – for Trump and others. I'd bet half of my pension fund that the Trump organization helped Wilder launder money and that his donations bought him government favors."

Like a new identity via the EB-5 program. "Who told you not to write the report? Your boss? He's a political appointee of this administration."

"Graham, this is Washington. My boss would never be on the record for telling me to do something that violates the law! It doesn't work that way. No, I got a call from an ex-Secretary of the Treasury, one of my original patrons, now long-retired. There were a lot of hedges, hypotheticals and hints, but what it came down to was, 'I'm telling you this for your own good. You've had' – emphasis on the past tense there – 'a great career at Treasury ... wonderful things to come if' – stress on the conditional – 'you can learn to be a team player.' It was a masterpiece of innuendo."

She sat down on a nearby bench and he moved alongside her. "So what are you going to do?"

"I genuinely don't know." She lifted her left hand. "On the one hand, I write the report. Then the blitzkrieg starts. The one called, 'If the facts are against you, attack the messenger.' I'm portrayed as a mean-spirited Obama holdover with a grudge against the new Republican administration. Fox News runs nightly character assassinations. My boss questions my professionalism. 'Why were you working alone, against our policies? Why didn't you share your investigative results? Jay Gould might be alive today if you'd followed procedures.'"

She looked closely at Graham. "There's also a good chance ... I'd say a near certainty ... that they'll discover that I was ... am ... sleeping with the husband of the woman who manages the agency that I was investigating. Think how that will play on Fox News."

She lifted her right hand. "On the other hand, I don't write the report. Put on my best 'Aw shucks!' accent and tell my team that it was one of those 'smoke, but no fire' leads, nothing that amounted to a winnable case. A cushy promotion is suddenly found for me; higher pay grade, less field work. Word is leaked that I'm on the short list for assistant secretary. And then I'll get an invitation to leave government work and take on the presidency of one of those prestigious think tanks that issue weighty papers on emerging policy issues."

She sat staring at the two hands held open in her lap, while Graham thought of a third possibility. *Somebody in Karnek's line of work gets a call from an anonymous client and, shortly after that, a senior Treasury official with a distinguished career is tragically killed.*

Have we come that far, that I can be having such thoughts? Yes, we have. He felt incredibly tired suddenly. *You're almost done.* He looked at the two keys that he was holding in his left hand; Karnek's parting gift. *Only three more puzzles to solve.*

He touched her arm very gently. "Take a ride with me. I want to show you something that may help you decide."

The Test

Graham tapped each of the four corners on the keypad at the entrance to the self-storage complex, just as Shanahan had done. The barred gate slid open and he thought, *That's one puzzle solved.* He drove to the unit with the sign reading 'Interment Products Limited' and parked with his headlights illuminating the blank door. He took the two keys that Karnek had given him an hour earlier, picked one at random and inserted it into the lock. When he turned it, there was a solid 'click' and he slid the door open. *That's two.*

Renee had said nothing since he'd said "Take a ride with me." Her silence and the way that she passively followed him without any seeming curiosity told Graham that the indecision and depression were hard at work within her. *I think that is about to change. But which way?*

She stood looking at the ranks of metal coffins lining the one wall. "Yuk," she said with considerable feeling. Then she looked accusingly at him. "Please tell me that you're not going to show me more bodies!"

"Not bodies. But I'm going to show you something that was buried for a long time. It's been exhumed, so to speak." He pulled out the third coffin from ground level in the fifth column and held the lid halfway open. He stood waiting while Renee walked slowly down the aisle and after giving him a mistrustful look, glanced quickly into the coffin and then grasped the rim with both hands and looked much closer. She reached in and raked her fingers through the small bundles, like a small child sorting through the contents of a piggy bank dumped out for her inspection. Graham wished he could see her expression.

"The light is poor in here. Are these all hundred-dollar packages?"

"Yes."

"This is Shanahan's stash? The cash he was laundering through NEW SF?"

He hesitated. "Yes."

"There must be nine or ten million here." *She's worked in Treasury for a long time. Probably pretty good with eyeball estimates.* He said, "I'll take your word for it."

Then she asked the question that he knew he couldn't answer. "How did you know it was here?" All he said was, "Shanahan told me." *She doesn't need to know the whole story ... the confession ... McDavid's living room ... Karnek giving me the key.*

"Did he say where it came from?"

"Yes, but I can't tell you. But I can say that it wasn't from narcotics or organized crime." After a pause, he added, "It's more like a lost and found situation."

"So nobody knows he had it ... or even that it exists."

"Nobody." *Except an itinerant assassin who doesn't want the money because it's too difficult to carry around!* He waited for her to go through the same sequence of thoughts that he had already cycled through a dozen times. When she remained silent, staring at the interior of the coffin, he said, "And nobody will miss it if we keep it for ourselves."

The words seemed to echo within the enclosed metallic space of the storage shed.. She simply looked at him. There was no indignation, righteousness, denial ... not even surprise. Like him, she was thinking of possibilities. *Let's make it even easier for her ...*

"Think about it. If you didn't turn in your report ... did what you were told to do ... having a few million bucks would go a long way toward making you feel better about caving in to the bastards, wouldn't it?" *No reaction.* "Or if you decide to write the report, the money would compensate for all the crap that's going to be dumped on you?" *Still no reaction.* He repeated, "Nobody will miss it if we keep it for ourselves," speaking very distinctly and watching her.

He could *see* her decide. One second she was pensive, almost brooding, looking at all those little green bundles cascading over one another. The next second, she was standing erect, letting the coffin lid fall back in place, looking like a woman who had no doubts about anything – duty, wealth or her place in a dirty world. She looked at Graham and said, "No."

He felt his muscles relax and only then realized how unsure he had been about how she would respond. *I will have to find a way to make it up to her, for doubting.* He nodded at her. "OK, there's one more –"

Her voice was accusing. "You could have taken all of it. You didn't have to show me. Or tempt me." She was looking at Graham, but he knew that she was talking for her own benefit, having to work out for herself what the real agenda was for this trip. "Graham, why did you bring me here? What is it that you want from me? Is this some kind of test?"

More questions I can't answer. But this time it's because I don't know myself. Am I trying to buy this woman? Here, have a few million dollars. Do you love me now? He waffled. "It can't be a test ... there are no right answers."

She pressed, "What would you have done if I'd said, 'Great! Let's do it!'"

"That's easy." He smiled, "I have a big empty duffel bag in the trunk of my car. I would have handed it to you and let you take as much as you like … help you carry it if it was too heavy." *I wonder how much nine or ten million weighs? Frank Shanahan would know.*

"Your share too?"

"Sure. Unlike you, I'm already rich, remember?" As he spoke, a new and disturbing thought occurred to him. *You're getting divorced. Splitting all assets 50-50. Would Valerie have wanted you to take the money? Would I even tell her about it? Would you have kept the money if Sergei hadn't knocked on your door and made you instantly rich?*

Moral dilemmas are stacking up all over the place! And it struck him for the first time that writing the book would involve much more than research and simple storytelling. *It will require a whole lot of self-analysis!*

She looked at him for a long time. Then she slid the coffin back in line with the others and walked back to the car. He trailed her and slid the metal door down, locking it once more. As soon as he turned to face her, she said, "OK, so we're both goody two-shoes. Insufferably moralistic and incorruptible. But what *are* we going to do with the money?"

"It depends on whether you turn in your report or not. If you do, then you can hold a press conference in front of a large stack of confiscated currency and announce a major bust of a money laundering operation, featuring Barry Wilder as the primary villain."

"Not many reporters will show up," she said. "Ten million dollars doesn't make for much of a photo op these days. But the Barry Wilder bit will get their attention. But what if I don't write the report? How do you explain how this" – she gestured behind her at the storage unit -- "rather large amount of cash was 'mislaid?' Or were you just going to bury it again?"

"That makes it much trickier. I figure –"

"Never mind." She reached for the car door. "I've decided to write the report."

Not much surprise there. A woman that has just turned down several million dollars of tainted money probably has a fairly highly developed sense of right and wrong.

He held his hand against the car door. "Renee? This really wasn't a test of some sort. You could go either way and I'd be OK with it." *I think that's true, but I'm glad she chose the way she did. It makes the next bit a lot easier.*

She tugged at the door. "Let's go. I've got a lot to do in the next couple of hours." She paused, one foot in the car. "But Graham? Thanks."

"For ... ?"

"Two things, actually. The money, of course. It means that I can get their attention ... show them real flames, not just smoke. More importantly, it means that the 'attack the messenger' strategy will be harder for them to pull off. And thanks for the test that you refuse to call a test. It's good to know that the high-minded ideas we have about ourselves aren't too far off."

"Hamlet."

"Huh?"

"Act I, Scene 3. *This above all -- To thine own self be true.*" He grinned at his own pretentiousness and tried to mitigate it.

"I think Shakespeare had in mind the bastards in their pinstriped suits and power ties."

"I never liked the tragedies. Too much of that in my real world. Look, can we go now? Please."

"Uh, Renee. There's one more thing you probably should see."

Shanahan asked Karnek if he was the one who had taken the money. He said, "Yes. But not far. It's very close. In three very large trunks. I've left a trail." Graham had a theory, but it was so insubstantial, so *unlikely*, that he did not share it with Renee. The theory required him to believe that Karnek had a highly developed sense of humor, a trait that did not seem to fit with the man's image in any way.

He asked Renee, "Suppose you wanted to physically transport a lot of cash in an inconspicuous way, on short notice, and using some kind of container that is readily available. How would you package it?" She responded within a few seconds. "Not in a coffin. That's certain. I'd get a few of those metal trunks that are used for tools or sensitive electronic gear. You see them on baggage carousels all the time."

He pointed at the sign on the adjacent storage unit to the left, the one with "LJS Luggage Wholesalers" printed in an Old English style font. "Trunks. A form of luggage, right?" She nodded at him and he could see the beginnings of comprehension in her eyes. "And if a child asked what's the best book ever written about a search for buried treasure?" It took her a few seconds longer to answer the question than it had taken him. *She's probably read a lot more books than I have so it's harder for her.* But she got to the same point: "Treasure Island, by Robert Louis Stevenson. Hands down."

"Last question: What was the name of the most memorable character in the book?" She knew where the game was going now, but was willing to let him show off a little. "Well, there was young Jim, of course, and Squire Trelawny and Billy Bones and Dr. Livesey ..." He waited, enjoying their game and at the same time fearful that he had it all wrong. She said, "But the *really* memorable character was Long John Silver. His initials would be LJS." She looked up at the sign with a severely exaggerated expression of discovery.

Graham was beginning to feel the slightest bit of fondness for Karnek. *Some time soon, I will have to reconcile my conflicting views of him. If I can.*

Graham took the second key that Karnek had given him, inserted it into the lock and turned it. The answering 'click' was enormously satisfying. *That's three.* He slid the door up and turned on the overhead light. Three large metal trunks sat in the middle of the concrete floor. There was nothing else in the unit. Renee slowly approached the nearest trunk and lifted the lid. There was no lock. They both stood gazing down at the portrait of Benjamin Franklin repeating itself across the rows and columns.

She lifted the lids of the other two trunks. The view was identical to the first. She breathed, "There must be eighty million dollars here."

She's close, Graham thought, remembering Karnek in the living room that night. *"The man wanted to know, so I counted it. Seventy-seven million, nine hundred and twenty thousand dollars. That's not counting the two million in the bag for Vargas.*

"That should make a proper background for a press conference. Probably get quite a few reporters out for that."

Renee closed the three lids and sat down on the middle trunk. Graham took the one next to her and, after three or four seconds, she leaned against him with her head on his shoulder and twined her fingers with his.

"What are we going to do now?" She asked.

He chose to misunderstand her question. "Speaking only for myself, I thought I would get a divorce, move to Washington DC and write another book." She did not reply, but after a few seconds, she brought her other hand across to lie on top of their interlaced fingers.

Epilog

Graham watched the press conference on television. It was staged in an auditorium in the New York Federal Reserve Bank for security reasons and co-sponsored by the Departments of Treasury and Justice. Renee Delgado was there but barely visible in the row of officials lined up next to a very impressive pyramid composed entirely of bundles of hundred dollar bills.

There were a lot of TV cameras and reporters, but it was not much of a press conference, even by the low standard set by the current administration. A mid-level official from DOJ took the lead and made a five-minute presentation, mostly about the Ross Sea Group, Barry Wilder's flight from justice and how an informant had tipped them off about the cash hoard once the murder-suicide became public. The theme of his remarks was the inevitable triumph of justice due to dedicated public servants.

The reporters did their best, asking all the right questions: Where did the money come from? Why was Wilder killed? Was he funneling the cash into any of the political or conservative causes that he favored? Was the Trump White House in contact with Wilder at any time in the last three years? Who authorized his entry into the U.S. under an assumed name? By Graham's count, none of the questions were answered. The repeated recitations of "no comment" or "that's under active investigation" or "I have no information about that" deflected the questions that mattered and eventually frustrated the reporters.

"Money laundering" was mentioned only once, a minor point in a longwinded answer. "There are some promising leads. We know that Wilder was slowly laundering the cash, converting it into corporate profits through an assortment of complicated transfers. A team of highly skilled investigators from Treasury is pursuing a number of avenues."

There was no mention of Renee Delgado, Jay Gould, Valerie Dodd or NEW SF.

Divorce papers were filed with the court and both Graham and Valerie testified that the settlement arrangements were mutually agreeable. The divorce would be official after a judge reviewed the papers and signed the final decree, probably within a few weeks.

Graham had not seen or talked to Valerie since the phone call in the Meditation Garden. When he thought about her, he was depressed when he realized how little he cared about her feelings, her affair with McNeal, her job at NEW SF or any other part of her life, as though the last forty years had passed with him in a trance. When she sent a text message asking, "What about all the stuff from the Palo Alto house that's sitting in storage?" He responded, "I don't want any of it" and was startled to realize that it was true.

He called Renee. "I saw you at the press conference. Just barely."

"That was part of the deal. My farsighted, tough-on-crime, relentless boss gets the limelight while I – the loyal subordinate working to further the new administration's crusade against corporate criminals – become part of the woodwork. It's fine with me."

"So, no blitzkrieg attacks against the messenger?"

"No. That very impressive stack of currency made it abundantly clear that this was not going to be swept under the rug. And Wilder's dead, so they can't offend him by naming him as the sole villain. That source of funds is gone, so they figure they might as well say 'we knew it all along.' Another set of alternative facts."

"You said the word 'deal.' What did you get out of it, in return for staying out of the limelight and uncovering all that cash?"

"A promotion, budget increase for my team and a promise of non-interference with future investigations."

"Can you enforce it?"

"I may have implied that I have access to audio recordings of Wilder talking with Shanahan just before he was killed. He was talking about past activities ... diverting money intended for black ops, funding dirty tricks for politicians, bribing certain Republican congressmen ..."

I told her about my iPhone recording. McDavid did in fact incriminate himself in multiple ways, but she's embellished quite a lot. "Renee ... If I write what I want to write, in the way I want to write it, all that stuff will come out. Your threat won't be worth much in that case."

"Go ahead and write your book. I'll either be retired or running the entire investigative wing of Treasury by the time it's in the stores. And there's a decent chance that the royal fool will be impeached before then."

He tried for the most casual tone he could summon. "I'll be in Washington tomorrow. How about dinner?"

"Can't. I'm at an international conference on digital crypto-currencies. The whole week is blocked out."

A very slight tremor of doubt skittered across Graham's consciousness. *Have I misjudged so badly? Confused what is possible with what is plausible? Am I just an older and more pathetic version of the classic middle-aged crisis being acted out?*

But then she was saying, "Where are you staying? Never mind, we both know what DC housing is like. I want you to stay with me until you find something – or someone – you like better. I'll text you the address – it's a townhouse in Georgetown – and I'll leave a key for you. I should be there by about nine tomorrow night."

"Renee, I …" He paused, embarrassed that he was about to stammer out some kind of pro forma protest … "Oh, I can't impose on you like that" or something equally inane, when what he really wanted to do was say how utterly grateful he was for the continuance.

It seemed that her intuition was more than a match for his self-doubts. "Graham. We're good for each other. In ways that we don't even know about yet. I'll leave the key under the third flowerpot on the left side of the landing. Bring a bottle of wine if you can."

He left Alden Acres on a Monday morning by simply walking away from the place. He called a moving service to pack his personal goods from the visitor's room and the apartment that he had occupied so briefly. His only detour on the way out was to stop to say goodbye to Sal and Butch.

He called Alison from the airport. "I'll be gone for couple of weeks. Once I've got things set up in DC, I'll be back and forth pretty regularly."

"Are you OK?"

"I'm fine."

"You didn't hear me. I asked, 'Are you OK?' It was a genuine question, one that every now and then, in certain contexts, requires a thoughtful answer. And this is one of those times."

Am I OK? On the one hand, I'm walking away from everything I thought I was ... toward ... what? Nothing solid. A perhaps relationship, an uncertain book, the opposite coast and the most insular city in the world ... I have no particular friends, hobbies or routines and I'm getting old, or at least older. Sounds kind of grim. But on the other hand, I'm healthy, have enough money to do whatever I want to do, and I have prospects ... that relationship and the book ... that I'm eager to explore. I'm better off in almost every way that matters than 99.9% of the world's population ...

"Dad?"

And I have a daughter that is worried about whether I'm OK!

"I'm fine, Alison. I really am."

Author's Note

My friends and relatives always ask, "How do you write your books?" which segues into a discussion of work habits (undisciplined), travel history (extensive) and all the minutiae of literary engineering (haphazard and self-taught). But the far more interesting question for me is "Why?" not "How?" In fairness, my psychoanalyst (non-existent) should answer that question, because it involves ancient maladies like compulsion, insecurity and arrogance; as well as more positive drives ... curiosity mostly, because I do not know where the story will take me and the only way to find out is to start writing and see where the characters decide to venture.

Fortunes of a Misbegotten War began as the offspring of a dinner conversation among friends, each of us confronting the "what next" question that haunts those of us who are done working and therefore contemplating real-life versions of Alden Acres. And since the inhabitants of such places are necessarily wealthy and successful, they are bound to have interesting secrets that can be exploited in fictional form.

Like today's talk show hosts, TV comedians and columnists for the *New York Times* and *Washington Post*, it is easy for the authors of political thrillers to find ample inspiration for writing about corruption and incompetence in the one-year old presidency of Donald Trump. My only hope is that at least some of it is, in fact, fiction.

The Author

Thomas Hofstedt is engaged in approximately his fourth career, each of which is partially reflected in the plots and settings of his writing. He has worked as a professor in major universities, as a management consultant all over the globe, and finally as an advisor and board member for not-for-profit organizations. He is the product of a Scandinavian heritage, a Midwestern upbringing, and a Northern California value system. He lives in San Mateo, California with his wife and most diligent critic, Sharon.

He has authored eight other books of fiction, all of which are available in paperback or ebook formats from Amazon.com.

Other Titles

A Conspiracy of Patriots
A Convergence of Evils
The Hundred-Year Storm
They Call it Tinseltown
A Small War in a Far-Off Place
The House on Russian Hill
The Wisdom That Comes With Winters
A Lethal Intelligence

www.ingramcontent.com/pod-product-compliance
Lightning Source LLC
Chambersburg PA
CBHW062125170626
46813CB00002B/576